The Savannah Stories

Tainted Love

J.L. LEMON

ISBN-13: 978-0-6151-6774-9

Published 2007 by Up At Midnight Publishing
www.geocities.com/upatmidnightpublishing

Other titles available in the Savannah Stories:

Blast From The Past

Payback

First Comes Love

Walking On Broken Glass

To my parents who continually cope with Savannah's antics and all my ideas for her. Thank you both for your patience and love.

And to everyone who has encouraged me to write – thanks to all of you. (That also includes Mom and Dad.)

*Some men are alive simply because
it is against the law to kill them.*

- Edgar Watson Howe

1

Residents used Walton Way as a shortcut from the Calhoun Expressway to the other sides of town. Visitors and tourists found it to be a scenic main street of Augusta, lined with houses built with Colonial, Neoclassical and newer Antebellum homes. To the outsider, Augusta was pretty and Walton Way a testament to the creativeness of the Southern lifestyle. The houses along the western end boasted no less than three thousand square feet and a grand old tree or two towered in each front yard. Their lawns were perfectly manicured, the homes meticulously maintained. Many of these homes were inherited from generation to generation and each changing of the guard began a civil war of its own between families – those who sought ownership against those who were gifted with the property.

To Savannah, however, Walton Way was nothing but a detour to hell. She couldn't blame the neighbors, who, by tradition, knew some of her family's secrets like hers knew theirs. As any Georgian knew, no one could claim true privacy in their neighborhood. Her childhood home certainly wasn't at fault. It weathered more storms inside than out, and protected her, at times, from a wrath comparable to God's. Unlike the neighbors and their Neoclassical dwellings, her family home was built in the Antebellum style in the 1950s. It was also larger in size with four thousand square feet, but the source of Savannah's private distress also lived there. The culprit was her father.

Her ultimate problem was his drinking and his temper, both of which fueled his efforts to let the place go to seed. He fastidiously stocked the liquor cabinet with hoards of scotch yet the lawn perpetually exhibited a shaggy, unkempt appearance, the porch pillars crumbled at their bases and the house itself needed painting. Since buying the house, it had been her mother's pride and joy. Now when Savannah visited, it pained her to see it in such disrepair. To the passerby the house probably looked fine, except the lawn. To her, though, she could nearly hear her mother crying.

On her last visit, Savannah jotted a note to call various and sundry repairmen to fix the pillars then to paint the place Charlene's personal pick of white trimmed in cream. Since she hadn't received a bill she assumed R.J. chased the men off the second they stepped onto the property.

The majestic magnolia tree that her mother cherished seriously required pruning, and the front yard needed a good mowing before the end of the month. As a girl Savannah pretended the beautiful house was Tara and spent hours leisurely propped against one of the four pillars framing the porch, daydreaming. Now the reality nagged at her when she visited. If she, Georgia and Seth didn't do something soon, they'd be standing in the remains of their own postwar Tara with only a scraggly looking magnolia tree to lean on.

Savannah was in the process of polishing off a Rocket Burger from the OK Cafe when the call from Bobby came. Her cousin, the Richmond County Sheriff, rarely called during her shift, especially with a sheepish, almost hesitant tone. She knew something was wrong – the trick was wringing it out of Bobby. It required plenty of prompting for him to explain her father stripped naked and plunged into the pool whereupon, after positioning himself on the pool's top step in full view of the neighbors, he took up singing "Black is the Color of My True Love's Hair" as loud as he could and proceeded to wave his middle finger at the lookers-on as they gasped in dismay.

"What?" was all her paralyzed brain could muster. The shocking mental image of R.J. flouncing around the pool in his altogethers rocked her back on her heels. It brought a whole new meaning to the phrase "what will the neighbors think". She really needed to sit down for this but when she did, the jalapeno peppers from the burger threatened a return trip. Needless to say, she stood right back up.

Evidently her voice carried through the office loudly enough that Ennis appeared at the doorway demanding to know what was wrong. Rolling her eyes, Savannah gathered the energy to shake her head, "My father is acting up again." But surely she'd misunderstood her cousin. R.J. never digressed to such bizarre behavior. She prayed he at least had his shorts on...

Ennis, apparently sensing the riot within her, rooted himself to the spot in front of her desk, waiting for the phone conversation to end. She pinched the bridge of her nose while the familiar pang of a headache tapped at her temple. Dealing with R.J. became unbearable quickly and with a raging headache, it soon became impossible. She checked her desk drawer for aspirin, "Bobby, tell me he's not entirely nude. He's at least wearing his shorts, right?"

Of course, the response wasn't what she'd hoped for, "Sorry, honey. He's putting jaybirds to shame." Bobby proceeded to explain the situation as she gathered her jacket and purse. She made sure to scribble a note to stop by for aspirin, though this situation might call for a real painkiller instead. She had a feeling this particular situation would create a headache for the record books. Her stomach cramped again giving her a quaint reminder that an antacid might be extremely beneficial. She wrote that down too.

"...it's my first call about indecent exposure, especially in January," Bobby continued. "Weird thing is he's stone cold sober. Not a drop of booze in the place. He never runs out of it so I don't understand what happened."

Savannah groaned, "I know what happened. My sister happened." Taking a quick glance at her watch, she sighed, "I'll be there in a couple of hours."

"I hate calling you about this, sweetheart, but he'll only talk to you."

"Don't worry 'bout it, Bobby. He always calls for me and I don't honestly know why. I'm the meanest one of his kids yet he still keeps relying on me." When she hung up from Bobby she debated about rounding up Georgia and dragging her along for the trip. After all, the whole thing erupted because Georgia hid the liquor from their father. Her sister meant well but didn't comprehend the dilemma she produced by hiding his stash. He literally marched room to room, tearing the place up searching frantically for the scotch. Savannah knew exactly where Georgia hid the stuff. It was a secret compartment in the older sister's closet. As a child, she'd crammed her diary and a few other items in the small cubby hole, successfully concealing them from prying eyes – all except Savannah's. Now Georgia had taken to stashing R.J.'s liquor there.

"Need me to come along?" Ennis offered quietly. "I don't mind."

In his eyes, she read the truth. He didn't want to go but wanted her safe. She shook her head, "Thanks but he'd only climb higher on the walls if he sees anyone but me."

"Call me then. Tell me how things are going."

"Soon as I can."

She managed to make the trip in record time, calling Georgia on the way, "You did it again, didn't you? You hid his booze and now he's marching around the back yard *naked* and singing that damn song." Before giving her sister time to fully explain, Savannah continued, "The neighbors called Bobby. They don't like the striptease Daddy's giving them. As usual he's called for me so I'm on the road to clean up your mess again, thanks very much."

By the time she arrived, the sun fell behind a bank of clouds, giving the horizon a reddish, nearly purple hue. She'd driven down Walton Way to her house, and the moment she stepped outside, she heard R.J. yelling at the top of his lungs. The most distinct sound of her name being shouted polished emphatically off with, "I want my baby! I want Savannah!" He continued the mantra nonstop until she figured the neighbors were about to skin her for not arriving sooner. She slammed the Camaro's door hard just as Bobby charged out the front door, a mixed expression of desperation and sheer relief showing on him. He'd been blessed with a large frame and perfectly distributed muscle along each bone. Since his teen years, people compared him to a linebacker, a comparison he took well despite the fact he hated football. Now he appeared more sheepish than imposing as he waved his hands frantically as if to ward off any thoughts of actually going inside, "Hold it, hon. He's still in the buff."

She started forward anyway. The sooner she shut R.J. up, the better the neighbors and she would feel, "Yeah, so? He's not putting any clothes on until he sees I'm here. I know where his booze is and he knows it. It's a stupid game but I'm the one who gets tagged to play."

Bobby's jaw slacked momentarily, "Why didn't you tell me where it was? I could have saved you a trip."

She shook her head with a smile of annoyance, "If I did that, the whole game is ruined. Someone hides the booze, Daddy gets all pissed then calls Savannah. You can't screw with destiny, Bobby. It'll kick you twice as hard if you try." She trudged diligently to the front door.

Bobby rushed in front of her, "At least stay behind me so I can *think* I'm preserving someone's modesty."

Savannah opted to stride alongside him instead. She appreciated his efforts but he obviously had no clue how difficult her father could be, "If he doesn't care that strangers see him naked, he won't care if I do. Let me make a pit stop to the bathroom, 'kay?"

The mention of a brief detour didn't set well with her cousin. A mild frown appeared and faded just as fast, "Please make it quick."

Savannah leaped the two porch steps and the instant her feet touched the entry's pine floor – or what she remembered to be pine floor – she skidded, nearly losing her balance. Two arms caught her from behind as Bobby steadied her, "I meant hurry, don't kill yourself."

After thanking him, Savannah glanced down to see a rug that started out at the front door but now sat three feet in front of her, "Must be a new welcoming device Daddy thought of. What he doesn't realize is, if he kills off me and Georgia, he's on his own."

She geared down to meandering through the living room instead of charging like a bull. The ache in her heart returned the moment she laid eyes on the living room. Her mother's English-style chairs and couch were buried in R.J.'s pants and various shirts he'd worn. The built-in wooden bookcases on either side of the fireplace held the classics as well as dirty shot glasses and crystal he'd used to drink from. Ring marks dotted the cherry wood coffee table where he'd spilled scotch then left the glass to sit. Not even Georgia's ingenuity could polish the table back to its glory days. Savannah's sister possessed the tenacity of a dog with a bone when it came to cleaning. She gave up when she gave out. With their parent's house, it didn't take long to wear oneself out. Georgia usually dedicated a day every two weeks to keep the place tidy and livable, probably more to preserve her mother's wishes of a neat house than anything. That's when Georgia pulled the sneaky trick of hiding their father's scotch, thus throwing Savannah into the fray later.

She angled past the couch, trying her best to overlook the heaps of clothes. She followed a secondary trail of pants and shirts, papers and magazines along the hallway floor and into the nearest bathroom. Poor Bobby, she thought. Not only was he forced to deal with her drunken father, he also had to mine his way through the once beautiful house to find the back door. Then to top it off, once she arrived she detoured to the bathroom, probably to pee, he thought.

Her purpose, however, was slightly more involved with their current situation. One peek at the toilet made Savannah's stomach lurch. Being boiled in oil sounded less horrifying than sitting anywhere near that porcelain throne. She dared to flush the contents with a quick prayer the toilet didn't overflow.

Prayers answered, she proceeded to rummage the linen cabinet, found a bath towel and tucked it under her arm. She popped out of the bathroom to Bobby's delight then jogged up the stairs to Georgia's bedroom – much to Bobby's frustration, "Where are you going now?"

"Be right down!" she called. Georgia's room always rivaled military cleanliness – at least during their childhood – but now it smelled musty and dank, like a room abandoned in time. Everything remained neat with the exception of R.J.'s maniacal pillaging spilling over into the doorway. Why he never suspected his oldest daughter of hiding his booze amazed Savannah. Seth never visited. Savannah did but not nearly as regularly as Georgia.

She opened the closet, shoved some old clothes aside to reveal the secret compartment. Savannah reached in her pocket for a coin to pry the door open. All she had was a dime but it would serve the purpose well. When the door popped loose, the innards revealed the truth. Georgia stuffed all of R.J.'s liquor into the cubby hole, no doubt with hopes he'd magically dry out and forget he was an alcoholic. Savannah snorted at her sister's ignorance and grabbed the bottles and didn't bother to replace the compartment's door. This was the last straw. Georgia had to realize their father needed professional help to dry out, not good intentions.

Skipping down the stairs with her arms loaded with the towel and two tons of scotch, Bobby nearly fell over upon sight of her, "God Almighty, girl. Where'd you find all that booze?"

"Georgia hides it from him sometimes when she comes over. That's why he goes crazy like this," she answered while restocking the wet bar for the umpteenth time. Logic told her not to bother actually placing the bottles inside the bar. She left them all on top because he'd be on the binge of a lifetime after this, especially when he figured out he'd embarrassed himself in front of all the neighbors. R.J. might have been a raging drunk most of the time but he also had moments of brilliant clarity. Those moments tended to emerge upon the infusion of liquor. Savannah estimated that in less than eight hours, R.J. would place phone calls to the neighbors apologizing for his behavior. Calls that no one would bother answering. They'd had enough of his drinking, just as his family had.

Savannah allowed Bobby to escort her to the back yard but not before she armed herself with the huge bath towel and a bottle of scotch first. They stepped outside to see R.J., his back turned to them, making obscene hand gestures to the older lady next door watching from her upstairs window.

"Uncle R.J., stop that," Bobby implored, his cheeks glowing from embarrassment.

Savannah stood behind her cousin's shoulder, allowing his body to block the majority of R.J.'s nudity. Thankfully she only saw her father's bare back, "Daddy, quit making a fool of yourself."

R.J. spun on his heel and Savannah instantly closed her eyes before being gifted with a scene guaranteed to mortify her. She blindly offered the towel to Bobby, "Here. Try to encourage him to wear it."

Bobby took the towel and from what Savannah gathered, he approached R.J. tentatively. She heard her cousin speak low but firmly, his footsteps shuffling slow in the dead grass. A different cadence in the grass tuned her attention – a faster, lumbering sound of her father approaching her, "My baby is here. Give Daddy a hug and a kiss."

Savannah held a hand out to stop him, her eyes still closed, "Not while you're in your altogethers." If he wouldn't listen to Bobby, maybe he would heed her words, "Daddy, you can't go flashing the neighbors like this. Put that towel around yourself then I'll hug you."

Bobby chimed in, "Uncle R.J., just wrap this around your waist and we'll go inside."

R.J. flared angry, "I'm not doing it and ya can't make me." He turned his attention to Savannah, "I didn't call you here to get a damn lecture. I called bec –"

"I know why you called," she interrupted, "and you're not getting any until you show some decency. Put the towel around yourself and I'll give you a drink. Until then, you run the risk of going to jail for indecent exposure and you will *not* get a drink in there."

The yard fell silent making her wonder what was happening. Modesty kept her eyes closed but something wasn't feeling right about this little meeting. R.J. never clammed up when a person spelled out facts he didn't want to hear. Instead, he got mad. This time proved no different when Bobby yelled, "Savannah, duck!"

She did but not before R.J.'s fist clipped her jaw. It felt like a rock slamming against her chin. The blow snapped her head back and knocked her sideways somewhat but thankfully the full result of his effort went unfelt. Considering the tears beginning to well, she'd hated to have felt the brunt of his attack. Luckily Bobby warned her in time to duck most of the swing. When she stumbled sideways, Bobby scrambled to her, trying to keep her upright.

Two strong hands wrapped around her and she clung to her cousin in an attempt to settle her spinning brain. Bobby inquired if she was okay. She nodded through growing tears. God, she hated coming home. It always resulted in a fight of some sort. And if Bobby didn't stop asking her if she was okay, she'd really break down and cry.

R.J. loomed over Bobby's shoulder. He pointed accusingly at her, "That'll teach you to disrespect your daddy. I didn't raise no smartass and I'll teach you to speak civilly to me."

His tone solidified her resolve only briefly. Savannah clenched her jaw and her fists. She really didn't need this shit, especially right now. She and Ennis were working on a difficult case involving child abuse. So the call this morning only served as fuel for the tears rolling down her cheeks.

The sight of tears spurred Bobby to sweep them away. His strong embrace wrapped her in a blanket of warmth, both literally and emotionally. Bobby spent most of his life protecting people from abuse and supporting them in the aftermath. At times, however, the most even tempered tended to tilt and Bobby did, "Uncle R.J., we're taking a little trip."

"Bobby, don't do it on account of this," she declared while trying to straighten her face. "He's hit me before."

"He doesn't hit you in front of me and get away with it, honey. Go inside and calm down. I'll be in after I get him in the car."

Still allowing tears to flow, Savannah's anger suddenly turned black as her father's. She stared straight into R.J.'s eyes and held the scotch bottle for him to see, "I *was* going to give you this but I'll be damned if I help you with it again. This is the last time, Daddy." Savannah angrily slammed the scotch bottle onto the patio, the ensuing crash giving her more joy than she'd felt all day, "You can dry out in the county jail for all I care." She marched back inside only for the shaking began. Speaking to R.J. so harshly felt good at the time but she'd pay later. No matter how old she got, the fear of her father's rage would light a flame of terror inside her. She merely prayed that he stayed in lockup for the night because she hadn't the energy to drive home.

Once Bobby drove off with R.J., she locked up the house and took out for Pump N Shop and Surrey Center Pharmacy. She topped off the Camaro's tank at the former then dropped by the latter to have a prescription refilled. Just as the outing began to look successful, the day turned backwards again when she joined the checkout line at the pharmacy.

"Well, if it isn't Savannah Prince. What brings you back to Augusta? Daddy call you again?"

Savannah didn't recognize the screechy, nails-on-a-blackboard voice right away. Only when it squawked again with a "Thank you and have a nice day" to a customer ahead in line did it register. It belonged to none other than Cynthia Donner, ex-cheerleader and ex-football-groupie extraordinaire. Cynthia, the nemesis of all common people at Cross Creek High School, made Savannah's life near miserable goading her about R.J.'s drunkenness. She reverted fifteen years in two seconds, caving to notions of pulling that silky blond hair from Cynthia's head. *Thou shalt not think evil thoughts*, Savannah admonished herself. Dealing with idiots was part of her job but she thoroughly detested dealing with them off the job.

Allowing the person ahead of her to pay out and leave, Savannah proceeded to unceremoniously toss her prescription on the conveyer belt, "You know, Cindy, coming home is always such a headache because of people like you." She pointed to the small sack in Cynthia's hand, "That's why I need that crap." And in case Cindy missed the badge on her belt, Savannah purposefully drew her jacket back and slid her hand in her pocket. Evidently the glint attracted Cindy's attention and her mouth shut instantly. *Better*, Savannah thought. *Much better.*

It only lasted so long when Cindy inquired, "So how's your grandpa?"

Withdrawing the cash, Savannah answered casually, "Still dead but thanks for asking. And your family?"

Cindy's eyes widened to dinner plates and her mouth gaped. After a goodly time, she snapped out of the fog and handed Savannah her change, "They're fine. Gene got married last month."

She grabbed the prescription and presented a half-smile, "Give him my condolences."

2

Once arriving back at the house, Savannah took a prescription painkiller, picked up around the living room then reclined on the couch, praying for relief. When the first pill failed to alleviate not only the pain but fade the memory of the day, she rummaged her purse for another. She rarely took two because they spaced her out and dulled her reactions to the point she feared death. She needed it tonight, though. Anything to kill off the day and if, in the process, she died from it, at least she'd avoid R.J.'s wrath later.

Her mother would have kittens if she saw the wreck R.J. managed to leave at times. He'd thrown blankets hither and yon, left food out for days at a time and never washed the dishes after eating. God help her, she even feared sitting on the toilet so she cleaned it. Over the past years, R.J. peed like a fire hose out of control so hitting inside the toilet wasn't exactly like Tiger Woods playing golf. A hole in one with R.J. never happened.

She robbed her bedroom of two blankets and a pillow and lugged them downstairs to the couch. Tossing his clothes to the hearth, she made a makeshift bed from the blankets and laid down. It took a good while to relax from the day's events and her chin panged occasionally just as an unkind reminder of what happened. Savannah was about to drop off asleep when her cell phone rang.

Dragging herself to a sitting position she clicked on the phone, "Prince." A nasty throb bolted through her jaw and she inadvertently groaned into the receiver.

"Are you finished bitching me out yet?" Georgia inquired then a momentary silence ensued. Then, "Why are you groaning?"

Savannah fell back against the couch, sighing, "Because I hurt."

"What happened and why were you so angry earlier? You know I always hide Daddy's stash."

Not now, please... She merely required some down time – everyone needed it – so why didn't hers ever kick in? She swore the entire world possessed a camera and microphone honed into only her, calling or banging on her front door when her energy and tolerance were at zero. "I know and normally I'd be okay with the cat and mouse crap but this time Daddy hit me for being disrespectful to him. All I wanted him to do was wrap a friggin' towel around him so his Benny didn't shine for our neighbors."

"I'm sorry, honey, I never expected him to get violent –"

Oh, she *had* to be kidding, "Well, that's what alcoholics do, Georgia. When they run out of booze, they get mean. Sometimes violent. You'd think growing up with him you might have tumbled onto that fact."

Handily ignoring Savannah's dig, she offered, "I'll come over and fix you something to eat."

"I'm at the house. I'll stay tonight then drop by and see Daddy before heading back in the morning."

"What do you mean go see him? Where is he?"

"In jail. Bobby saw the whole tragic event take place before his very eyes and arrested him, even against my will."

"Don't be a smartass. If he hit you, he deserves to be in jail."

Savannah apologized. It was at that moment fate answered her prayer to relieve her of this tenuous conversation. The doorbell rang. "I gotta go. Someone's at the door."

"Stay on with me until you find out who it is."

She rolled her eyes, "Yes, Mama." Climbing to her feet, she carefully wandered toward the general vicinity of the front door. She did it mostly by feel and slightly by memory considering the room was pitch black. Success loomed near until she stubbed her toe on a foreign object by the door, "Shee-yet," she hissed while cringing at her new inventory of pain. Switching on the light revealed an iron doorstop in the shape of a terrier. "Stupid doorstop," she griped, barely containing the urge to heave it out the door.

"Turn the light on, Savannah," her sister instructed in a vaguely irritated manner.

Past the point of being ultimately cross with Georgia, she still retained enough oomph to let her know the comment wasn't entirely appreciated, "The light *is* on, Georgia." She pulled the door open, "Who moved the damn thing that close to the door anyway?"

"I did."

"Well, thanks for trying to kill me…" Savannah's vision went from her throbbing foot up the legs of her visitor. Long legs encased in jeans that, as she followed the body to the face, recognition slowly dawned like the sun from behind a storm cloud. The handsome man standing before her was Roy Carlson, her boyfriend from high school. A man that, by her current calculations, should've worn a ring in the neighborhood of the third finger on his left hand. Glancing at his left hand gave her a rousing jolt along her spine. Roy wasn't married anymore. Or, her wickedly sadistic mind taunted, he was still married and just chose not to wear a ring.

She heard Georgia reply to her statement. A smart aleck remark, no doubt. But her attention focused solely on the slice of heaven standing before her. He still towered over her, still possessed that rugged masculinity she'd always gotten weak-kneed over. And that chocolate brown hair and those beautiful green eyes. To die for...

Roy tilted his gorgeous face and smiled, "Heard you were back in town. How about a drink?"

"I gotta go, Georgia. I'll see you later." She clicked off absently while basking in Roy's killer smile. The smile she fell for in third grade. She often thought it should've been illegal or immoral to be that handsome. She still thought it even as she stood staring back at him. Nature gifted her with a sharp tongue – it usually came in handy on the job. However, faced with a man she'd dreamed of every night from third grade to graduation, she found herself strangely speechless. All she could manage was, "Cindy tell you?"

Surprisingly he shook his head, "Heard it from her brother. Said your dad walloped you again."

Savannah instinctively flinched, the joy temporarily sucked from the moment. "Welcome Home" flashed briefly in her mind. The past never faded in a town like Augusta. Driving past the city limit signs thrust people back to their youth when friends knew plenty more about a person than was comfortable. Roy saw her through plenty of scares and beatings in her childhood and teen years. She'd cried many tears in his presence and he'd comforted her as best he could.

That was the problem with towns like this, she thought. Gossip traveled faster than the speed of light. Information raced from North to South, East to West like a net cast for fishing. It encompassed all because if a person resided in Augusta (or was born there), the ringleader felt it their honorable duty to inform the masses when a returning resident breached the fortress. In this case, the ringleader was a former cheerleader who babbled it to her brother who then babbled it to Roy who himself plunged headfirst into a lake of fire by saying, "Honey, you look awful."

"I hope you're not expecting an invitation inside after that statement." It was half honest, half not. She'd like to catch up on old times but no woman should be subjected to hearing how bad they looked after a long, hard day.

His hand swung from behind and held up a package of Yoo-Hoo, "I was hoping to bribe my way inside, Detective Prince. I also have pizza on order." He glanced at his watch, "'Bout another ten minutes and we can eat."

"You took a chance on that, didn't you? What if I wasn't here?"

He shrugged, "I'd be forced to drive to Atlanta and track you down with all that cold pizza in my truck."

"I suspect that would make your wife slightly unhappy."

Roy waved his left hand at her, "I'm dee-vorced. Free, white and thirty-one. So what do you say? You're not turning me down *again* are you?"

"If you keep quiet about how bad I look, you can come in. Otherwise you'll be limping home – without your pizza." His reference to turning him down again stung a part of her soul. He'd proposed to her an hour after graduation and she'd refused him. In retrospect, the decision probably wasn't her finest but the desire to finally leave Augusta and her father proved too strong. Roy wanted to stay with his father's landscape company and she wanted out of town. The thought of staying within shouting distance of R.J. depressed and angered her. Seth signed with the army the day after graduation. Georgia picked up and left for Atlanta after hers. Savannah expected a brighter future anywhere but Augusta. And no one, not even Roy, would stop her. So she moved to Atlanta to enroll in the police academy, much to Roy's surprise. She suspected he doubted her abilities to be a cop. When they met again several years back, he discovered she was a detective and she discovered he was married. He went home impressed, she went home depressed.

Roy stepped past her and glanced around the living room, "Wow. Pretty much the same after all these years except somebody's been camping in the living room."

"Mostly Daddy. Normally it looks worse but Georgia cleaned the place recently. You're seeing it in a modestly disheveled state." She offered him a seat on the couch, "The kitchen is deplorable so we'll have to eat in here." Savannah scooped up the blankets and pillow she'd used to make room for them to sit.

Roy watched her dump the mass into a nearby wingback chair, "Why are you sleeping on the couch?"

"Easier. Trudging up those stairs again today would be the death of me, guaranteed." After placing the cell phone on the coffee table, she settled in next to him, ensuring to maintain a respectable space between them.

Roy, on the other hand, slid closer and put his arm around her shoulders. When she gave him a tentative look, he pretended not to notice but tilted her chin to the side, "He didn't nail you so hard looks like. Not like he could have."

"I'm thankful. Hate to go back to work with a dinged up jaw."

The mention of her job drew his attention to her badge and gun on the coffee table. She'd stacked her jacket and purse together, leaving the gun, badge and cell phone within easy reach. On the side sat an open Coke and Yoo-Hoo. He reached forward and took the badge in his large hand to study it, "I'd have never guessed you for cop material when we were in school. Thought maybe you'd follow in your mother's footsteps."

His suggestion made her laugh, "A beauty queen? Never. Georgia inherited the grace and looks from Mama." She noted Roy's silence and as she looked to him she felt the gentle stroke of his knuckles on her arm.

Roy nudged her closer, "You're plenty graceful and a knockout to boot. You're also approachable. You've done real well for yourself,

Kitten. I'm proud for you."

Savannah's blush engulfed not only her face and neck but heated everything south until she feared spontaneous human combustion. She'd forgotten the nickname he'd pinned on her in grade school. He'd done so because her brother called her Tiger and Roy insisted she was a kitten to him.

When he returned the badge back to the table, he noticed her rosy cheeks, "Nice to know I can still make you blush." He enticed her so close she laid a hand on his leg to prevent him from pulling her into his lap. Roy, it seemed, interpreted the move as eagerly receptive, not hesitantly preemptive, "God, I've missed you."

Whether it was the words, the painkillers or the feel of his embrace, Savannah didn't know. She only knew she relaxed a bit in his embrace. The warmth from him sank deep, his smell so tempting it brought back memories of curling in his embrace many times before. She let herself fall into the past, grateful Roy came to check on her, thankful he still cared.

As though reading her mind, the corners of Roy's mouth curled into a tiny smile as he leaned in and kissed her.

She tried to pull away but Roy cupped the back of her head, refusing the attempt. With more determination she pulled back, finally breaking the kiss, "Roy, don't."

Realization apparently dawned through his haze of passion, "I feel another male presence between us. What's his name?"

"Ennis," was all she said.

Roy lifted her left hand to his vision in a hasty manner, as though he'd never thought of her as betrothed to anyone. That itself pricked her ego. He hadn't imagined her married or engaged at all. He stroked the knuckle of her ring finger with a mischievous sparkle in his green eyes, "He's not claimed you yet. Seems to me you're as free as I am."

Savannah stared at him, wordless. Oddly, his statement made no sense to her whatsoever. She *felt* claimed, ring or no ring. She wasn't about to break the trust between her and Ennis. Not for Roy, not for anyone.

His tone softened as he neared again, "There's nothing wrong with kissing. In fact, it feels pretty right to me."

The caress of his thumb on her finger now traveled to her wrist while he leaned in to kiss her palm. The rasp of his rough cheek gave her a shiver when he kissed it once more. She tried to free her hand from his grasp, "Roy, I can't do this. I told you I love Ennis."

"No," his deep voice corrected, "you never said you loved him."

His warm lips journeyed to the inside of her wrist, causing her to withdraw her hand more forcefully, "Well, I do so stop."

"You love *me,*" was the firm reply.

His tone set off alarms inside her but before she reacted his large hands braced her shoulders and shoved her flat against the cushions, his weight settling atop her.

"Roy, don't," she said, the fear in her voice evident. She bit back a cry as Roy squeezed her breast like he tried to crush a beer can. "Stop it," she warned in a stronger voice. Her fight against him proved pitifully ineffective with strength and weight favoring him. "You love *me,*" he insisted. "You said so."

"That was years ago now get off of me!" Savannah realized reasoning with him wasted time and energy so she focused the latter on wriggling beneath him for leverage. Instead she managed to lose more ground in their battle. He wedged his knees between hers then burrowed to widen her legs, his arousal nestled against her lower belly.

For the first time since knowing Roy Carlson, Savannah truly feared for her safety, "Get off of me right now or else."

Her eyes welled with tears at the pressure on her breast and at the disappointment of her friend's motives. She thought of all people Roy would be genuine with his intentions: to have dinner and relive old times – the non-sexual ones. Even in high school his size belied his handling of her. He was a master of gentle, not a brute.

She hated hurting him but he asked for it. Ignoring her pleas to stop only upped the scale of her anger. Savannah pushed her left foot deep into the cushions, forcing it beneath his leg. Amid his fervor he clearly didn't notice or care – until he felt her knee snuggled against his crotch.

Savannah felt him stiffen as she applied pressure to his engorged genitals, "One last warning. Ignore it and you're on the floor in more pain than I am."

Roy fell deathly still. His eyes instantly centered on her narrowed blue ones. The words finally penetrated his passion-laden brain until his grasp released her wrist and his other hand withdrew from her blouse, "I guess you were serious."

"Very serious." She waited for him to remove himself from atop her before bolting to an upright position. Savannah put a good amount of distance between them before allowing herself to react to the pain in her breast. A few choice expletives fell from her lips as she cradled it then, "Don't you ever do that again. I mean, for God's sake, what's wrong with you? You've never acted like that."

Roy's vision swept down then back up her body with a rapacious hunger. The only sound in the room was his awkward breathing. Savannah allowed herself only a brief glance southward to his crotch. The unmistakable bulge outlined his arousal, giving her pause. Maybe she *should* take the drive home that night. She felt wide awake even with the two painkillers and seeing Roy in such a sexual frenzy didn't instill comfort. Now that she'd basically threatened him off of her, he probably wouldn't take kindly to the rejection. No man did. She'd said "no" to him in the past and he'd taken it well. But, as life repeatedly taught, years passed, people changed and Roy Carlson wasn't a happy man right at that moment.

He noticed her fleeting glimpse of his nether region and adjusted himself, grimacing as he did so. "It's Finus, isn't it?"

"Ennis," was the stern correction. "I love *Ennis*, in case you didn't hear me before." She pointed to the door, "Roy, you'd better leave. I'm not in the mood to fight anymore people today. Two's enough."

He held his hands up in instant capitulation, "Let me stay. I'll behave, I swear."

Her head tilted sideways a degree, "I look that stupid to you? After what just happened? Are you out of your friggin' mind?"

A fountain of fast, nearly unrecognizable speech from him, "It won't happen again, I promise, just don't kick me out. Please don't make me go…"

Trying to catch all the words bursting from him equaled trying to catch twenty fastballs at once. She caught most of it but what caught her attention was his voice wavering at the end. Her mouth opened to reply when she witnessed further bizarre behavior from her former lover. Savannah watched his eyes, wide and tear-filled shift in the direction of the coffee table. Besides an artificial ivy, three objects remained on it. Her cell phone, badge and gun. Common sense warned her he had no need or want for the plant, phone or badge. Roy's two long strides confirmed Savannah's sixth sense, especially when he reached down for her holstered gun.

Her reaction time shocked them both. Her hand sped to the weapon faster than his, her grip firm and unrelenting as it wrapped around the gun. She didn't pick it up but would if forced to, "Don't be foolish. Back off and leave."

He withdrew his hand hastily and as instructed, backed off a step, "I was going to hand it to you, honest. My point was, if you feel safer with it, keep it close. But don't kick me out tonight."
She heard the emotion in his voice except somehow she remained unmoved. "First you try to maul me then you race for my gun then you want to stay? What, to finish the job? My mama didn't raise a turnip." She again pointed to the door, "Go home, take a cold shower and screw your head on right. Both of 'em."

Roy's shoulders slumped in defeat. He ambled to the door with another apology, "I wish you'd reconsider."

"And I wish you'd shown better judgment." She followed him and before closing the door behind him she said, "Good-bye, Roy."

3

It was a nettling feeling and one she wasn't accustomed to. Savannah sensed someone watched her. Even ascending from deep slumber the sensation intensified instead of waning. Her hip and leg hurt too for some unknown reason. Her brain too happily reminded her of R.J.'s stunt but drew a blank on her lower half's calamity. It really began to ache the more consciousness crept in. Helping that along, a noise in the room brought her eyes wide open to see Georgia standing behind the couch, her arms crossed. Her Rita Hayworth features sported a disgruntled expression, an almost furious one. The color of her cheeks practically matched the radiant purple of her sweater. If she hadn't been hurting, Savannah might have laughed. Georgia's "mad" surpassed comical.

Holding off on divulging any sign of humor, Savannah blinked to clear her vision because her sister wasn't alone. Tilting back, she caught sight of Ennis standing three paces behind Georgia. He'd dressed more formally than normal and if he hadn't resembled a whipped puppy, he'd have been sexy as hell in the double pleated khaki pants and heather crew neck sweater he wore. It was his face that soured the fantasy. His best poker face neglected to hide the obvious hurt he felt. But hurt over what? It seemed she'd awakened in some parallel universe that sleeping made pains appear and waking pissed everyone off, "What are you two doing here?"

"Funny," Georgia griped in response, "but we could ask *you two* the same question."

Thoroughly confused and not one bit happy about it, Savannah rose from her reclining state. She found it rather difficult since something pinned her in the position. Glancing down, she saw the top of Roy's head staring back, the weight of his head pressed like a weight into her stomach. Confusion ruled her slumberous brain. Hadn't she kicked him out the night before? Yes, she was sure of it. But how did he find his way back inside the house? She locked the door...didn't she? She thought so. However with the strong painkillers she took, God only knew if she locked it or even closed it adequately.

Looking at Roy now, lying beside – and slightly atop – her on the large sofa and covered with a blanket, fear commandeered the confusion. From Georgia's and Ennis's angle, it appeared she'd had a late night tryst. Savannah swallowed hard with the realization of how it looked to them. Especially Ennis. In case she missed the fact, Georgia sternly reinforced it with a whisper, "What the hell are you doing? Do you know how this looks to Ennis?"

"No," Savannah bit back, "tell me." She wrestled with Roy's weight, trying to wake him up and at the very least remove the visual sting for Ennis. "Roy, get up."

Roy took a deep breath then moaned. *Well, that didn't help the situation at all*, Savannah lamented inwardly. "Roy, dammit, get up."

Clearly unaware of their sudden guests, his head lifted and he smiled an unhurried, dreamy smile at her, "Hi, gorgeous. That was some night, wasn't it?"

Savannah gave up, falling back to the couch with a sigh. *Kill me now 'cause I can't stand the agony of Ennis's disappointment.* Fear rejected the idea of glancing at him. Every word Roy uttered she could literally feel her partner boiling. She gave the most overused and least believed excuse in the book, "Nothing happened last night." She would pray her sister and partner would believe her but reality told her another long day had begun and would probably last much longer than the previous one.

Roy's brow dipped slightly, "We finally reconnected again. I never felt better about getting my divorce than last night."

"Roy, please shut up," she pleaded in a way he'd have been brain dead to misinterpret. Ennis continued boiling and from the corner of her eye, Savannah now observed Georgia percolating up a storm as well.

Wearing a wide grin, Roy bobbed his brow, "What, I'm just waiting for your sister to speak up."

Finally Georgia's angered appearance splintered momentarily, giving way to surprise. Roy propped on his elbows and glanced back, "I saw your reflection in the fireplace doors. How are you, Georgia?"

"I was worried about her since she never picked up her phone," she made her way around to the coffee table. Picking up Savannah's cell phone, she gave it a hard look, "No wonder. It's turned off. You have three messages from me and four from Ennis."

"Sorry. Roy surprised me last night." She frowned at the judging glare Georgia flung at her, "He brought pizza and Yoo-Hoos and the last I saw, he left before I went to bed *alone*. We only had dinner together. That's it."

"What can I say? She sold out cheap," Roy chirped while handily ignoring the reference to sleeping alone. He flinched good-naturedly when Savannah grasped a fistful of hair and directed his attention to her.

Trying to instill the gravity of the situation without thoroughly hurting his feelings, she stated, "You're killing me here. I'm past tarred and feathered – now they're gonna shoot me too. Ennis carries a gun, you know." She wriggled beneath him, "Please get up."

"Don't squirm, babe. There are consequences to that action and we don't want to add fuel to that fire." He planted his hands on either side of her, effectively revealing the barrier of blankets between them as he swung to a sitting position. Standing up, he allowed his blanket to fall to the floor, which effectively threw Georgia into a tizzy. She gasped and whirled her back to him.

Witnessing her sister's show, Savannah clenched her teeth, "Miss Modesty, he's fully clothed as am I." She reluctantly grasped Roy's offered hand and spoke as he lifted her to her feet, "Nothing happened between us. Just dinner."

"Much as it wounds my ego, it's true," Roy concurred. "I tried my best moves and she kept me at bay. Again."

"Again?" Ennis finally spoke, making Roy wheel to see him. Her ex-boyfriend pretended to be surprised at the presence of another man. She wasn't entirely sure if Roy was playing anymore. Maybe he did want to make trouble for her and break her and Ennis apart. In an attempt to diffuse further inflammation of the situation, Savannah quickly introduced the two – Ennis as "her partner" and Roy as "her childhood friend."

Not content to leave the introductions as is, Mr. Carlson threw in his two cents and answered Ennis, "Take it from me. She's harder to snag than a greased pig."

"Thanks for the compliment," Savannah shot back with sheer irritation. "Can you shut u –"

"Anytime, Kitten," Roy continued. "Yeah, once upon a time she and I were nearly married."

Savannah choked out loud. Where she found anything but frustration to choke on, she didn't know. She did quickly realize no one felt compelled to render aid in her time of need. After a short barrage of coughing, she gathered herself and wiped the growing tears from her eyes. Then she leveled a frown from hell on Roy. It wasn't the best time to mention their near-marriage. They'd just been found in a compromising position and no one believed a word she said. Ennis still looked injured to the bone by finding them that way and Georgia was being a good little ally by stilling her with a critical glare.

The reference to marriage certainly stimulated Ennis's attention better than an owl tracking a mouse, "Married?" He then, of course, looked to Savannah for an answer she knew she should give, but didn't. Roy would make stew out of it anyway.

Georgia added, "Did Roy call you 'Kitten'? That's not a friend's name. That's –"

"Roy," Savannah virtually skewered him with his name, "tell them the truth. The real truth – not that shit that'll get me lynched."

He extended his hand to Ennis, "Truth is, if you're not Ennis then she's slipping around behind your back with someone with that name."

Unable to restrain herself any longer, Savannah hurled a pillow at Roy, smacking him across the back, "You've always been impossible." She stole a peek at Ennis's face. Still pissed, still confused, still ready to bite nails. But she saw his hand ease out and shake Roy's, his only words being, "Ennis Rutherford, Savannah's partner."

"Ah, there's that word again. Partner. She never expounded on the exact meaning of your relationship." Another pillow, this one thrown significantly harder than the last, bounced off Roy's wide shoulders. He rethought his statement, "Well, maybe she did say you were involved, after all."

Savannah grumbled as she straightened the blankets. Wondering why the hell Georgia not only entertained the idea of bringing Ennis along but also acted on that idea. She voiced her question as her sister neared, "Why the hell did you bring him here?"

Georgia's steel exterior showed no fissures or weakening in any respect, "Possibly because he was worried out of his mind about you." She turned to spy Roy still gigging Ennis. She muttered under her breath, "Why, I don't know. Looks like you had your hands full all night. Or Roy did."

Savannah bolted upright to square off with her sister. Her keen hearing caught every syllable Georgia spoke. It took every cell in her body not to react violently to the insinuation. When she ground her teeth, the pain from her jaw settled her temper slightly, "You really don't want to go a round with me, Georgia. Neither of us can afford it. I told you he left and I'm telling the truth." She noticed Georgia's attention drawn to the men. Savannah watched as they wandered toward the kitchen. Both girls knew the condition of the room and were mortified by the chaos and grimy condition. As if on cue, both girls preached in unison, "Stay out of there."

The men stopped in their tracks, taking time to give them a questioning glance. Savannah hitched her thumb toward the door, "Go outside if you two want to talk."

Bowled over at the declaration, Roy mentioned, "But it's downright freezing out there."

Savannah smiled sweetly with a touch of frustration, "Then it will be a brief conversation. There's not that much to talk about."

Roy volleyed the same smile back, "I see you haven't changed either." He returned to her partner, easing the tension in his expression, "Savannah's afraid I'll tell all her secrets. Like the fact I was her first −"

"Roy, for God's sake," Savannah sincerely implored. One glimpse at her sister revealed the true depth of refuse she stood in − and it was rising fast. Georgia couldn't be that naïve, she thought. As long as she and Roy were together in high school *something* was bound to happen between them back then. Neither had exactly concealed their attraction to each other. It wasn't her best decision to sleep with him back then but, by God, she wasn't doing penance over it now…

"Her first kiss," Roy blurted in the form of a question while locking vision with her. He shrugged innocently at her like "what did you expect me to say".

She battered him with a narrow gaze, "Stop educating Ennis on our past." She clipped her badge to her belt then slipped the gun in her holster, "Or else."

He watched the gun slide leisurely into the holster, as if she might actually follow through. Evidently he detected the gravity of her mood, "Yes, ma'am." Roy pointed at Ennis with a wink, "You've got yourself a prize there, Detective. Don't let her get away like I did." He rounded the couch for his jacket then while passing Savannah, slid his arm around her waist and brought her in for a brief kiss, "See ya, Kitten. Let's not wait so long to meet again, 'kay?" His voice lowered to a whisper, "You can bring Mr. Chatty with you if it'll make him feel better."

Forcing a smile, Savannah softly punched his gut, "If you've screwed me and Ennis up, I'll come for you and not in a good way. By the way, how'd you get back in?"

Roy leaned in to murmur, "You forgot how resourceful I am." He paused then, "Actually the door didn't catch when you shut it. Since you looked so tired, I thought I'd be your guard dog for the night."

"Thanks. Now I can share the dog house with you because my sister is mad enough to blast me to the moon. Ennis will probably light the fuse for her too."

Roy gauged Ennis's expression and shrugged, "I don't think he's pissed at you so much. I think it's me he's ready to skin."

Savannah wasn't a genius but her IQ certainly surpassed the intelligence of dirt. Ennis was pissed off at her and from the scene he and

Georgia walked into, he had every right to be.

She thanked Roy for dinner and waved him off as he left. The instant she turned around, she faced the two most confused and somewhat riled features of Georgia and Ennis. "Oh, come on. You don't honestly think I slept with him, do you?"

Georgia declined to answer but shifted her green eyes toward Ennis. He, in turn, placed his hands on his hips and sighed, "My only question is, how in hell did you not feel him slither in with you?"

Fine. Defending her honor wasn't in her plan that day but if proof was in order, so be it. She stomped back to the coffee table, rummaged her purse and withdrew the bottle of painkillers, "I took a couple and I zoned out but not before asking him to leave and he did. He said the door wasn't latched so he came back inside because I looked tired. He wanted to make sure I was okay. After yesterday, the last thing I felt like doing was the horizontal mambo, especially with an old flame." She shoved the pills back in the purse and plopped down on the couch, "Thanks for the trust." Her heart hurt now, damn it, and that made her angrier. If it wasn't one thing aching, it was another. She was so pissed off, she wanted to cry. Why the intense anger boiled up so violently stumped her. She'd never cared what anyone thought of how she lived her life. Why now? Why did it matter that Ennis believe her? Good God, she verged on rage *and* tears and making sense out of it all was beyond her.

Taking an assessment of herself in the fireplace doors, she admitted she looked like a stubborn brat with her arms crossed and eyes watering with tears. And she didn't care. Only when she glimpsed

Ennis's image in the fireplace did it honestly matter. He gradually ambled behind her, his large hands still clamped to his hips. Well, the moment of truth. She expected either a pat on the shoulders or complete strangulation.

A gentle touch on her shoulders stiffened her momentarily then eased as Ennis kneaded the muscles. She heard the rattle of dishes in the kitchen telling her Georgia busied herself cleaning the house for the umpteenth time. Good. Let Nosy Rosie clean up a mess for once, instead of making one. Savannah did a fine job of immersing herself in hot water, she didn't need her sister joining in.

Ennis's soft touch dug firmly, not hard or roughly. It still failed to stop the nagging weepy sensation inside. She *wanted* Ennis to trust her, wanted him to wrap her in his embrace – hell, *he* was who she wanted last night, not Roy. She sniffed back most of the tears but one managed to escape and roll down her cheek. Angrily, she wiped it away. Crying made her weak and she hated weakness in herself.

As though Ennis read her mind, his fingers continued their movement over her shoulders then he bent down and placed a gentle kiss at her temple, "I'll agree that walking in here today took the breath out of me," he began. "But once he started yammering, I realized I needed hip boots. He's jealous and I know it."

The urge to cry a river bubbled dangerously near the surface. In his words she detected hope. Maybe he was beginning to believe her, "Ennis, I swear nothing happened but dinner. I didn't even invite him, he just showed up."

He rounded the couch and extended his hand to her. Savannah

stared at it a moment then clasped her hand in his. Without any effort on her part, Ennis brought her to a standing position and cinched his arm around her waist.

She continued her campaign, "I went to sleep on the couch alone and –" Ennis cut her account short by diving in for a kiss. A kiss that she felt all the way to her toes. A kiss that dried her tears and made everything okay again.

4

The girls spent an hour tidying up the house and washing dishes. An hour well spent yet hard to see a marked difference. Without dedicating weeks to thorough cleaning, the house stood on the liberal edge of adequate. At least, Georgia lamented, the kitchen was tidy and the bathroom sanitary again.

Once finished, they decided a visit to R.J. was in order. A decision made by Georgia with a generous amount of backpedaling and faltering on Savannah's part. Nothing like an older sister to guilt a person, she grumbled. The most enthusiasm she mustered equated to obligatory resignation. After thinking on it, the guilt melted with anger at R.J.'s tirade he threw at her. That's when she informed Georgia in a tone the sister could not misunderstand that she'd drop by to thank Bobby for all his help and nothing more.

Georgia, on the other hand, intended to spend a while with R.J.. Talking about what, Savannah never got an answer and she really didn't give a rat's ass. So long as Bobby still had R.J. caged, that's all she wanted while she was present.

Ennis just wanted to forget yesterday happened. He rode with his partner who drove in brooding silence, taking roads completely foreign to him, making turns at a reasonable speed and traveled the labyrinth of Augusta, Georgia in such a manner as to totally confuse him. He only knew his heart went out to Savannah. The other two siblings basically dumped R.J. in her lap, saying she was the only one who managed to control him. Ennis wanted to hit Seth and shake sense into Georgia. Besides being unfair, leaving R.J. to his youngest festered into a boil that evidently exploded the day before. He'd come with Georgia with two primary goals. To comfort Savannah and flail the shit out of R.J., whether physically or verbally. Savannah torpedoed the latter by insisting he behave himself – slap a hand over his mouth if necessary but do not incite R.J. in any respect. Against his best judgment and his raising, he agreed to keep quiet. She'd clearly had a difficult day before so pissing her off wouldn't exactly be prudent.

They walked in the Richmond County jail and all Ennis could do was follow. Georgia and Savannah evidently knew their way around so he let them lead. They meandered left down a hallway past the noise and commotion at the front desk. The longer they walked, the softer the noise up front faded but the resonance of off-key singing rose from somewhere in the back of the building. Just as they slowed, the door to an office opened. A tall, burly man in a gray uniform stepped out. Ennis rarely saw this size man outside the Nebraska football team. Thick, powerful arms and legs joined to a tree trunk body and his neck had vacated the premises probably around adolescence. His face appeared friendly, minus the stress, and his copious brown hair had been cut

properly for the likes of the U.S. Marines. Ennis suspected few people
tussled or argued with him.

The man recognized the girls because his arms opened wide for
both upon spotting them, a giant grin split his once serious face. He
managed a big bear hug for both Savannah and Georgia at once, one arm
curling around each and squeezing. Ennis decided to stand back until
summoned.

It didn't take long. "Bobby, this is my partner, Ennis
Rutherford. Ennis, this is my cousin Bobby Prince."

Holy shit, he thought. *They're related.* How could a Redwood
tree be kin to the delectable slice of heaven he slept with at night? Had to
be a rogue gene... Shaking the notion from his brain, Ennis thrust his
hand out and the two exchanging their "glad to meet you" greetings.
Bobby slanted him a look, "So you're the guy I keep hearing about.
Why, I've never heard Vanna go on about a fella like she does you."

Ennis expected a blustering, semi-stammering rebuttal from
Savannah, denying any feelings except related to work. What he got was
a blush and the sweetest words he'd heard from her lips short of "I love
you". She linked her arm through his, smiled and replied, "He is pretty
fantastic. I think I'll keep him."

Ennis accidentally allowed his weight to settle more in her
direction. Not even the irritating singing in the background registered.
His knees suddenly felt wobbly and weak from her words. Savannah
noticed the shift in his stance and Ennis hurried to right himself, her
declaration still making his brain spin. That, in his mind, was as good as
a solid commitment. He raced to second the emotion, "I *know* I'll keep

her."

Cutting his eyes to Savannah, Bobby smiled a knowing smile, teasing, "I knew it would eventually happen. Cupid shot an arrow where Vanna couldn't reach it." As if anticipating her reaction, he pulled back at the same time her hand swatted at his burly arm. She missed by a mile.

Bobby placed a large hand on her shoulder to bring her close. He whispered something to her, something too low for Ennis to discern. When she stepped back, her partner noticed the fierce blush on her cheeks, neck and forehead. Ennis swore the blush probably migrated south all the way to her toes. The grin she gifted him with was priceless despite the fact he had no clue what was said.

Hesitantly, Bobby veered the conversation toward their presence, "If you're here to see Uncle R.J., I'd turn around and go home. He isn't ready for company. He's been pretty vocal overnight." He rubbed at his forehead, giving Ennis the feeling he suffered the similar headache that Savannah always developed when dealing with her father. Bobby cringed and confirmed, "Had this blasted headache all night."

"Bet it started yesterday afternoon," Savannah stated quietly.

Bobby glanced at her, surprised. "Yeah. How'd you know?"

"Because it has a name. Robert Jefferson Prince. If you need anything stronger than aspirin, let me know."

Ennis's hand scrubbed his jaw, annoyed, "I'll need something if that idiot doesn't stop singing that damn song. He's wrecking me." For some reason all three of his companions turned their vision on him. Ennis never claimed to be a genius but it took a fool not to feel the drop in temperature around him.   To top it all, he suspected even a child could interpret the expressions.   Georgia seemed slightly offended. Savannah looked surprised.   Bobby appeared to be judging the other two's reactions.   Ennis unknowingly stepped in a pile of stink.   The challenge – a hefty one – was scraping it off.

Savannah saved him, thankfully, by addressing Bobby, "What do you mean vocal? About me or his miserable life in general?"

Their cousin glanced away.   All caught the weight of the silence, the significance of it.   Savannah took a deep breath and started forward, "Well, he has to face me someday."

Bobby blocked her path, "I'm not telling you how to deal with your father but I am making a strong suggestion.   Both you girls need to leave him alone right now. He's not himself."

Ennis touched her shoulder, bringing her attention to him, "Let's listen to him. We'll get our paperwork done on our case then call Bobby tomorrow. I'll bring you myself." He nodded to Georgia, "I'll bring you both, if you like."

The sisters exchanged concerned glances.   Georgia shrugged a bit, "I'm willing to wait if you are."

Savannah's blue eyes shifted downward, "What's he been saying?"

A pained frown flooded Bobby's face, turning it as red as hers had been moments ago, "Just trust me, Vanna. You don't need this, especially after yesterday. He's not himself because he's drying out. It's not pretty."

She seemed to consider his statement.   Still not making eye contact with anyone, she slowly stepped past them, "Drying out or not, his true feelings are gonna come out. At least this way he can't belt me."

Ennis's gut told him to stop her. Savannah was the hardest headed woman he'd ever matched wits against but she wasn't so closed down she wouldn't listen to reason. He'd learned that repeated proposals or suggestions finally penetrated her stubborn brain. When it came to family, no one's head screwed on tight enough. Everyone wanted acceptance, especially with their parents. Savannah obviously worked overtime for R.J.'s and he held it just out of reach – or withdrew it during convenient times.

Contrary to his instinct, he followed behind her instead of halting her journey. Georgia and Bobby fell in behind him, evidently resigned to the situation as well. Ennis noticed she traveled the halls by memory until stopping short at a doorway. The boisterously awful singing took center stage now, revealing the fact the lousy singer stood only around the corner.

A preliminary glance into the room told Ennis this was the jail area. A deputy sat behind a desk, his weary features showing signs of stress due to the wailing in one of the cells. Upon sight of visitors the deputy shot rod straight in his chair with an attempt to show a pleasant smile, "What can I do for you folks?"

Savannah didn't answer directly. Instead, Bobby weaved his way to the front, "Wes, they're here to see R.J. Prince."

Wes heaved a grateful sigh while reaching in a desk drawer, "I'll draw up the release papers."

"No," Bobby corrected. "They're here to *see* him, not bail him."

Ennis saw the stress lines trench deep into Wes's face again, defeat slumping his shoulders while the singer wound up for another chorus of the old Southern song, "Black is the Color of My True Love's Hair".

"I love my love and well she knows," the voice wailed, "I love the ground whereon she goes, and how I wish the day would come, when she and I can be as one, black is the color of my true love's hair."

They rounded the corner of the jail area. Ennis instantly discovered why Georgia wanted to smack him moments earlier. He'd called their father an idiot. R.J. was the person singing at the top of his lungs and doing a horrible job of it. If Ennis could have crawled in a hole he would've but upon second glance of Savannah's face, he decided any degree of embarrassment was worth staying by her side. The look on her beautiful face broke his heart. From his distance, he still saw tears welling in her eyes, still saw the little girl looking to her daddy for love and acceptance. What she got was entirely different once R.J. locked vision with her. The singing mercifully ceased but what replaced it served only as fuel for her tears.

His haggard face showed signs of a week's length of whiskers, no sleep and plenty of venom. "What the hell are you doing here?" her father demanded. "I don't recollect asking you to come."

"I wanted to see how you were doing," was the brief reply. Ennis heard the tremble in her voice even if no one else did. But he knew Savannah. She would die before falling apart in front of a crowd of people. She'd suck it up, walk out with tightly restrained dignity then cry her heart out later when she was alone.

"Why? You don't care. You let Bobby cart me off like trash yesterday. Best get out of here before I do. You won't be so full of yourself when I'm finished with ya." His dark, weary eyes settled on Georgia and his attitude brightened considerably, "There's my girl. See, here's the one I can count on. Georgia'll get me out of this godforsaken cage."

With arms crossed, Georgia shook her head hopelessly, "Daddy, don't talk to Savannah like that. She's only trying to help you. We all are."

He rose to his feet. Despite standing a good ten feet from R.J., Ennis felt Savannah step back, nearly flush against him. He settled a hand to her shoulder for reassurance. He wasn't sure but thought he detected a faint shivering in her, telegraphing the magnitude of fear of her father. Strangely, R.J. appeared totally competent and fully aware of his surroundings and most importantly his words. The "drying out" symptoms Bobby warned of were not obvious to him in any respect.

R.J.'s huge hands grasped the cell bars, "Her kinda help'll only put me in the ground." He looked to Savannah again, his tone low and threatening, "Tell you one thing. My kids just shrank to two. I got a son and a daughter and her name is Georgia." He stood only a moment as if waiting for a knee-jerk response from her. When it didn't immediately come, he inflamed the situation further by spitting on the floor, "You're dead to me."

"Daddy," Georgia cried, stunned. "You don't mean that..."

While the older sister's disbelief carried over into an admirable attempt to scold R.J. while salving Savannah's feelings, her words barely registered with Ennis. He'd busied himself with biting his tongue. He promised – a promise now he wished he'd never made – to keep his mouth shut around their father. Savannah stood, boiling with rage and trembling with tears. Emotions clashed with such purity and strength, Ennis wasn't sure how she'd react to R.J.'s tirade. For the moment she looked completely stricken by his comments. Georgia and R.J. bickered back and forth but Savannah appeared shut down to it.

She swallowed hard as Ennis squeezed her shoulder. He wanted to grab her into a hug but felt her body stiffening against any further attacks and, unfortunately, any support he might try to provide. It was self-preservation, he knew, bracing herself to either respond to R.J. or walk out as dignified as possible. She sniffed back the tears once then rotated on her heel and proceeded past everyone, including Ennis, toward the front door.

Ennis and all the others followed behind like baby ducks trailing their mother. The halls fell silent as the small group wound their way to the entrance. If Savannah noticed, she overlooked it while keeping her vision straight ahead, her strides long and steady.

Once at her car, the first sign of temper flared as she threw open the Camaro's heavy door. The barriers she'd erected in front of R.J. crumbled quickly. Ennis saw her hands shaking to the same tempo as her bottom lip. He reached for her before she slid into the driver's seat, "I'm driving."

He hadn't intended to start his own firestorm with her but judging from the set in her jaw, he stood precariously close to doing just that. He plucked the keys from her trembling hand, "I'll drive like Grandma on Sunday morning but you're not getting behind that wheel."

She tilted her head back to look directly at him, "I'm fine. I've been through this with him before."

Ennis felt his temper swell in his gut. It churned sourly inside him, encouraging him to go back inside and belt R.J., "He's said things like that to you?"

Savannah remained quiet. She lowered her vision telling Ennis that no, R.J. hadn't ever been that brutal to her. He sensed her control splintering then, as the lagging group caught up, her mood shored up and solidified. Bobby was the first to speak, "Honey, he's drying out. He's not himself and he wants to blame someone for how he's feeling. Give him a while and he'll be okay."

Ennis watched tears swell in her eyes. These weren't going away. They grew at a speed that ignored any attempt to restrain them, "Well," she told Bobby, "thanks for not saying 'I told you so.' I can't take being disowned and being labeled a fool in the same day."

"Hon," Georgia offered softly, "Bobby's right. Daddy didn't mean it. In a day or two he won't even remember what he said."

Savannah hurriedly wiped away falling tears, her voice showing first signs of the pent-up emotion, "But I will."

5

Ennis drove home at the solid objection of Savannah. After a good twenty minute discussion, she capitulated and slid into the passenger seat of the Camaro – with the promise from him not to drive like the devil was after him.

Abiding by his vow, Ennis drove sanely if not painfully slowly at times. She wanted to get home in a decent amount of time. He pulled up to her house fifteen minutes short of three hours.

Savannah's residence wasn't anything spectacular. The modest two bedroom standalone house was really part of a "neighborhood" of such small homes. So small she insisted on calling it an apartment. The rent she paid covered maintenance fees for lawn mowing and hedge trimming and the meager manicuring the small front and back yards required.

The exterior of the place looked quaint, even to her. Mostly brick with trim painted in eggshell, it sported shudders on the windows and a genuine cobblestone walkway that drove her positively batty when her feet hurt. The inside wasn't as picture perfect but it served her purpose well.

Everything measured on the verge of Lilliputian for two people but she and Ennis managed. She decorated, not as Georgia did in paintings of impressionist glory, but with family photos and cottage paintings by Carl Valente. Space limited her on the amount of furniture so she bought pretty but functional pieces when on sale. Her biggest splurges were the burgundy recliner in the living room and the oak bedroom ensemble, all bought from Ashley – and not on sale. The single biggest drawback to the bedroom suite was that between the queen size bed, nightstand and dresser, everything swallowed the majority of the bedroom. She always valued a good night's sleep and the money she paid for the bed practically guaranteed it. If it weren't for her job, she'd have dropped off asleep every time her head hit the pillow. Tonight though, she feared, would be another sleepless night.

She hung her jacket by the door and Ennis followed suit. She wandered to the bedroom to put her purse on the dresser. Next to it sat a Rubik's Cube, Rubik's Twist and several other puzzles similar to them. They'd never been solved but it relieved tension for her to play with them anyway.

She noticed Ennis peeled off from the living room toward the kitchen while she angled to the bedroom. Shucking her slacks, she caught site of herself in the dresser mirror. She looked like utter shit. The sadness in her face didn't measure up to the pain in her heart. It did, however, manage to convey how devastated she felt. Tears welled in her eyes causing her to bury her face in her hands. The stress of the last day built up to stellar proportions and had discovered a crack in her carefully displayed features. The agony breached her armor, sending her into a crying jag to beat all crying jags. She fell to the bed, sitting and crying uncontrollably. A few moments later, she heard Ennis express his most sympathetic, "Oh, sugar." Then only a second passed when his arms enfolded her, bringing her against his chest while she cried.

On the job Ennis was hard as stone – except with her – and when they were alone, he was Prince Charming. He worked ceaselessly to please her, comfort her and make her smile. When he held her, she felt his sincere desire, his love. And now, in a heap of tears she hadn't shown but once to him, she felt his concern and affection for her.

His voice was soft, "Cry it all out, sweetheart. I'm not going anywhere."

She did and he didn't. Ennis held her until she cried herself dry, then he leaned forward and grabbed something from the dresser. Savannah glanced up, seeing a double fudge Yoo-Hoo staring back at her.

Ennis offered it to her, "I brought two just in case you needed a bracer."

Savannah gave him a half smile and took a sip of the drink. She thanked him to which he replied, "I'm not done. After I get you naked, I'm drawing up a hot bath for you."

Much as it sounded like heaven to her, she shook her head, "I'm just gonna go to bed. Consciousness isn't a good thing right now. Lets me think." Her voice broke over on the last sentence and a tear rolled down her cheek.

Ennis's hand settled at her bare knee, his other at the small of her back. His fingertips pressed into the tense muscles of her back and moved in tiny circles, "Precisely why I'm staying. I can keep your mind busy thinking about a hot bath."

Savannah wiped the stray tear away, "I'm not much fun tonight. I'll just end up crying again."

The hand on her knee lifted and drew her face around to his, "Hey, I'm in this relationship for the good, not-so-good and the downright awful. You're stuck with me. We'll just kick off our clothes and crawl into bed if you want."

"Sounds like –" The cell phone rang, cutting off her agreement. Tonight she wished Elvis would shut up. She was all for "A Little Less Conversation" but the action would have to wait. "Sounds like we'd better hold off on any plans," she finished, resigned. Assuming it was her father calling to bitch her out again, she tentatively answered it, "Prince,"

"Aunt Savannah?" the little voice questioned. "What's wrong with your voice?"

It was Lindsey. Not as bad as her father calling but now she'd have to whip up a quick explanation for her plugged up nose, "Hi, honey. I've been sneezing like you do when you're around certain flowers. What did you need?"

"I need a gerbil."

"A gerbil?" *Oh, if life was that simple now*, she mused darkly. "Don't you have one?"

Lindsey's joy evaporated only to mope, "Belle died. Didn't Daddy tell you?"

"No, honey, 'fraid not. I'm sorry she died. I didn't know anything was wr –"

"That's okay," the little girl brightened like a flash, "Mama and

Daddy said you can get me another one."

At this point Savannah heard a commotion in the background. It was a combination of Seth and Leah's voices clamoring to be heard. Finally, Seth appeared on the phone, "Sorry, sis. We were hoping you could take her to find a gerbil but we'll send the money for it." His voice lowered, "At the rate they're dying, I might as well send enough for a dozen."

Savannah giggled a bit, "Sure, I'll take her. I'll even buy this one. Just don't let her get the notion of a horse or you'll go broke in a hurry."

"These hairballs are breaking us as it is. Hey, are you alright? You sound sick or something."

"Nah, I'm fine. Just a sneezing attack."

"U-huh," he didn't buy the excuse for a second but didn't let on, "well, stay away from whatever you're allergic to, read me?"

"Loud and clear, Major. Lemme talk to Lindsey right quick." There was a significant pause after Seth agreed to relinquish the phone. She heard him talking to his daughter in whispers and she strained to hear while Ennis's hand stroked her back lovingly. She hadn't realized his light, rhythmic caresses had calmed her considerably just the few moments she'd been on the phone.

Savannah heard her niece's attempt at covert whispering but discerned her "Okay, Daddy, I will," as clear as day. Then the girl's voice boomed loud and boundless into her aunt's ear, "Can we go tomorrow?"

Savannah cringed at the timing, "Uh, well, honey –"

"She'll be there, Lindsey," Ennis spoke over his partner's shoulder. "What time?"

Savannah turned to him with an unmistakable "what the hell are you doing – we've got work to do tomorrow" expression. Ennis merely pressed his fingertips into yet another tense muscle and massaged.

Blissfully unaware of the motions transpiring between her aunt and Ennis, Lindsey barreled on, "They open at eight. Can we go, Aunt Savannah? Please, please, *please*..."

"Of course we can go, sweetheart. I'll be there at eight and we can get your gerbil."

"Thank you, Aunt Savannah," she gushed as if Savannah had saved her from impending death. "You're the greatest." Savannah clicked off the phone, repeating the words without the enthusiasm, "I'm the greatest." Somehow she doubted her father would agree. She turned her attention to Ennis, "And you, partner, are stuck with paperwork while I scout the city for gerbils."

"I've managed paperwork before. I can even sign my name with my toes if need be." Ennis tenderly nuzzled her neck, "What all did the munchkin say?"

Savannah smiled quaintly while allowing him free reign on her flesh, "I'll just bet you know. This whole phone call smells of a setup. Did Seth call you or was it Georgia?" She winced slightly when he accidentally nipped her, his cover obviously blown. Ennis tilted away with a ring of astonishment, "You think I set you up?"

"No, I think my siblings did it but you had your hands in the mix."

He eyed her cautiously, however Savannah knew he couldn't read her that well yet. When called upon, she possessed a steel poker face, one that not even her sister could penetrate.

"Oh, hell," he finally sighed. "Georgia wanted to know when we'd get home tonight. She said Lindsey would be calling for something." He glanced at her, still uncertain, "You can't get mad at the kid. She's trying to help."

"Ennis," she cupped his cheek and answered with a soft smile, "I'm thankful for every one of you. Even the more wily ones of the brood."

6

After less than thirty minutes with Lindsey, Savannah decided the little girl was more effective medicine than Valium. Thoughts of her father rarely reared up thanks to the dilemma of gerbil-hunting. They dropped by the closest pet store to scour the gerbil stock which gave Savannah opportunity to observe her niece in action.

Lindsey inspected every rodent with meticulous care as if she were shopping for the perfect divan pattern. She held each one, petted them, spoke to them and held them to her ear. Savannah suspected the kid listened for a name. After three gerbils, Lindsey sighed, "I dunno. None of them answer to Cinderella."

The declaration, delivered with pure downtrodden sincerity, still brought a lifted brow from Savannah, "You're asking their names?"

A shrug followed a firm nod, "But none of them are her."

Times like this fueled Savannah's yearning to have a child. Their innocence and creativity knew no bounds. Plus, they were just fun to listen to. Guaranteed a genuine gem of a reply, Savannah inquired, "Well, who are they?"

Precisely pointing to each one Lindsey replied, "Sylvester,

Merryweather and Flower."

Savannah held a hand to her mouth in an attempt to hide her amusement. Instead, her expression displayed the same dire concern as the girl's, "Not a Cinderella among them." She bent down further, critically observing the other specimens. After a short time, she pointed to a white one with gray fluffy feet, "How about that one? She looks like she might be Cinderella."

Lindsey scooped up the small gerbil, spoke to it then listened. Her aunt waited patiently. Suddenly the girl's eyes grew wide, "Aunt Savannah, listen." She held the hairy creature to Savannah's ear. She felt the tickle of tiny whiskers as it nosed around her ear and she smiled, "Did she say Cinderella to you 'cause it sounded like it to me."

Lindsey drew the animal closer to her own ear again. A brief silence ensued then an exuberant, "It *is* Cinderella." She held the gerbil between her hands, not about to let her down, "Let's get Prince Charming too. I think he's the one over there."

Now Savannah's grin waned. Seth and Leah only approved one gerbil, not two. If she dragged in two, one male and female, her brother would hang her upside down by her toes and rightfully so. "Your mama and daddy only signed off for one gerbil. I'll need verbal and written authorization before I agree to this."

"Please, Aunt Savannah," she whined and nuzzled Cinderella closer.

Savannah shook her head. The sweet talk worked for an extra ice cream cone, not an extra creature that Seth didn't want in the first place.

Lindsey, sensing imminent defeat, changed tactics, "Call Daddy."

I may look stupid but I'm not, Savannah thought. "I need your mama's approval too, sweetheart." Just as she thought, her niece's lip puffed out – the sign of a wicked kid plan foiled by a quick thinking adult.

"But why?" Lindsey whined, "Daddy will say yes. Mama won't."

Savannah knelt down face to face with her, "Do you want me to continue coming over to see you and your brother?"

The girl snuggled the gerbil against her cheek, hoping to milk pity for all its worth. She nodded, her lower lip still two sizes larger than her upper one. Her brown eyes rounded, giving her a most forlorn, almost hopeless appearance.

A basset hound's got nothin' on this kid, Savannah thought then tried to explain frankly but gently, "Honey, if I bring home two of those instead of one, your parents will likely refuse me entry into the house ever again." She stared at the sad, sulking face until she capitulated and reached for her cell phone, "I'll call Seth."

Lindsey bounced up and down excitedly, thrilled beyond any words except, "Thank you, thank you, thank you."

Savannah really dreaded calling her brother about this. He hated animals in the house, especially the rodents his daughter found so adorable, "Careful of Cinderella, honey. And you're welcome *but* I'm calling your mother as well. If they agree to this, I'll buy Prince Charming and his cage."

"I'll just put 'em together."

The mere thought of it halted Savannah's fingers on the keypad, "Oh no, you don't. Those two aren't married, not even dating, so you're not housing them together until your parents say it's okay."

Lindsey giggled, "Aunt Savannah, you're funny. Gerbils don't date."

"These do. I'm not going to be responsible for a population explosion just because Prince Charming didn't have his own digs." She dialed Seth's self defense studio, praying he was busy or on break. Unfortunately he answered on the second ring. After uneasily clearing her throat, Savannah eased into the subject, "Lindsey found Cinderella. She's holding her right now."

"Good. Thanks for taking her, sis. She's really missed seeing you."

The statement struck her as odd but she didn't mention it, "You know I always enjoy spending time with the kids. Even when they want a little extra, like a second gerbil."

"What?" her brother's tone developed a thread of alarm. "Another hairball?"

"M-hmm. Cinderella needs her Prince Charming, you know that."

Savannah counted a solid five seconds before his hesitant reply, "Did you?"

"No. That's the reason for the phone call. I wasn't about to haul in a tribe of 'em and risk being excommunicated from the family." The last few words suddenly hit home like a knife in the back. Her father's words echoed in her brain even as Seth softly reassured, "Hey, you know that would never happen." Then he added, "We'd just pack up the extras and send them home with you. You and Ennis need a pet or twelve."

"Now you've gone to meddlin'. We're too busy to keep goldfish alive, much less rodents. So are you and Leah gonna skin me if I spring Prince Charming from his gloomy prison cell? I've already promised to provide his own condo."

"Just don't buy the one with mirrored ceilings and heart-shaped bed. We don't need hordes of 'em. It'd be different if you could make coats outta the things."

Savannah smiled down at Lindsey who proudly displayed Cinderella for her to see, "I'll dispense with passing that information on to your daughter. She's happier when *they* wear their coats." She stroked the gerbil to appease her niece, "So Leah's not gonna clip my wings either?"

"If she clips yours, she'll surgically remove mine for agreeing to this. Go ahead and get her the thing, I guess. Could you maybe slip a Princess Charming into Prince Charming's fur? Better to deal with two females than the alternative."

The question caused her to pause. "Uh," she whispered, "how do you sex these things?"

"Beats me. Just do what you can and it'll be fine. The things don't live that long anyway."

"Should I buy three?" she joked.

"Now you're talking grounds for divorce. Leah would have my ass if she saw that many rats running around."

7

It took a grand total of four hours and eighteen minutes to choose, purchase, and deliver the happy rodent couple to their new abode. Lindsey cooed to them and stroked them as all new mothers make over their babies. Surprisingly Leah wasn't home to receive the new occupants but Seth was. Savannah had the house key in hand when the door opened to receive them and his smiling face appeared around the door. Seth's features favored R.J. to the point of being a younger version of him. The girls took after Charlene but if Seth was any indication, all sons born to R.J. would have been his spitting image. As if he realized whose image stared back at her, Seth greeted her with a far too congenial, "Hey, sis. Come on in."

Erasing the shock from her features would take longer than normal. Seth was a great brother, but his personality couldn't be described as "chummy", even with his sisters. Today Seth was chummy and that put her on edge, "Hey," she replied uneasily. Immediately she swapped topics to something more comfortable, "Lindsey found Cinderella and Prince Charming. I also got a ladder for His Royal Highness. Apparently, gerbils love to play on ladders."

Lindsey proudly displayed the newest gerbil in his cage, "Prince Charming needs toilet paper, Daddy."

The declaration stunned Seth momentarily enough to look to his sister for an answer, "They're not that friggin' smart. What do they need toilet paper for if they don't—"

"She means the tube. They play in the toilet roll tubes. Glass jars, empty egg cartons, things like that."

Her brother forced a smile, "Will it keep them alive longer or hasten their demise if we gift them with these objects?"

Savannah shrugged as she and her niece entered the house, "Who knows? But if you have any questions, Butch at Animal Land will happily answer them."

"I'll make a note to call him."

"Her. Butch is a woman and she lives up to her name." Savannah loved to confuse her brother sometimes. At least it proved he had more expressions than his normal brooding one. Her cell phone rang, redirecting her attention. Staring at the number produced no hint of the caller. The name did though, and it produced a lengthy groan from her.

"Bad news?" Seth inquired.

"Roy Carlson. High school sweetheart turned pest." She answered her phone, "Hi Roy."

"Can you meet me at your house?" His voice sounded almost alarmed, "Like right now?"

His mood brought back memories of the night she ordered him off of her. His words ran together frenetically, so fast she wondered how his tongue kept up, "I'm not in Augusta, Roy. I'm –"

"No, your place here. I'm in Atlanta. I'm sitting in your driveway."

She caught the words "in Atlanta" and "in your driveway" as clear as crystal. Her expression darkened significantly, prompting Seth to frown and listen closer. She turned away from Lindsey who detected the sudden drop in room temperature. Savannah lowered her voice, "How did you find my address?"

"It wasn't from your sister, that's for sure. She's a piece of work when she's pissed off. Outright accused me of sabotaging you and your partner. I asked around the police department and some guy named Bailey coughed up your address. I told him our history together and he was more than helpful."

It figured. The desk sergeant liked her okay but still enjoyed ruffling her feathers once in a while. She'd made detective in record time, leaving him to toss sideways glances when she walked by. Lately they'd gotten along fine, she thought. Now she wasn't so sure. "I'm busy right now. I'm visiting my brother and niece."

"Listen, Kitten," Roy's voice not only careened into a panic state but lifted in volume as well, "this is a matter of life and death here. I swear I didn't track you down to monkey up your relationship with Finus."

"Ennis," she corrected calmly.

"Whatever. I need you right here, right now."

At this point, Savannah turned to face her brother. His concern plainly etched deep in his brow. Lindsey's vision swung between her father and aunt, unsure of the unfolding events. She snuggled Cinderella under her chin while gluing her wide eyes on her aunt. In an attempt to ease the worried posture of her niece, Savannah smiled at her. Lindsey stroked the gerbil but her attention never wavered. Seth's daughter was too much like him in that respect. Indeed, Seth was the hardest sell of all. He loomed close by, waiting. To pounce, it looked like. Hands perched on hips with a frown dark enough to scare off demons. Savannah took a deep breath, her words directed into the phone, "Tell me what's going on."

"Not on the phone," Roy responded with the same amount of determination.

"Roy, I had a really crappy day yesterday, crappier than you can imagine. I don't have the time or patience for this. What is the problem?" When her vision shifted to Seth, she saw it spread across his features like wildfire. The guilt of knowing R.J.'s tirade. Georgia told him everything their father said at the jail. It was written all over Seth's face.

Roy didn't help matters by raising his voice so both she and Seth heard every syllable falling from his lips, "I'll tell you what a crappy day is, Kitten. It's when the police try to frame you for murder. That trumps *your* crappiest day by a mile."

She broke visual contact with Seth to stare disbelievingly at her phone. If snakes crawled out of it or flowers grew from the antenna, she couldn't have been more stunned. Roy accused of murder? Sure, his mischievous nature provided enough ammunition to accuse him of a plethora of offenses but not murder. He didn't possess the qualities of a killer. But as the other night reminded, he was a different person than when they attended high school together. People changed over the years. She certainly had.

Seth pointed to the phone, "Sounds like you need to attend to this problem. Need some help?"

Savannah shook her head, "Calm down, Roy. I'm leaving now." She clicked off her phone to say goodbye to Lindsey and Seth when the phone rang again. *So help me if it's Roy again…* One glance revealed Ennis's name and she immediately calmed, "Hey,"

"Hey. Who were you on the phone with?"

She didn't feel comfortable telling him the truth. If Roy was telling the truth, involving Ennis wouldn't help the situation, "The pet store. We found Cinderella."

"Good," he replied then hesitated a moment. "Has the Augusta PD contacted you yet?"

The mere mention of it closed her eyes in defeat. Roy *was* telling the truth. Still, she hid the fact she'd spoken to him, "No, why?"

"They're looking for your friend Roy Carlson."

"And they immediately thought to contact me?"

"Well, they weren't exactly forthcoming with information. I don't know why they want to talk to you. Only thing I overheard was something about a murder investigation."

"Thanks, Ennis. I'll be on the lookout for them." She disconnected again and clipped the phone to her belt with abrupt resolve. One slow intake of breath later, Savannah turned her attention to Lindsey, "Sweetheart, I've got to go. Now I expect a full update on how

Cinderella's getting along with her prince. Remember what the lady at the pet store said. Leave them in their own cages because they probably won't like each other yet."

A spark of recognition lit the girl's face, "You mean like Daddy and Grandpa?"

Not knowing exactly how to answer, Savannah looked to Seth then back to Lindsey, "Sort of but not quite." She wrapped her arms around the girl, "Love you, sweetheart. And remember, call me."

Lindsey hugged her neck then whispered, "Be careful. That man sounded mad."

Just the words brought the insightful youngster tighter in her embrace, "I'll be careful, don't worry."

8

When she rounded the corner, the sight of Roy's brand new red Dodge pickup greeted her vision. Not just a glaring piece of mechanized ego, she thought, but a beacon to the Augusta Police that their suspect kept company with a cop – at her private residence. She could only imagine what they'd say if they stumbled onto the scene...

Upon approaching her driveway, she discovered parking in it was futile. The mammoth Dodge swallowed the thing whole. With its wide bed and dual rear wheels, Roy might as well have parked a city bus at her house. Parking at the street, she observed Roy sitting, his head propped in his hand against the driver's window as if catching a few winks before her arrival. She also observed residue of mud along the bottom of the truck and the cloudy scum covering the once shiny wheel covers. Roy needed to learn the fine art of washing his truck properly. A half-ass wiping down only did a disservice to the vehicle. That's why, Savannah grimly added, she never washed her Camaro. It usually received plenty of attention from the clouds when it rained.

She killed the engine and the instant she slammed the door closed, she witnessed Roy jerk awake like someone shot at him and barely missed in the effort. The closer she got, the more the truth unfolded. Roy hadn't been asleep, he'd been hunkered down in his truck, hiding. His wide-eyed deer-in-the-headlights stance hardly waned once he saw her. It only spurred him into action.

He shoved the truck door open, making Savannah hastily sidestep or get bashed. Roy began speaking before his feet hit the ground, "You gotta help me, Kitten."

She breezed past the unnerved hunk she once considered saying "I do" with and saw him throw wary glances up and down the street. In an attempt to refocus his attention, she waved him inside after opening the door, "Why do you need my help? You didn't kill anyone did you?"

Roy brushed past her, his face pinched in a frown but she barely saw it. She was too busy checking the street for detective's cars, mainly from Augusta. His tone, however, left no doubt, "You gotta be kidding. I'm the one who rescues injured dogs on the road."

Savannah heard his voice gradually grow nearer until he stood behind her, his hand on her waist, "I'm the one you came to when your father beat the hell out of you. Did I present myself as a threat to you then or the other night when we were alone?"

She chewed on that one. He wasn't threatening per se, however convincing him to take "no" for an answer proved harder than bending steel. Determined and horny he was. Potentially lethal he wasn't, at least not to her. She assumed her ability to arrest him weighed heavily in the equation.

Impatient for a reply, Roy's shaking hands turned her to face him. They rested on her shoulders while he resumed his plea, "Baby, I need your help like you needed mine years ago."

The sensation of his trembling hands, once so stable and strong, took a toll on her. His words took the air out of her. Roy never let her down, never shut her out when she needed him. He needed her now and it didn't feel right to ignore him in his time of need. "Tell me what's going on."

Overwhelmed with relief, Roy planted a quick kiss on her lips and thanked her. Savannah nodded and offered him a seat, "Calm down, Roy. Sit and I'll get you a drink." She stepped past him only to feel him grasp her arm, his voice still heavy with distress, "Forget the drink. Just listen. The cops think I killed this woman living on Walton Way."

The hair on the back of her neck stood at attention. She thought it odd since Walton Way was a basic main street in Augusta. It traveled for miles. "Where on Walton?"

Roy's thumb sawed back and forth across his bottom lip. His vision dropped from hers. She noticed his right leg fidgeted at the question. It refused to stay still.

"Roy," she prompted, now watching his teeth gnaw on his thumbnail.

"Two blocks down from you, okay? But I didn't do it."

She would have sat down but needed to tend to the window. They were living on borrowed time at this rate. The Augusta police were probably already headed to her house. "Who was she and how did you know her?" Savannah pointed to the sofa where he fell in the seat with a deep, exhausted sigh.

"I met her doing work on her house. We, uh," he glanced away to finish, "hooked up for about three months."

If the situation wasn't so serious Savannah might have laughed at his reticence. It didn't matter to her who he'd dated in the past but he shied from the subject as if she were his wife accusing him of an affair. "Who broke it off?"

"She did. Only because she found someone else." He'd added the last statement as balm to his wounded ego. No man voluntarily admitted to being dumped, unless their life or freedom depended on it. Still, there was no need to cut his legs off in the process.

"Do you know who?"

His teeth trimmed nervously at the thumbnail again as he shook his head, "Wouldn't tell me. Guess she was afraid I'd do something stupid."

"When was the last time you saw her?"

Roy's teeth worked double-time on the thumbnail and changed to his index finger. With the passing time, his demeanor steadily grew more anxious. She found out why when he answered, "Day she died. I went to see her."

If she broke up with him, why would he need to see her again? Savannah asked as much. Roy shrugged, "I wanted her back but she said no."

Knowing Roy's perseverance, she made an educated guess, "How often did you visit her after the split?"

"'Bout three times a week."

"So you didn't take the breakup very well," she stated as matter of factly as possible, much like at work.

Roy, though, took the gruffness personally, "'Bout as well as when you turned me down for marriage. I didn't dance naked in the streets but I didn't off you, did I? What is this, a trial before my arrest?"

Savannah rolled her eyes, "Take a breath, Roy. I'm trying to help and asking questions is part of it. Just explain how you reacted to the breakup."

A flash of shame screwed his mouth to the side, he hesitated then, "I got mad – but I didn't hurt her. I yelled and uh, sorta punched a hole in the wall."

Savannah's eyes bugged, "You what?"

"Okay, two holes." He winced at the disbelief in her expression and finally confessed, "Maybe three. Dammit, Savannah, stop lookin' at me like that."

She shook her head, aggravation replacing disbelief, "Besides attempting to understand male behavior, I'm trying to figure out why you need my help."

"We had pizza and drinks the other night, didn't we?"

Suddenly the grilling flip-flopped to designate him the interrogator thus putting her on the spot. Savannah did a double-take, "Yes, pepperoni pizza, Cokes and Yoo-Hoos."

"And I stayed the night with you, didn't I?" He frantically waved off her scowl, "Nothing happened between us but I was there all night, right? I mean, we woke up on the couch together." His voice lifted hopefully, "Hell, Georgia and Finus found us there, remember?"

Unfortunately, yes. The definition of joy wasn't reliving that morning. But Roy's behavior cast a blindingly clear light on the situation. "The murder happened the night we had pizza?"

"Yes, and I *need* you to verify I was with you that night."

She would except the painkillers she took that night rendered her basically dead. She could only truthfully confirm they'd seen each other and the still unnerving reality that they'd awakened together the next morning. To reinforce her displeasure of the latter, she reminded him that she'd sent him packing and he felt compelled to break in later that night. She all but explained that to him, finishing it with, "Technically you were trespassing, you know."

He waved off her annoyance which only increased, "After you broke in, did you happen to leave at any point during the night?"

His features lit up like Rockefeller Center at Christmas, "What the hell kind of question is that?"

"One I will be asked by the Augusta Police. 'Was Roy in your presence all night?'"

He plopped his hands on his hips, disgusted, "That's when you answer 'Yes, Detective Dumbass, he was.'"

"Were you?"

Roy's edginess returned full force. He paced again while his thumb worried his bottom lip. She watched him take four small steps left, turn, then make the return trip, over and over, "Roy," she urged.

"No, I went to the truck for a beer." His wide eyes met her narrowing ones, "But I came right back."

"How long were you gone?"

"Twenty minutes," he judged her suspicious expression then admitted, "thirty at the most."

"For a beer? What'd you do, drink it from an eyedropper?"

Roy now took to rubbing the back of his neck, "I went to Peabody's for a six pack. I was frustrated, okay? Getting coldshouldered by a beautiful woman does that. I needed something to relax me."

She ignored his needling, "Peabody's. Then the clerk will remember you. There's your alibi for when you left me alone for someone to walk in and slaughter me. Did you leave my door open while you paraded around town?"

"No, I left it unlocked so I could get back in. And that alibi ain't pannin' out. I went back to the place and the clerk quit the next day. He went back to Wazoo, Michigan, or something. I'm screwed unless you vouch for me, Kitten. Help me."

"Roy," she shoved a hand through her hair then, to prevent herself from thoroughly pulling it out by the roots, she hurriedly bound it in a ponytail. "What were you thinking running out of Augusta like that?"

He recoiled slightly at the show of temper, "I had to see you, get your confirmation of our story."

"There is no *story*. You were there, at my house, we had dinner and flaked out. I will tell the police that when they arrive. Yes, they're looking for me and it's about you."

"You're not gonna tell them you kicked me out, are you?"

"I should." Her words induced sheer panic in his features, forcing her to backtrack, "I'll avoid it if possible, okay? How did they find out about that night? How did they know to look for me?"

Roy shrugged with the same amount of confusion as she had.

"Shit," she sighed while glancing out the window. "Well, it doesn't matter now, does it? The Augusta police are here." She watched the gray Ford sedan park directly behind the Camaro. Two men, one tall and thin, the other built like a fire hydrant, surveyed her property from the sidewalk then pointed to Roy's pickup. *Shit, indeed*, she thought.

Roy shot from the sofa, eyeing the parted curtain as though it were a snake about to strike, "Savannah, you gotta help me. You gotta hide me."

"Don't be foolish. Face them, answer their questions or they will target you." She turned to face him, "Believe me, I know because that's what I'd do."

Two shaking hands grasped her shoulders, "Promise to tell them we were together."

"Roy, settle down or you'll look guilty. That's not exactly advisable for innocent parties." She angled to the front door as the sound of two short bursts of the doorbell chimed through the house. Savannah opened the door to Mutt and Jeff. Mutt, who looked amazingly like a young Vincent Price, displayed his badge and spoke before giving her the opportunity for a greeting, "Savannah Prince?"

His demeanor felt warm as a Minnesota winter. The tone and phrasing shouted the fact he held no special love for her, her name and definitely not her title since he conveniently left it out. In normal circumstances, she'd have slammed the door in his face for being disrespectful. Today, however, forced her to pretend he was polite company, "Yes, *Detective* Savannah Prince. And you are…"

The little fat one opened his mouth only to have Mutt answer for him, "Detectives Pierce and Dunne, Augusta Police Department. We'd like to ask you a few questions about Roy Carlson."

Savannah appraised the two men. Jeff, or Dunne, looked familiar but she couldn't recall from where. He sported the reddest hair this side of Bozo, buzzed short and flat in a military cut. He wore a gray suit, nothing real expensive but utilitarian and topped it off with a maroon tie with subtle pinstripes. Maybe it would eventually come to her, where she knew this man. For now, she invited them inside, "Ask away."

Dunne thrust his hand out to her as he passed, "Savannah, it's good to see you again."

She gave his hand a firm shake and when he smiled, her mind instantly reverted fifteen years, solving the mystery of his identity, "Owen Dunne?"

Proudly he nodded, pleased that she remembered, "The terror of Cross Creek High, at your service."

"Well, this is a surprise. Come on in, have a seat."

"You're as surprised to see me with a badge as I am you. Who'd have thought a Prince would decide to be a cop?"

The butterflies in her stomach slowed but stood long short of flying away. She'd seen this little dance before since partners adapted to their situation. Dunne's assignment was to pull her guard down, make her at ease and more willing to talk. Pierce's, in contrast, consisted of diving in for the kill – and he looked lethal enough already. The twisted version of good cop/bad cop played out every day in every city – and she was as guilty as anyone of participating. "Being a cop was better than the alternative. I picked enough fruit on my grandfather's farm to choke a mule."

She noticed they gave her abode a thorough visual sweep. Somehow it felt intrusive being on the other end of the questioning and the innuendo. It nearly gave her hives... Then she realized Roy was nowhere to be found. She left him standing at the window, essentially paralyzed with fear. The scent of his Polo cologne still hung in the air – a detail Pierce noticed instantly. The way his nose flared reminded her of a bulldog getting a whiff of dinner. Or a bloodhound locating a hot trail...

He scanned the room, his pale eyes periodically settling on her. A sore attempt at appearing casual, he smoothed his black tie to his crisp white shirt while bending over her coffee table. Two issues of the Atlanta Journal Constitution remained folded where Ennis left them. Pierce picked them up and thumbed through them.

He searched for a particular something, she assumed. A note perhaps, or some shred of evidence Roy had been inside her house. Fed up with his snooping, Savannah offered, "Today's paper is on the dining table. Want me to get it for you?"

Pierce straightened and only presented a minimal grim smile, "No thanks."

Besides herself and the detectives, the house sounded strangely quiet. Just another reason to worry, she inwardly griped. Roy's actions weren't endearing to anyone, her included. All she could do was pray Roy ran to the bathroom and not out the back door to leave in his pickup.

Okay, let's get down to business... She'd wasted enough time pacifying the two so she barreled into the meat of the visit, "What about Roy Carlson? And why did you come to me for information? I hardly know him anymore."

Pierce cut his eyes to her. "That so?" he asked in a manner saying he'd believe that when they found Elvis alive and well.

"Yes, that's so," she answered brusquely with hands on hips.

Dunne waved his partner off, "Don't let him rile you. We're just needin' to know a few things like when you last saw him."

Savannah saw Pierce's vision flick to the picture window back to her then he smiled. The hairs at the back of her neck bristled again. His smile reminded her of her cousin Randy. He smiled a similar crooked smile just before he launched an attack. The best defense is a good offense, she always maintained, so, "You mean before today?"

Pierce folded his arms, "That truck outside belongs to Carlson."

"I'm delighted to know that since he was in the driver's seat. He was in here a moment ago. Probably went to the bathroom. Roy," she called, trying to draw him out.

The house remained quiet. A sense of panic rose in her stomach. Panic that he'd bailed and left her to clean his mess. She called his name again with a "get out here now" tone, all to no avail. The absence of noise or movement drove her to the bathroom, the two detectives trailing behind.

Pulling open the door revealed the truth. The only sound in the room was the lacy curtain flapping in the breeze of the now open window. Roy was nowhere to be seen. Incredulity lifted her brow. Not only had he bailed but he'd somehow managed to squirm his enormous frame through the modest sized window.

The distinct roar of a large engine ripped through the house. Roy was running again. For an innocent man, he sure excelled in giving the opposite impression, she reflected.

Turning to head back to the living room, she gasped upon smacking dead into Pierce who refused to step back. The tall detective merely palmed his phone while inquiring, "I can assume the Atlanta police will assist us in locating Mr. Carlson?"

To hell with manners, "Get out of my way," she demanded, and pushed past him to punctuate her point. By the time she arrived at the living room window, any indication of Roy's presence disappeared. The driveway stood empty, aside from skid marks Roy left for a speedy departure.

"Ms. Prince, we will have your department's cooperation, will we not?"

That did it. She rotated on her heel, facing the young incarnation of Vincent Price and declared, "I'd appreciate a little professional courtesy. Address me by my title or all you'll get is my shoeprint on your behind as I kick your ass out my door."

Dunne chuckled under his breath but Pierce's jaw tightened, "Professional courtesy? You were harboring our suspect."

Savannah squared off with the condescending cop, "I was having a conversation with him. If I was 'harboring' him, I wouldn't be dumb enough to let him park his vehicle in my driveway, nor would I have admitted to seeing him today."

Dunne stepped forward, leveling a look at his partner that

instructed him to back off. Turning to her, he spoke in an even tone, "We're not accusing you of anything, Savannah. Why was Roy here today?"

Taking a deep breath, she calmed down but not enough to honestly notice. "I was with my niece and he called me, very insistent that we meet here." She pointed the remainder of her statement at Pierce, "The desk sergeant gave him my address. Until then Roy didn't know where I lived." She looked back to Dunne, "*And* until a couple of nights ago, we hadn't seen each other in about ten years."

Dunne reached in his coat for a notepad and pen. He jotted something down, "A couple of nights ago. When was that?"

"Thursday night. I had to make a run to Augusta and Roy magically appeared on my doorstep with pizza and Cokes and we had dinner at my house. I thought he was still married until he explained they'd divorced. Owen, why are you questioning *me*?"

His complexion reddened to match his hair, "We're investigating a murder that occurred down the street from your house. Roy dated her for a while and was noted for his temper, especially when she broke it off. In fact, what's that bruise on your chin?"

Savannah rolled her eyes, "It's not Roy's work. It's the result of a family disagreement."

Owen paused, clearly waiting for her to elaborate. Sighing again, she whispered, "It was Daddy."

Realization dawned on him as she finished, "Bobby Prince is my cousin and the Richmond County Sheriff. He was there and can confirm it." By his demeanor, she imagined Owen already knew about the fight somehow. If they'd contacted Bobby, he'd have called her so their source was someone different.

She crossed her arms in an indicative manner that all communication ceased until further notice then repeated her question, "Why are you questioning me about this murder?"

Pierce made no bones about the fact, "Because you were seen with the suspect the night of the murder."

Slanting him a scathing glare, she aimed her words at Dunne, "And you knew this how?"

"One of your neighbors told us. A," he thumbed through his notepad, "Mrs. Johnson. Neighbor west of you."

Ah, yes... The old lady Daddy was flipping off just hours prior to Roy appearing at the door. His actions just keep giving and giving when it comes to me...

Dunne continued, "Said Carlson stayed a while."

She prayed her decision didn't bite her in the ass, "Far as I remember, he stayed all night and no, nothing happened between us. Sounds hokie but it's the truth. We were together in high school and that's where the love affair ended."

Owen met Pierce's skeptical frown. "And you're positive he stayed all night? Didn't leave for any reason?"

Before answering, Savannah slowed her thoughts down. Tossing out answers at this point felt like navigating a minefield. She retraced her actions that Thursday night... Her reply wouldn't ultimately please Roy, "I took some painkillers for my jaw and conked out. If he left, I wouldn't remember it. When I woke up, he was still in my living room asleep."

"Where? On a bearskin rug with you?" Pierce offered. "And nothing happened, eh?"

Pierce's insinuation brought out her claws, "Back off, Detective. I'm trying to help but you're making it very difficult to want to." Turning to Owen, she instantly calmed, "It surprised the hell out of me, truthfully. I never asked him to join me."

"Savannah," Owen took her aside, his voice low, "do you know why Roy and his wife split?"

"No, he didn't tell me and I didn't ask."

Owen hesitated then went on, "It was common knowledge that he had mood swings. She'd end up calling the police to have him removed from the house."

Visibly stunned, she inquired, "Why?"

"There were reports of physical violence as well as sexual violence. After a point, he was committed for observation and was diagnosed with bipolar disorder."

"Roy?" she fell short of calling the detective an outright liar, which would have been unwise at best, terminal at worst. Picturing Roy with manic depression equated to seeing Ennis in a chicken suit, a badge clipped to his wing. It didn't compute.

Her thoughts registered with Owen who gently proceeded, "That's why they divorced. Now, I'm gonna ask you this and I don't want you getting offended or upset. If anything happened between you and Roy, was it consensual or did he force you?"

The recollection returned of repeatedly pushing Roy away using a great deal more strength than should be required. He'd been extremely aggressive in his efforts, requiring her to be equally vigilant in hers. "Um," she started off slowly, not wanting to bury her friend due to lack of proof, "he was very amorous that night but I told him I was involved with another man."

Owen blinked. His brow slowly migrated downward, "Very amorous? Describe that for me and don't be shy about it. If he forced you, or tried to, we need to know it."

"He was insistent." She watched Owen scrawl some notes and finished, "Nothing a good shove didn't fix, though."

Still writing, Owen nodded. Savannah excelled in reading upside down and caught a few key words of his scribble. "Not that I'm questioning her story but did his ex-wife's account pan out as credible? I mean, Roy bipolar? It's hard to believe."

Pierce began to speak only for Owen to shush him with a raised hand. Her classmate nodded, "I know but you haven't lived in Augusta in several years. Big as it is, it's still got a small town mindset. The hospital kept him long enough to be sure of the diagnosis, especially knowing who Roy's wife was."

The acid level in her stomach intensified beyond any relief Tums could provide. Savannah forgot Roy married the ex-mayor's daughter. The man had money to burn and she highly doubted if he approved of his debutant daughter hitching herself to a landscaper. "Okay," was all she said in response.

He presented a sympathetic half-smile, "I know you and Roy were tight in high school. The illness didn't appear until his early twenties and according to his employees, he's not acting right. You know, like he's not on his meds. That's part of the reason I wanted to talk to you." He tossed a critical glance at his partner, "Not to accuse you of anything."

9

Savannah plopped down on the couch, Yoo-Hoo in hand. Two exhausting hours later, she'd seen the detectives off, hopefully back to Augusta and out of her hair. Less than ten minutes later, the fatigue of the bizarre day remained heavy on her mind. She decided conclusively that interrogations from that end were not only unpleasant but unnecessary in some cases. Firstly, it didn't matter if she and Roy had sex. Their case hung on a murder, not her personal interaction with him. It didn't seem to faze either detective when she took up for Roy. Strangely, it irritated Pierce greatly to hear good and decent particulars about her ex-boyfriend but then she, in general, seemed to create an itch he couldn't quite scratch. Besides token interaction, he'd remained silent with only a foul frown wrinkling his brow. His distaste for her gave her pause for thought. Nearly as much as why Roy split the scene so quick without confronting his accusers. Something stunk about the whole situation. No one was telling her the entire truth or even the whole lie.

"What are you thinking about?" a voice inquired.

Savannah jumped, sending the Yoo-Hoo to and fro in her now fumbling hands. Once the bottle rested solidly in her grip, she sighed to

Ennis, "Just shoot me, why don't you?"

Ennis slid beside her, "Tough day, eh?" His arm curled around her shoulders to pull her closer, "What happened?"

Grateful for the ally and the hug, she abandoned the Yoo-Hoo to the side table and leaned against him. If she could curl up in his lap like a rescued feline, she would. She did feel rather abused once Pierce chewed a few hunks out of her ego, "It's a chaotic mess. Besides being accused of sleeping with Roy – an accusation I'm rather weary of lately – I found out my neighbor involved me in this murder investigation."

"How?"

"She's evidently our neighborhood watch. When she saw Roy arrive that night, I'm sure she wrote meticulous notes as to how long he stayed and if my hair was properly placed when I left." She snorted, "Nosy old bat."

"If she's that thorough, the police know you aren't involved." Ennis stroked her ponytail lightly, producing a little tickle down her neck.

She felt a tiny smile threaten with his action but the day's events prevented it from emerging, "That's another thing. One of the detectives seems to highly dislike me for some reason. He was crass and pushed every one of my buttons."

"Tall, skinny dude, looks like a young Vincent Price?"

She nodded and felt him tug at the ponytail as he finished, "Don't take offense. He raked the desk sergeant and Josh over the coals. I have a feeling Augusta PD doesn't have the sensitivity training Atlanta does. Either that or he naturally lacks manners. Believe me, he left no friends at the station."

Savannah snuggled in closer. Reliving the encounter gradually took a toll, "Well, if we see each other again, *I'm* not the one gonna be doin' the shithouse shuffle. I think he believes Roy and I killed that woman together."

Ennis tightened his embrace, "Stop thinking about him. In fact," he rose to his feet, offered his hand, "run along for your shower. I have plans for you tonight."

"Ennis –"

"Savannah," he mimicked her tone, "don't argue. Just conform."

As Ennis instructed, she indulged in a long, hot shower. The steam and heat relaxed her enough that the ugly events melted to the back of her weary mind. She toweled off but before she could throw a robe on, the phone rang. The incessant ringing retightened some muscles and brought some of the day screaming back. Ennis knocked on the door then proceeded to let himself in. For a few priceless moments, he stood speechless with phone in hand as he stared at Savannah's nude body. He explored her visually from head to toe and back again, then swept his tongue across his lips. "Uh, it's Lindsey," he managed in a deep, gravelly tone.

She took the phone from him, amused at his reaction. Ennis was the funniest man she'd ever met. Anytime he spied her naked, he was struck dumb. His reaction may have inclinations of a young man seeing his first nude woman but his actions in bed told a whole other story.

Ennis made love like the world was about to end. He was patient and controlled enough to take his time but when passion overwhelmed him, she swore someone spurred him. As the steam settled, she saw him readjust himself much like Roy had the night she backed him off. Ennis stepped behind her, leaving no question what his plans were. A soft kiss pressed at her shoulder then her neck while inquisitive fingers danced along her belly. Ennis Rutherford also possessed an insatiable appetite for sex. They'd been together no more than three days ago and every time they frolicked he left her barely able to complete a conscious thought – a fact he crowed regularly about. His self-esteem certainly rose to the occasion at those times, a lot like another part of himself.

While she spoke to Lindsey, Ennis tenderly drew his hand up Savannah's spine. The sudden action brought her to her toes, her breath catching in her throat. If Ennis's goal consisted of drawing her attention away from the day's events, it worked. It would also incite curious questions from her niece if something didn't wrap up quick. Lindsey proudly reported that all seemed well on the gerbil front, news that faired well in Savannah's brain and stomach. At least something went right that day. Once she finished talking to Lindsey, Ennis gleefully tossed the phone through the bedroom and into a chair in the living room. In shock, Savannah warned him good-naturedly, "If you just killed my phone, I'll be forced to deal with you in a harsh manner." She suddenly yelped as her legs went from under her and she found herself weightless in his arms.

Ennis bobbed his brow, "And I'll deal with you right now." He dove in for a kiss and the instant their lips touched, she forgot about everything except his tender hold and sweet taste. The kiss went deeper, rougher as passion overwhelmed them and Savannah found herself clinging to him and savoring every moment. Only when Ennis bent to lay her on the bed did she part from the kiss, "I like the way you deal with me."

"You ain't seen nothin' yet," he promised.

She watched him disrobe in a matter of seconds, his shirt and pants falling to the floor, his shorts dropping quickly behind. "You get any faster," she said, "and I'll have to call you Superman."

"Sugar, you can call me Superman any day and it won't bother me in the least."

Savannah's blue eyes slid down his muscular body. She never honestly cared about how a man looked naked but Ennis changed her mind. The wide chest sprinkled generously with wisps of coarse, dark hair nearly made her weak. His chest tapered to a trim waist and heavily muscled legs. Every part of him seemed sculpted. The bone and muscle worked in concert to contour a heavenly hunk of human male. His parents deserved a Thank You note for creating such a specimen.

Once her eyes fell below his waist, she swallowed and pointed, "That looks painful."

"Try walking with it," he crawled in next to her.

She ran her hand along his arousal, "Oh, you've found other interesting ways to exercise it."

Ennis closed his eyes and once her fingers wrapped around him, he sucked in a quick breath, "And I'm gonna be twisted into a pretzel if you keep doing that." He reached behind her to slide her closer against him. Savannah took the hint and surrendered her hold.

Descending on her, his mouth covered hers hungrily, ravishing
and thoroughly devouring along the way. Savannah responded to the
eager kiss until she felt weak and breathless. No other man affected her
like Ennis. His touch heated her skin, his kiss stole her breath. The rasp
of his day old beard scraped her skin, and she knew by experience her
chin wasn't the only thing in store for whisker burn that night.

Rolling her to her back, Ennis settled between her thighs,
unwilling to part from their kiss. His right hand glided down the curve
of her waist then back up, his thumb brushed her taut nipple.

Savannah arched slightly and moaned. She felt him smile against
her lips. Ennis barely parted the kiss, "If you're not ready for this
tonight, we'll stop."

She nearly burst out screaming. She recognized the easy out he
gave her, but damn, he'd gotten her hot and bothered and then decided
to present it. His thumb still played at her nipple, distracting any
thought but unfettered, raw sex. "What's the matter?" she goaded gently.
Inside, she prayed he was joking, "Started something you can't finish?"

His eyes flared, the pupils widening, "That sounded like a
challenge." Before allowing time for her answer, Ennis descended once
more for a kiss, his hands pinning hers beside her head. She felt his
arousal hard and ready as it pushed against her stomach. Before he got
too worked up, he'd have to attend to the condom – or let her. They'd
not engaged in unprotected sex since getting together and tonight would
be no exception, no matter how horny he was.

Ennis reached over to the nightstand to pull the drawer open.

Savannah felt his hand slip off her wrist to brace himself. It slid under his pillow while his other hand searched in the drawer, evidently unsuccessfully for a condom. Suddenly she felt his body tighten unnaturally. "Ennis? What's wrong?"

Slowly, he withdrew his hand from beneath the pillow and the contents of his hand startled both of them. He held a .32 caliber pistol and a note. Savannah struggled to a sitting position, "What the hell is going on?"

Ennis laid it gingerly on the bed, "Dunno, but I believe I'll leave it there until I can handle it properly." He unfolded the small note. They both recognized the paper as a partial sheet from a notepad on her dresser. In Roy's handwriting it read, "I'm leaving this with you for safekeeping. I'm innocent but I need you to keep this for me."

"Ah, shit," she groaned. The phrase tumbled from her weary lips too often these past few days. If the sky fell in on her, she wouldn't have been surprised. The week just predicted disaster from beginning to end.

Ennis climbed from the bed with a sigh. Meandering to the kitchen, she heard him utter, "Tell you one thing. That boy knows how to kill a moment." He returned with a large plastic bag and an ice pick. He slid the ice pick through the trigger guard and dumped the weapon unceremoniously into the bag.

Even in the midst of the current hell, Savannah found it rather arousing watching a naked Ennis maneuver the gun into the bag then seal it. He caught a glimpse of her near grin, "What are you smiling at?"

"Ennis Rutherford in his altogethers playing police detective. Very sexy."

He winced as his arousal lengthened and hardened, "Don't get me too riled. I might just attack you whether you like it or not. Plus," he lifted the bagged gun, "we've got this to deal with."

Savannah fell back again, "Can't we wait until morning? Roy's at least unarmed, as far as we know. Dunne and Pierce are at home doing whatever they do. Why can't we forget about this for six or seven hours?"

"Because the longer this little gem stays in our possession, the more Vincent Price will suspect us. I'll make you a deal. You call Dunne and I'll call Josh. I'll tell him we need some time to sort this mess out."

She rolled out of bed, more exasperated than angry, "I'd be more inclined to help these goats if they'd be upfront with me. I don't even know how the woman was killed." She traipsed out naked as the day she was born, still preaching as she went, "Hell, Ennis, they didn't even want to divulge her name. To me, a detective, for God's sake."

"Where are you going?" was the befuddled question from the bedroom.

"Before I do anything, I'm finding out the basics." She sat down at the computer which emitted its own pains for awakening so late at night. It whined and whirred until finally connecting to the internet service. She looked for the Augusta Chronicle and backdated it to Friday's late edition. A search for Maria Saxon produced the front page of the local section. "Local Woman Strangled," the headline read.

Ennis's voice sounded from behind, "Guess you know how she died now."

Scanning the screen, Savannah caught sight of a small picture of Ms. Saxon. A genuine pang of jealousy vibrated through her. To her, the woman qualified as beautiful.   Not cute, sweet or pretty but downright beautiful. She possessed the kind of beauty that started wars between men. Shifting her vision covertly to the side, she noticed Ennis staring at Maria too – or maybe he was just reading. Her ego chose the latter. Reality shot that theory when her common sense explained that the Latino lady with dark wavy hair oozed sex appeal where Savannah's specialty was sarcasm. Either way, this woman was deceased and not by her own choice. That fact seeded her brain with a hefty load of guilt.

"Scroll down the page," Ennis requested, "unless you're not finished reading."

"I'm not," she answered softly.   Truth was she hadn't *begun* reading yet. Savannah leaned forward a tad, blinked and tried to focus. She blinked again, leaned forward more and squinted. Then she finally heaved a sigh and reached in the upper desk drawer. A pair of glasses withdrew to Ennis's shock, "What in the…"

With clear, unadulterated self-consciousness, she slid them on her nose. It positively galled her to wear glasses, even for the simple task of reading. All her life her vision remained sharp, focused – until the past few months. She'd held off longer than she thought, struggling to read without the delicate wire framed spectacles. Showing her colleagues and partner that her vision was flawed wouldn't exactly thrill her but ultimately the optometrist was correct – she'd eventually have to drag 'em out and hang 'em on her face.

Ennis screwed his head around to see her, "When did you get those?"

"When I got old and couldn't read the computer screen without putting nose prints on it." Looking up from the monitor, she glanced to see his reaction. A slow, gentle smile curved his lips, making her slightly touchy about the subject, "If you're gonna laugh do it now so I can kill you without witnesses."

To her surprise, he bobbed his brow, "Actually, I like 'em. Makes you look –"

"The word 'distinguished' is grounds for justifiable homicide too, Rutherford, so be careful."

Ennis frowned at her, "I was gonna say they make you look more beautiful than you already are. So here," he thrust the bagged .32 at her, "kill me now."

She paused, thought a moment, then replied, "Nah, I think I'll keep you. You're handsome as hell, sweet as a Moon Pie and great in bed."

Ennis flinched, she noticed, and his arousal regained hope, "Had to bring that up, didn't you? What did you find? Anything?"

"Not much but that's the story of my life this week. She was a stockbroker but that's not exactly a dangerous profession." She rethought that, "Well, unless she bilked clients out of money."

"That has been known to happen. And it's also been known to drive people to kill." He bent down to read over her shoulder, his fingers kneading her shoulders tenderly. Ducking lower, he took note of the writer's name, "We could give this fella a call, see what he's holding out – if he is."

"Then we risk further involving ourselves on the wrong end of a murder investigation. Pierce is sniffing for an excuse to put me down and I don't know why."

Ennis straightened, yawned, "Back to square one. I call Josh, you call Dunne. That redheaded imp shouldn't get a jump on sleep if we can't. 'Cause I can already tell I'm not getting to jump you tonight."

10

Savannah huddled, trembling in the corner of her closet. Normally claustrophobic to an insane degree, fear drove her to bury up behind closed doors, hidden. Her father's rampage began after a look at her report card. No matter how Charlene attempted to diffuse his anger, it boiled into a tumultuous storm – a storm that stomped up the stairway one heavy footfall at a time.

It was a "C" in math that triggered him this time. She struggled nonstop to learn the figures, fractions and equations to no avail. Even as R.J. raged downstairs, his deep, loud voice carried every syllable skyward to her room on the second floor. "No kid of mine is gonna flunk out. I'll teach her those numbers myself if I have to…"

Savannah heard her mother's calm voice answer him. R.J. interrupted before she finished, "I *know* she ain't stupid. She needs to concentrate, needs motivation and I'm gonna give it to her. *Savannah*! Get your ass downstairs now!"

She didn't dare move. If the earth began to shake she'd stay rooted to the spot. Being only nine, she was old enough to have bore the brunt of R.J.'s rages and too young to realize that hiding only made it worse. Now he tromped up the stairs, every footfall sounding louder, harder than the last. "*Savannah!* Get your ass out here now, girl. We need to talk."

Talking to R.J. meant a beating. He'd talk as he swung his fist, sure, but while most kids cried when their daddy berated them for a bad grade, Savannah cried while hers worked her over. She heard him stumble around the room, mumbling, "Hiding under the bed?" then he moved to the closet. Her heart leapt in her throat, the coursing blood and pounding made it difficult to hear him yell for her one last time before the door flew open. A shaft of light penetrated enough for her to see his legs. They moved closer, effectively smothering the beam. She held her breath.

She cringed when large fingers wrapped in the shirt she wore, the surprise forcing a gasp from her. R.J. effortlessly hauled her out from behind the hanging clothes and over the stash of Barbies and toys she put away. Battling to regain her footing she heard his anger ripen to the rage from downstairs, "Hiding from me again? You little coward. At least your brother and sister are adult enough to face their punishment. But you, you're always thinking you can outsmart me." His fist quavered in the shirt, his anger still mounting. "When are you gonna learn to respect me or do I have to beat it into you?"

Clearly R.J. felt the latter was in order, even as tears began flowing down her cheeks. He brought her up short by the neck and threw her across the bed, against her mother's pleadings. He yanked his belt from his pants with such force, Savannah heard the leather zip through the belt loops. Crying in earnest now, she struggled to the far side of her bed only to feel him grab her ankle and drag her back, "Stay still and don't you cry. I'm not having a dumb coward for a kid. And I'll be damned if I'm having a disrespectful shit for a daughter. You'll take this whippin' like a woman or you'll get it ten times worse."

Savannah clawed at the covers, desperate to escape. When she felt R.J. strip her pants past her bottom, her fight began in earnest. The first lash caught her by surprise and she screamed. R.J. brought the belt down faster, harder, "Told you to *be quiet!* Every time you cry you'll get ten more..."

Ennis heard Savannah's moans transform to genuine cries of pain. Her lips moved in a slow manner not allowing him to make heads or tails out of her words. All he knew was she was hurting – in reality or in a nightmare. He propped to one elbow and shook her gently by the shoulder, "Savannah, wake up."

The cries became louder, more intense. The words finally distinguishable, "No please, Daddy, I'm sorry."

Ennis squeezed her shoulder harder, "Wake up. You're having a nightmare." His action evidently affected her dream because she began struggling and fighting. He watched as her fists balled in the covers, her arms shaking as if she was freezing. When her legs drew up, Ennis realized the nightmare wasn't surrendering that easily so he shook her harder, "Savannah."

A deep gasp filled the room and Savannah's eyes popped wide. They searched wildly for a second or two then locked on Ennis. By her expression, his grasp remained steadfast. *If looks could kill, I'd be lying on the floor.* Risking another physical battle, he whispered, "You were having quite a nightmare."

Her breathing slowed telling him she was, at last, in the here and now. Even the murderous look evaporated once she realized where she was, "Sorry."

Ennis rolled to the side, taking in his own deep breath. He knew Savannah's normal physical strength – or thought he did. She was stronger than any woman he'd ever encountered, even growing up on a ranch. He'd seen small and average size women buck hay, rope steers and brand cows. He was pretty damn sure the spitfire beside him could out-buck, out-rope and out-brand any female in Texas. Taking stock of his own strength, he understood Savannah fought fervently against her father, whatever transpired in the nightmare. Ennis literally feared touching her yet. He didn't need a black eye, "You okay now?"

She stretched and winced as the strained joints fought to regain their familiar positions. A moment later she nodded, "Yeah. Just reliving my wonderful childhood."

"Damnation, girl. What the hell was going on?" He wasn't stupid, of course. He'd heard her pleading with her father and apologizing for whatever transgression she'd committed. In his heart, Ennis was hoping she'd finally open up to him. She'd never shared the painful part of her childhood with him, only choice stories where R.J. was "unhappy" with her. She made sure to wrap the story in just enough fluff that he'd feel crappy for asking more details – which he didn't. Tonight might have broken the dam.

"Daddy was disappointed with my 'C' in math," was all she said.

Well, so much for forthcoming… "But you're good with numbers."

She slanted him a knowing look. Ennis used it as his key inside, "He beat you until you raised your grade."

Now she looked away, closed her eyes. After inhaling a deep breath, she confided, "He demanded to see every paper, every grade, every day and he whipped me mercilessly every day for two weeks. Only thing that stopped him was my mother pleading with him to stop."

Ennis heard the emotion in her voice. He softly stroked her arm, let her finish.

"I finished the year with a 'B' in math." She chuckled plaintively, wiped a tear and said, "He still wasn't happy but at least the whippings stopped."

At that point Ennis became speechless. He'd grown up in a loving household where spankings were saved for misbehavior and whippings were for major misconduct. Never did his father or mother put lasting marks on the boys. This kind of brutality angered him to the edge of losing every manner his mama taught him. He wanted to hurt R.J. Prince. Truthfully, he wanted to kill him with his bare hands. Ennis leaned in and kissed her cheek. Immediately he noticed tears welled larger and faster in her eyes. He couldn't resist drawing her close, "Oh sugar, don't cry. You know I'm here for you, don't you?"

"That's *why* I'm crying," her voice quavered. "Besides Roy, you're the only man to stand by me during these times. Roy was my first crush, my first relationship. You, you're…" she trailed off with the thought, which effectively gave him a heart attack. He was what? Ennis was about to speak when she completed the sentence, "You're so much more to me. I feel like we've known each other all our lives."

Now that sounded better… Plus, it trumped "first crush" any day. Ennis wouldn't spoil his happy little moment with the mention of marriage. God knew he wanted to. Even his family mentioned they acted married, their mannerisms, their ESP to each other's thoughts and actions. It scared Ennis how attuned they were to each other.

He rested his hand on her hip, bringing her to her side to face him, "I know just how you feel. For the record, I wouldn't trade you in for a Ferrari or a Hilton girl for anything."

While wiping tears away, Savannah nearly smiled. Nearly. He needed to try harder. Eventually he'd break through but tonight seemed to take an enormous emotional toll on her. He'd back off for now. Instead he stroked her lower back slowly and tenderly. He knew his partner from head to toe now and currently his index finger rested about where the tiger's nose was on her tattoo. Her eyes glittered in the moonlight as his fingertips brushed over her skin. Out of the blue she stated, "That's part of the reason for the tattoo. To cover his scars."

The many times they'd been together, Ennis noticed the elongated scars across her bottom and lower back. He hadn't mentioned them since he knew about R.J.'s abuse. The smaller scars across the backs of her arms caused his temper to flare when he saw them. The sign of uncontrolled rage, a drunken rage, taken out on an innocent kid. He could nearly see the little girl flailing to protect herself only to feel the stinging bite of the leather belt across her arms. It took every ounce of self control not to unleash the same wrath upon R.J. Prince.

"Well, it did a good job. Can't hardly see them."

Her vision narrowed as she tried to fish out a lie. He wasn't lying outright, he was covering a white lie. A person could still see the scars but the tattoo artist must have been a genius since most of the scars aligned with the stripes on the tiger. "Don't try to ferret," he warned good-naturedly. "I'm telling the truth."

She relaxed then. "I didn't want that large a tattoo. The artist said it would take it if I wanted to cover most of the damage. I was tired of coming out of the shower and seeing Daddy's work all the time. So now I see a tiger."

Ennis purred while his fingers traced the length of her back, "Personally, I like kissing that cat. Running my tongue down his stripes…"

"Daddy didn't just use a belt. You know that tree out back? He'd break off a limb and when he hit you with it, it felt like a bullwhip slamming against you. That's what caused most of the scars."

The off-topic remark brought his vision back to hers. She was still measuring his reaction to the information. Savannah always gauged people's response, their body language, facial expressions and their eyes. Especially their eyes. Ennis gradually settled into the conversation with the realization she wanted him to know details about the abuse. Not for sympathy but for his education. She was explaining what molded her into the woman she was today, what influenced her personality and outlook. So he took the plunge, "That what made the marks on your arms?"

She nodded slowly but deliberately. Until now the object creating the scars was a mystery. None measured longer than two inches in length. Some looked slightly jagged like lightning bolts, others had smooth edges. He'd counted them once. Twelve. Thirteen if he counted the tiniest one closest to her elbow. His mother asked him about them when they spent time in Texas. Ennis couldn't explain other than to caution his mother about the home Savannah grew up in.

"Georgia and Seth have these too?"

Again she nodded, "I don't think they have the ones on their arms though. They managed the impossible. Withstand Daddy's whippings and beatings without fighting back. If you resisted, you were disrespectful and," she shrugged, "you got a worse deal."

Disrespectful. The word grated on him now. The very description R.J. labeled her when she tried to clothe him just days earlier. While stroking her hair, Ennis stated the obvious, "You've had an insanely tough week, sugar. It's no wonder you're having nightmares. Why don't you take something to help you rest?" Offering her a drink to calm her only served to anger her. She avoided alcohol like the plague because of R.J.. Since they'd partnered, Ennis hadn't seen her drink a drop, even on her toughest day. She did, however, indulge in a sleeping pill or painkiller at her worst times. Hell, he thought, every cop had their potion. Liquor or pills, if it worked and didn't endanger anyone, why not? He liked a beer now and again. Savannah didn't berate him for it. She merely lifted her glass of Coke and toasted to a bad day gone bye-bye.

She seriously contemplated his offer then, "I'd better not. I have to face Dunne tomorrow and I need a clear head."

11

The meeting with Owen Dunne went smoother than she anticipated. Without Pierce breathing down her neck, turning over the gun became a matter of two cops interacting, not a cop and a swine. Dunne asked few questions thankfully, keeping it mainly to business.

She planned on going home but a twinge of guilt reared its head, forcing her to drop by Roy's landscaping business first. The least she could do was inform him of what she'd done to prevent him from being blindsided later.

She exited the Calhoun Expressway to make her way to Fifth Street. The Carlson Design & Landscape sign looked newly painted which pleased her. During her childhood, the old sign took a beating from weather, leaving most people to find the business from memory.

The building still retained the original charm and rustic appearance. In her mind, she knew what every room contained and remembered Roy's father owned two beat up 1975 Ford pickups that parked in front. The landscape business back then mainly consisted of mowing lawns and trimming bushes. That's where Roy cut his teeth on the company. He often bragged that he was the vice-president of mowing. Trouble was, Roy really liked the title. He clung to his father's every word, worked his ass off for the few accolades his dad gave. Sadly, Savannah reckoned that was partly why she and Roy hit it off so well. Their fathers incessantly rode them hard and gave little praise for results.

Savannah turned into the small angle parking lot to realize the old trucks that once inhabited the place were replaced with brand new Ford F-150s like her brother's, only accessorized with ladders, shovels, fertilizer and the like. An employee stood at the back of one truck, loading equipment. Her mama might have used her favorite term for him – strapping. Indeed, if his front looked as fine as his back, the ladies of Augusta never lacked for exceptional scenery. When she pulled next to the other truck with hopes it was Roy's, she noticed the handsome specimen turned in her direction. The instant the car door swung open, he startled her by darting toward her then offering her a hand, "Good morning, ma'am. How can I help you?"

The name embroidered on his Carlson Landscape shirt read "Nate". The lilt in his tone told her that yes, Nate knew he was stunningly handsome and no, he probably never spent a night alone. Savannah allowed him to help her out and when she stood up straight, she noticed just how tall he was. Did Roy only hire men who stood as tall as him? She tilted her head back to make eye contact, "Is Roy here?"

She sensed a flash of disappointment in his expression then optimism replaced it again, "No ma'am. Haven't seen him this morning. Anything I can do for you?"

"I need to leave him a note." She pointed to the office, "May I?"

"Of course," he walked her to the door, opened it for her and

Savannah felt the hint of a touch at her back. While being the chivalrous one, Nate also treaded on thin ice. Most women likely didn't care if a strange handsome man took the liberty of touching them, but it raised her blood pressure and not in a positive way. She felt his hand guide her in the door and once inside she realized things drastically changed over the course of the years. Gone were the extra mowing blades hanging on the back wall, as well as the picture of President Carter. Replacing Carter's photo was an aerial picture of Augusta and, on the back wall, was the hall of fame consisting of photos of completed jobs for prospective customers to peruse. The place, though cleaned up to sparkling, still emanated a sadness she couldn't put her finger on. Maybe it was simply that, like the shop, times had changed so much. Everyone had grown up and moved on whether they wanted to or not.

Behind the main office was another, smaller office. Savannah spied another man sitting behind a desk. A phone rested against his shoulder as he spoke and intently pecked away on a computer keyboard. From her distance, she saw he wore an emerald green polo like Nate but couldn't read the name. She noticed he was decently older than Roy by at least ten years and, like Nate, slightly favored her ex-boyfriend in build, hair color and the cut. She tried not to stare however just before she looked away, his vision shifted slightly and she knew instantly when he made eye contact. Her body went cold and an unexpected shiver ran through her. The man's brow sank upon seeing her, as if he knew her and really didn't like her. On the last point, they were even.

"My name's Nate, what's yours?"

"Savannah," she answered uneasily. Shaking the mystery man's chilly stare would take a while.

"Nice to meet you, Savannah. That's Mr. Stephens in there," Nate offered while scrounging the desk for paper.

What does he do, kick dogs and eat small children for dinner?, she asked herself.

Noticing where her vision strayed, Nate explained, "He's always in a bad mood. That's why Roy gave him the back office." He presented her with pen and paper, "Want me to give your note to Roy?"

She gave Nate credit. He appeared helpful enough though she wouldn't wish Roy's wrath on anyone once he read the note. "I'll just leave it for him but thanks for the offer." Bending over the desk, Savannah contemplated the words to use in the note. Finding a phrase that connected with him without alerting prying eyes would be a trick. After viewing Roy's "partner" in the back, she mulled over even leaving a note at all.

A sensation of being watched never faded and now she detected someone edging closer to her. Savannah cast a glance to the side. Nate stood within a foot of her but he faced the door. Quickly, she scribbled her note, "Roy, the surprise you left has been delivered to the appropriate individuals. It really is for the best. Savannah." Folding it twice, she inquired, "Where can he find this? It's important he sees it when he arrives."

Nate spun on his heel, his attention now fully hers again, "I'll take it to his office in the back. He always checks his messages." He took the note then pointed outside, "That's a really nice car. Had it long?"

"Bought it new," she observed him trail to the back and turn left.

She couldn't help but glance at Mr. Stephens again. His stare penetrated her to the bone. He'd stopped work on the computer but continued speaking lowly into the phone, glaring directly at her.

Nate appeared again, a smile adorning his pleasant features, "Ever thought of selling it?"

Her Camaro always turned men's heads. The red sports car had that effect and when they noticed the features inside, they melted like butter. Problem was, she'd grown very fond of her vehicle. They'd been through a lot together. So, in response, Savannah returned the smile, "Not once."

He feigned injury by covering his heart, "Come on, Savannah. I'll pay you what she's worth and I'll treat her good, I promise."

He opened the door for her again. This time there was no mistaking his touch on the small of her back. "Sorry, Nate," she replied. "Me and the old girl have been together a long time."

A shrug of acceptance lifted his broad shoulders then he sighed, "Well, if you ever want to sell her, come to me."

She grabbed the door handle but his hand covered hers, gently removing it, "Allow me, please," he offered.

Savannah stepped back to watch him open the car door for her. His hand extended for her and she accepted it while sliding into the driver's seat. She hadn't seen this degree of chivalry since – well, since never. Nate poked his head inside to scan the interior. He nearly groaned, "If I had this baby, I wouldn't sell either." Nate grinned and topped it with a wink, "Don't be a stranger, Savannah."

She stopped at the Whistle Stop on Greene Street for a celebratory milkshake to soothe the grumbling her stomach began at noon. A blip of her meeting with Nate brought a smile. The guy was quite a charmer and a lot like Roy in high school. With the exception of Ennis, they sure didn't make guys like that anymore. Courteous, sweet and handsome, to boot.

While at the café, she spent thirty minutes getting affirmation why she'd moved to Atlanta. Augusta was just too small for her. Overhearing conversations about family gatherings and the gossip associated with them proved too much so she packed up to leave at three o'clock.

Forty-five minutes into the ride home her cell phone rang. Figuring it might be Ennis, she answered on the second ring. It wasn't Ennis.

"What the hell are you doing to me? I *trusted* you with that package and you hand it to the cops?" It took a bona fide idiot not to hear the fury in Roy's tone. Between his seething came labored, heavy breaths like he'd been running. The anger boiled so fiercely, he barely sounded like Roy. Savannah shook her head with the realization he'd run from the cops *again*. Would he ever learn that fleeing only marked him as guilty?

Forgoing the admonition, she switched conversational gears to ease his concern while explaining, "Roy, calm down. Ennis found it last night, not me. I'm not going to involve him in this." Okay, in her heart she felt basically serpentine for giving Owen the gun but her ethics as a cop weighed heavily too, "What made you think I wouldn't turn it over to the police?"

He ground the words between his teeth, "Only because I saved your ass a few times with Daddy. Did they train the compassion outta you at the academy? Used to be I could count on you and vise versa but I know the score now."

"Hey, I'm not against you so don't –"

"No, you're just covering yours and Finus's asses, I understand. Just hope you'll understand when this little stunt comes back to bite yours. Because it will, I promise."

Savannah pulled the phone from her ear and stared at it, puzzled at his wording. Was this really Roy Carlson, the gentle giant she remembered from high school? The inference left plenty of interpretation, none of it palatable to her. He'd phrased it plainly enough. He'd threatened her and Ennis. The former was bad enough, the latter intolerable.

Returning the phone to her ear, she expressed herself as frankly as he did, "Do not threaten me or Ennis. I'll arrest you myself if this is how you plan on dealing with your situation. I'll help you but you've got to stop running and stop –" She paused when he hung up. "Acting so damn guilty," she finished with a sigh and the distinct realization she'd just pissed off not just a physically powerful man but an enraged man with a mental disorder. The week just kept getting better and better.

Savannah parked her car in her driveway. Getting out after the long two hour trip set her bones into a hard ninety degree angle. Where was Nate when she needed him? Pulling herself vertical was getting more difficult these days and she eyed the red Camaro maliciously. Maybe she should mildly entertain Nate's offer then buy a car more suited to her aching back, or at least a car not so low to the ground. She shook off the thought to weariness and stress then slid her key in the front door lock. Ah, the sweet sound of home. She planned on consuming scarcely enough food to satisfy her hunger then she'd forego a shower for an extended, luxurious bath. By that time Ennis would probably be home and she could prepare something more substantial than sandwiches for dinner.

Once inside, she turned to close the door then locked it. After her little exchange with Roy, she double checked the lock. Her friend threw quite a curveball earlier. She'd never heard him so angry – especially with her – and up until that point she'd believed him incapable of such wrath. Content that the door was indeed secure, she tossed her keys and purse onto the small oak entry table. Next she headed for the kitchen. That was until her cell rang, delaying any of her secret plans to relax. She uttered a short prayer that the caller wasn't Roy again.

"Savannah, it's Owen. Make it home okay?"

"Yeah, why?"

"Because we tried to grab Roy at work and he ran. He knows about the gun and he's not happy."

Gee, I hadn't noticed... She wanted to say it but settled for, "I didn't expect him to totally lose it when I left that note for him."

"What are you talking about? Pierce told him about the gun

while we were chasing him down. Needless to say, Roy didn't speak well of you. In fact he led me to believe he was coming to see you."

Her vision automatically went to the front door lock. Of course as flimsy as it was, one good shove from a man Roy's size and he'd be inside. He ran the risk of being shot dead if he tried, she hoped he realized it through his rage-filled brain. "I figure he's hiding out somewhere and doesn't want to be seen by anyone but I'll be careful, Owen. Thanks for calling." She clicked off and sat the cell phone on the side table. Still, she couldn't understand why Pierce hated her so much. To give a murder suspect motive for committing another crime? He either had signs on his ears advertising Space for Rent or his little red choo-choo jumped its tracks...

Her stomach panged, reminding her of her original intent. Ingesting food. Her feet welcomed the carpet from the day's walking on hard concrete. *Damn*, she thought. *I must be getting old.* Wandering onto the hardwood floor of the kitchen incited another riot from her feet. They much preferred the carpet. She opened a cabinet for the bread then remembered she needed a new loaf from the pantry. Once she had that, she meandered to the fridge where a shiver wracked her from head to toe. She must be getting older because the house felt particularly cold. A distinct draft blew across her shoulders when she walked past the kitchen. She hadn't noticed it immediately since her brain consumed itself with problems of the day. Finding the draft presented a minimal puzzle. It either originated in her bedroom or the infinitesimal cubicle serving as a guest room. She bet on the former.

Savannah sat the bread down to search the house. Sometimes she or Ennis opened the bedroom window for a breeze on warmer winter days.   Laying it off to Ennis forgetting to completely close it before leaving, she started on her way to the bedroom.   Two steps past the fridge, she felt another shiver working through her.   Not due to cold but the reflection in the refrigerator's narrow handle.   The harsh reality of someone standing behind her finally kicked in, particularly when a jacketed, muscular arm fell across her vision.   She managed a mere pathetic yelp before a suffocating handhold choked all sound from her.

Automatically she reached for her gun but felt the man slide the weapon from the holster and saw him fling it across the room.   Although her hands were free, no matter how she clawed at his hands or face or jammed her elbow in his stomach, he refused to let go.   Her heart pounded throughout her body, rioting panic, and trying to rally an adrenaline-based battle.   Struggling and gasping for air proved futile as she battled the strength gripping her throat.   The man never spoke, grunted or made a sound.   Savannah made another attempt to dislodge the assailant – whom, by process of elimination, she assumed was her ex-boyfriend – and she stomped the living hell out of his instep.

Instead of releasing her liked she'd hoped and expected, his grasp constricted.   Rage fueled this man and overpowered whatever pain she inflicted.   Her fight began to ebb a degree as a curtain of gray slid over her awareness.   Now she wanted a look at the bastard – just to look in his eyes and realize who this brutal fiend was for sure.   Craning her head Savannah managed to snatch a glimpse of chocolate brown hair, cut exactly like Roy's.   The emerald green jacket the assailant wore matched the same color Roy wore a day earlier and the realization finally hit her.

Roy Carlson, the man who'd kissed her so passionately days before, currently attempted to end her life. She felt his thumb move slightly forward that sent her into another round of panic. The blood choke would kill her in less than a minute. She poured every remaining ounce of strength into her fight – flailing, kicking, punching and clawing at him but he stood stone still, his hold staying true until she felt her knees give. She remembered sinking to the hardwood floor just before consciousness betrayed her.

12

"Window's broken in the bedroom," a voice stated. "Whole damn thing's gone. I want to know who did this and how they managed to jump her and take her gun. If this asshole's running around with her weapon, I want to be the first to know."

Savannah's brain swirled and ached. Even hearing Josh's voice hurt. Her captain possessed a soft baritone voice but at that moment, it sounded like trumpets blaring. Without opening her eyes, she could imagine his stance. His tough, lean frame stood, hands clamped to his hips. When Josh Hunter was pissed, that was his posture. Eight years Savannah's senior, his face sported a stubborn self-confidence she found comforting at times, maddening at others. That day, it was the latter. Judging by his tone, no intelligent human would argue with him unless they had a death wish.

"Hey, she's moving," someone else mentioned. That voice unequivocally belonged to Detective Mathis, from her precinct. The hardwood floor sank slightly as the rotund detective stepped closer, "And lucky for us all the ambulance is about here."

Her eyes gradually parted to greet Ennis's worried expression. He touched her cheek, "Hey there, sugar. Good to see you awake." Before giving her a chance to speak, his nervous chatter habit took over, "Owen Dunne said you got home about 5:30. He also mentioned an incident with Roy at his workplace."

Even beneath the surface of concern, Savannah read her partner's mind. He hesitated to imply Roy attacked her so he tentatively continued, "Also said Roy wasn't too pleased with you turning in the gun. Did, uh," he cleared his throat, "Roy do this?"

"Yes," she eked and instantly regretted it. Her throat pained her something terrible. It felt like an elephant stomped on it. Even moving her jaw hurt.

Ennis bristled, "I knew it." Now Josh and Mathis closed in to listen. Mathis leaned down, his pudgy, friendly face flashed a semi-smile while glancing over his glasses. He lifted a notepad and pen and readied them to take notes, "I missed that. Who'd you piss off?"

Hands on hips, Josh's handsome face slanted the heavyset detective a warning glance. Mathis, in turn, shrugged innocently. Ennis grimly informed them of everything from the murder and "convenient" night Roy spent with Savannah to finding the gun and her turning it over to the Augusta PD.

"So he broke in and attacked her for doing that?" Mathis inquired, his hands now hanging at his sides. Clearly, Savannah thought, Mathis doubted the scenario and didn't think it warranted notes. In his mind, it fell into a generic domestic problem and some cops dismissed those as negligible. Growing up in a 24/7 domestic dispute, Savannah always treated them with utmost importance. After all, domestic issues spawned plenty of murders as she'd learned over the years.

Like Josh had seconds earlier, Ennis flashed Mathis an annoyed glare, "He's manic depressive and obviously something's gone screwy with him."

Mathis sobered considerably at that point. Josh whispered, "Could explain the note too." He leaned down to her, "You're going to the hospital."

She tried to sit up but wavered back down, her hand holding her head, "No hospitals. I'm fine." God, she wished she didn't have to speak. However staring at three determined male faces forced her to.

Josh narrowed his vision, "Detective, you *are* going. No arguments."

She momentarily capitulated, "What note are you talking about?"

Ennis's jaw clenched hard enough to break rocks while he pointed near her head.

She shifted her vision to the side to see something long and shiny jutting up from the floor. Focus came slowly. When it did, her eyes widened in shock and dismay at her Forschner butcher knife no more than an inch from her ear. Her line of vision connected with the two and a half inch blade that, on one end tapered to pin point, the other ended in a rosewood handle. It stood straight up from the floor basically staring at her. It didn't take a genius to figure out how the knife was standing so tall and regal. *No, not my hardwood floor...* When she moved in, she'd worked like a veritable Trojan restoring the old hardwood floor. She'd spent weeks on it and now it was a pin cushion. Savannah shoved herself to her elbows, spun internally a few seconds and with Ennis's help, propped on her side. The assailant stabbed the butcher's knife into the floor to hold a note. She tilted her head slightly to read, "Next time I'll finish the job."

A shiver worked its way through her aching body. Savannah cradled her head in her hand in a futile attempt to settle her rioting brain. Roy cut the blood off to her brain long enough to knock her out but not kill her. Sifting through her fuzzy thoughts, she considered it odd that he didn't finish the job at the time. Why bother giving her a warning when he had her, literally, in his hands? It didn't make sense. What did penetrate her haze was the fact Roy wasn't merely wanted for murder now. He was wanted for attempted capital murder on a police officer. The thought made her queasy all over again.

"What'd you do?" Mathis inquired, his pen finally putting words on paper. "Pick this guy special from the rock farm? He's not real bright trying to kill a cop."

Josh called him down while moving aside for the EMS workers. He reinforced his earlier instructions, "Don't give these guys a hard time. Go to the hospital. It'll make us all feel better."

"Josh, I'm fine, really." She pulled her legs beneath her and reached for the fridge handle. Halfway up, it appeared successful so she pointed across the room, "My gun is by or behind the TV." Then her knees buckled, legs went limp and she fought to keep her footing. The EMS attendants fell in behind to hold her, "It's best to let a doctor look at you. You've got some nasty looking marks on your neck."

"Well, I guess it's no surprise since someone tried to kill me," she smiled sickly at the man who wrapped his arm around her waist. He led her to a gurney where she parked it. She'd save the complaints for when they attempted to haul her to the hospital.

Mathis held her weapon for her to see, "I found your gun. I'll have it printed and see if this bastard's stupid enough not to wear gloves."

She thanked him but didn't bother telling him the attacker used his bare hand to handle the gun. The man was running on pure mad as evidenced by her neck and sore throat. She did croak the fact she clawed Roy's face. She displayed her hands with blood beneath the fingernails.

Josh instructed Mathis to bag the note and knife, "Meanwhile," he turned to Savannah, "I'm putting surveillance on your house in case he shows again. Let these guys run you to Crawford and I'll get forensics to process you. Don't worry, I'll let Georgia know what's happen –"

"*No, you won't,*" she was pleased with how firm it came out. The last thing she needed was her sister hovering over her. "Don't tell anyone."

"Gonna wear turtlenecks for the next two months?" he shot back.

Now she frowned, "I'll tell her in my own time. You know how she is."

Josh considered that. "I'll hold off for now but you'd better tell her."

"What the hell's going on? Where's Savannah?" a new voice entered the living room. A panicked male one and a voice that brought Savannah to full attention and wishing she had her gun, prints or no prints. Her aching head still prevented rapid movement but she continued visually searching for a viable weapon to swing with.

Ennis, on the other hand, lit out like his butt was on fire, "You son of a bitch, I'm gonna rip you apart."

"Ennis, stop," Josh called him down. He waved Mathis and a uniform to restrain the enraged detective. The two, seeing the gravity of the scene unfolding, raced to grab him. Just as Ennis's fist started forward, Mathis looped his arm over his colleague's, stopping the assault. He and the uniform cop battled hard to pull the burly detective back. Seeing their struggle, Josh yelled, "Rutherford, cut it out already!" He glanced down at Savannah who'd given up the search for a weapon and settled for just turning pale. "This Carlson?" he asked.

She nodded slightly. Josh started forward, cuffs in hand, "Roy Carlson, you're under arrest –"

"What for?" He searched Savannah out, "What happened? Where is she? I want to see her."

Ennis lunged forward, "I'll just bet you do, you sick bastard. Coming back to see if she's dead." He pulled against Mathis and the uniform officer, "If I get my hands on you, ain't nobody gonna find you."

Inside Savannah smiled. Ennis's Texas twang seemed to always burst forth when his temper rose. His face a deep crimson and fists curled into human rocks, Ennis truly meant to kill Roy. Savannah prayed Mathis and the cop were stronger than him and that their strength endured. Otherwise they'd *really* have a killing on their hands.

Josh cuffed Roy who still pulled toward the woman sitting on the gurney. The EMTs urged her to lie down only to hear her refuse. If Roy came any closer, she'd be forced to stand and run – a task she doubted would succeed. Thankfully, Josh pulled Roy up short, "Close enough."

The instant Roy caught sight of Savannah, his eyes bugged and jaw dropped, "What the hell happened? Are you okay?"

"You know how it happened," she basically croaked.

His brow jumped with a distinct "I do?" look to his face. Ennis jerked his head toward him, "Ask him about those scratches on his face."

Savannah couldn't exactly make direct eye contact with Roy. Nearly being bumped off by him shied her away from the idea. She did lift her vision to his forehead and cheeks. Red streaks crisscrossed his complexion. Just another nail in the coffin as far as she was concerned. Panicked, Roy glanced from one detective to another, "What? I'm a landscaper. I got caught by a rosebush this afternoon. Damn thing fell off the truck, smacked me in the head."

"Something smacked you in the head," Ennis agreed. "My partner's fingernails while you were trying to choke her to death."

Roy's head spun lightning fast back to Savannah, "And you think it was me? God sakes, Kitten, why would I try to kill you?"

At that particular moment, a detour to the hospital didn't sound so bad. Her neck joined her brain in dancing the samba on her nerves. Between all the shouting and stress, she could really use a shot of something potent to knock out the pain and calm her shaking. She laid back on the gurney as EMTs surrounded her, blocking Roy's access to her. With all the testosterone shielding her, she answered, "I remember a certain promise that turning in the gun would come back to bite me. And the note left here pretty well reflects your anger toward me."

Like Ennis, he strained for freedom – only in Roy's case his demeanor screamed panic, "What note? I said what I did because I was upset with you, not because I wanted to kill you. Savannah, you gotta believe —"

"I advised you of your rights, remember?" Josh held firm while Roy labored against him. "So maybe you should clam up. She's not listening."

With Savannah aboard, the EMTs rolled the gurney out of her once private, once perfectly messy abode. Now it stood with her captain, two detectives, a beat cop, and a very confused, dangerous man inside. Instead of messy, it now resembled what she considered total chaos after all the foot traffic, warm bodies, and cutlery used as darts and her beautiful hardwood floor as the dartboard. Damn.

13

He'd heard the voice loud and clear from his office. The deep tone flavored with a copious amount of disgust were difficult to miss, judging from other expressions he passed. Every creature, large and small, alive and dead heard R.J. Prince. It was that voice that sent Ennis into immediate action and in doing so, managed to solidly clip his hip on the corner of his desk. He didn't take time to cuss or kick the offending stick of furniture. He had to get to Savannah before the stress of the previous day blew sky high. She'd stayed the minimal time at Crawford Long, and spent a goodly part of it demanding to go home. By the time they arrived home, Ennis mentioned she should call Georgia and explain what happened. It took a split second for him to shut his trap. The glare she laid upon him described in detail how ugly she'd make his demise – if he mentioned contacting her family again.

Ennis hot-footed it down the hall to her office. R.J., as usual, fussed about something and in a rather expressive, loud way. A faint shadow from her doorway revealed a flail of hands and arms as her father spoke. Sidling up behind a tall fellow, he excused himself before barreling past the man. Once inside the small office, Ennis took stock of the situation. Savannah sat, head in hands, thoroughly frustrated with the scene but remaining quiet nonetheless. To her right stood Georgia, hand on her sister's back whispering to her. R.J. stood just inside the door creating a verbal melee. The man Ennis hurriedly pushed past was Savannah's brother Seth who stood close to R.J., his face pinched and eyes narrowed at their father.

Ennis opened his mouth to speak but R.J. beat him to it, "See? I told you coming here was a waste. She won't even look at me. You dragged me outta bed to apologize and for what? To be ignored by the insolent little –"

"What the hell's going on?" Ennis interrupted before R.J. finished his insult. He was tired of Savannah getting ripped and today he intended to put every one of them on notice.

Seth answered, "Georgia thought if he apologized to Savannah, it would fix the rift." He turned to Georgia with his arms folded, "Of course it hasn't because Pops won't shut up, like I told you he wouldn't."

Ennis wanted to grind his reply between his clenched teeth. He wanted to explain that apologies didn't work sometimes. Sometimes it was too late. After a deep breath, he managed in a much steadier voice than he imagined, "Take him home. She's had a bad week and this is making it worse."

R.J. centered on Ennis, his face darkening and hands fisting, "*I'm* making it worse? That what you said?"

The drunken old man stomped on his last nerve. Ennis saw Savannah look up just as he stepped closer to R.J., his hands fisting in response as well, "That's what I said. Coming here right now was a mistake. You can leave or be escorted out. Savannah doesn't need this shit."

Seth bolted forward at the exact time R.J. pulled back to punch. Ennis caught his fist in his hand and deflected the attack, much to R.J.'s surprise. Ennis gripped her father's fist mercilessly, his vision directly aligned with his, "Hit me and you'll go right back to jail. Only our lockup isn't as cushy as Richmond County's."

Savannah rose from her desk, her tone weary and brusque, "Just take him home. Ennis is right. I don't need this right now."

Her partner saw Georgia curiously eyeing the turtleneck sweater Savannah wore. The situation slid toward grievous in a big hurry. Ennis handed R.J. off to Seth so he could step between father and daughter. Unfortunately though, it was Georgia who opened Pandora's Box, "What's with the turtleneck? You hate them."

Savannah fidgeted with the collar, "It's cold outside. I decided to expand my taste."

"Whoa." Seth, the ex-army ranger, evidently possessed a sixth sense or he'd seen something. He warned R.J. to stay put then proceeded on his way to his youngest sister.

Savannah tried standing her ground. She held the indignant pose until Seth closed in which forced her backward a step to retain some space. When Georgia appeared at Seth's side, their sister's eyes widened as they traveled from one slibing to the other. Their close proximity overwhelmed the claustrophobic in her. Ennis shook his head. Had she taken his advice and called one of them last night, she could have avoided this situation today. She hadn't and now she was paying. He'd stay out of it for now, allowing her to answer questions she should have answered on the phone, *away* from the overbearing siblings.

Seth watched Savannah fiddle with the collar and squirm under his scrutiny. "What are you hiding?" he asked.

At that point, Georgia ganged up on her too, assuming the motherly hands-on-hips stance. From the corner of his eye, Ennis saw his partner angle her head in an attempt to catch his attention. She pleaded for help from the wrong person. After Seth shot a questioning glance over his shoulder at Ennis, he returned to his sister, "What is it, Savannah?"

Ennis imagined she was close to breaking by now. Being surrounded by both siblings – and the Prince siblings had a way of intimidating each other that bordered on the perverse, in his opinion – she had no choice but break soon. She made another effort to gain his line of vision and attention. Again Ennis chose to ignore her. He heard a weak reply from her – just a mere, "Nothing."

Ennis rolled his eyes and shook his head, "Not gonna tell them what Roy did, huh?"

Georgia and Seth wheeled to face him while Savannah glared straight at him. No missing those little arrows, he thought. She shot 'em true.

"What about Roy?" Seth suddenly gave his sister all the room she needed. He approached Ennis, the anger in his voice showing twice as lethal in his expression. Anger Ennis wanted no part of but her brother intended to get answers. "What did he do?" Seth's voice developed a hardness reminding Ennis of R.J.'s anger. No doubt the two were father and son, at least from Ennis's point of view.

At first he thought he'd done the right thing. In retrospect, Ennis doubted he should have opened his mouth. Judging from Savannah's heated appearance, he realized *he* might have opened Pandora's Box, not Georgia. "He, um, broke in her house –"

"And he caught me from behind," Savannah concluded, her vision still locked on Ennis. She yanked the turtleneck down to expose the bruises, "He didn't kill me, obviously, so there's no reason for this circus."

Even as Georgia and Seth swarmed to get a closer look, Savannah wouldn't break eye contact with Ennis. Oh yes, the deepest shit this side of the White House. He'd probably spend quite a few nights alone after this. "I told you," he whispered, "to call them last night."

She spoke in her normal voice to reply, "I was a little too involved getting coddled by the hospital staff at the time. When I got home, if you remember, I just wanted to go to bed."

"Where is Roy?" Seth demanded.

"Behind bars so you can't kill him," she said. "It wasn't a big deal –"

"Here or Augusta?" he asked.

Savannah said "Augusta" at the same time Ennis replied "Here". Seth and Georgia both looked to Ennis for the truth. He crossed his arms, "He's here but you can't see him." He acknowledged their anger by saying, "I wanted to kill him too and so did Josh and Mathis. Roy's going back to Augusta today. They're questioning him about a murder."

"Murder?" Georgia blurted like someone pinched her. The blood drained from her cheeks and Seth put his arm around her waist to guide her into a chair. Mouth agape in shock, she barely eked out, "And he broke into your house and tried to kill you."

"No," Savannah corrected. "He could have killed me but chose not to." Even in her own mind it sounded stupid but she was tired of being grilled.

"Don't defend the bastard, Savannah," Seth replied while inspecting the bruises. "That looks like a blood choke and you could have died in a matter of seconds."

"A blood choke?" Georgia asked, her expression still stunned and pallid.

"Applying pressure to the carotid arteries. The victim goes down quick and quiet."

Georgia uttered an expletive so foreign to her character, it forced Ennis to do a double-take to ensure it fell from her lips and not Savannah's. After the briefest of silences, the eldest sister declared an edict, "You're staying with me until this mess is sorted out. I have a gun –"

"Hello," Savannah pointed to her hip, "so do I."

"And why didn't you use it?" The question came from her brother. She cut her eyes to him and narrowed them, annoyed. She knew he was goading her into admitting that she'd had no time, that the blood choke disabled her instantly – and that staying with someone else was prudent.

Again, Ennis watched her ice blue eyes swing to him. She blamed him for starting this firestorm. "Because," she squeezed through clenched

teeth, "he caught me unawares and disabled me with the hold. There."
She aimed the remainder of her tirade at Seth, "Are you happy now?"

He folded his arms, "It would be smart to stay with one of us.
It's a matter of time until Roy makes bail. His family will pony up the
cash then what will you do?"

"She goes home for one thing," another voice said. It was Josh.
He shouldered his way into the room to face his female detective, "I told
you to stay home this week. Go with one of your kin, Savannah. You
need recuperation time." He headed Georgia off when she lifted her
head, hell-bent on confronting him, "She swore me to secrecy about the
attack, promised me she'd tell you. Clearly she didn't. Take her home,
will ya? Read *her* the riot act."

Savannah could have bitten nails she was so pissed. Being dissected
publicly had been bad enough but for Ennis to instigate the dissection...
Well, she needed time to mull that one over. More to the truth, she
needed time to cool down. Ennis grew up in an entirely different family
atmosphere. His brothers protected him – to a degree. Savannah's
siblings took protection to a nearly suffocating level. As a kid, they'd
swept her safely upstairs when R.J. came home drunk. Many times
they'd endured the merciless beatings meant for her. Now, when danger
threatened her, Seth and Georgia reverted back to their young selves.
Nice as it sounded in theory, in reality it truly became a nightmare as
they converged, demanding and bullying.

She'd walked out on all of them, leaving Josh and Ennis stunned, and Seth and Georgia throwing orders around like Nazis. Somehow her father managed to remain quiet during the chaos. He hadn't offered a word or helping hand – but at least he hadn't made the situation worse. She half expected him to label her a coward for walking. She totally expected him to call her useless. The instant she shoved the Camaro into Drive, she aimed it in the direction of Piedmont Park. Now she sat alone on a park bench sorting out the whirlwind called her life. Pulling the coat's heavy wool collar around her neck, she burrowed deep to cut off the biting wind. January was turning into December's twin with the day's high only reaching the mid twenties. It figured, she thought. All she needed was a good old fashioned blizzard to top off her week.

The wind bit into her hands, forcing her to pocket them for warmth. Savannah watched people scatter as the cold front hit, the feel of snow in the air. She needed to go home and be alone. She'd treat herself to a warm bubble bath then a hamburger and a Yoo-Hoo. Afterward, she'd indulge in the cupcakes she'd stashed in the upper cabinet for just such hideous occasions.

Unfortunately, going home was out of the question. Visions of Seth and Georgia hunkered in corners, waiting to pounce, filled her brain. Ennis probably stood to the side, lasso in hand, ready to rope her like a damn heifer. To ward off that event (and her hunger), she stopped and grabbed a cup of coffee and yes, a donut. Two donuts to be exact, with three in a take-out bag on her front seat.

A couple dressed in heavy winter coats ambled by, unaffected by the weather. Between them, their young son finished singing his rendition of Jingle Bells. Although it was January, Christmas clearly lingered fresh in his mind as his little boy voice started the song again, "Jingle Bells, Batman smells, Robin laid an egg..."

She smiled for probably the first time that day. She nearly laughed as the mother attempted to divert his attention to another song.

Savannah remembered when she butchered Christmas carols as a kid. She'd sung "Deck the Halls with Buddy Holly" forever until Georgia finally corrected her. The thought reminded her that her cell phone was turned off. No doubt her brother, sister and Ennis tried contacting her the last hour but she hadn't prepared herself to do anything past vegetate on the park bench.

Enough time passed she could probably answer the phone without yelling at the caller so she turned it on without bothering to check her messages. No more than thirty seconds lapsed when it rang. Savannah hemmed and hawed about answering it, knowing it couldn't be anyone she actually wanted to hear from, at least right then. It rang incessantly until she clicked on, "Yeah?"

"Are you all right?" Ennis inquired. "Where are you?"

She harrumphed, "Like I'd tell you, Benedict. Thanks for ratting me out at the station."

"You said you'd call them."

"Yeah, well..." she rubbed her forehead, frustrated. "I didn't but still I wished you'd kept quiet. Seth's temper rivals Daddy's. Now he's on the warpath and Roy will be lucky to live through the week."

"Don't you think he deserves some frontier justice after what he did?"

Savannah hesitated to state her opinion. After spending all night and all day thinking about it, she couldn't honestly identify Roy as her attacker. The man looked like him from the limited angles she got – he even wore a Carlson jacket – but if push came to shove, distinguishing Roy from another man with the same haircut and build would be iffy. She'd reviewed her attack as well as Owen's information until her brain threatened to explode. She knew a few facts herself. Roy tended to cling to certain women, even after a breakup. He owned a gun that he'd tried to hide from the police. He certainly sounded menacing on the phone before her attack, whether he followed through or not. And the biggest nail of all – he was bipolar and she wasn't entirely sure he was taking his medication.

"You don't, do you?" Ennis sounded put out again. "You still think he's innocent of everything, even your assault."

Savannah wavered between bitching him out or dissolving in tears, "Ennis, I don't know what to think. I hardly know Roy anymore."

"That's right. Remember that. Now come on home. No one's forcing you to move in with them. Your actions spoke louder than words."

14

Savannah drove up to see the unmarked police car stationed at her curb, Ennis's truck and Seth's Ford F-150 snugged into her usual roost. Recollections of pouncing and lassos reared their heads. At least two of the culprits lurked inside *her* house, waiting for her to stupidly stumble into their trap. *Not today*, she lamented then pulled the Camaro into Reverse to leave. Taking a quick glance behind her, she began to ease the car into the street again.

A banging on her window scared her so bad she jumped, stopping the car with a lurch. Whirling around, she saw Seth motioning to kill the engine. He had to be joking. She wasn't voluntarily getting waylaid so she let the car roll further toward the street. Seth followed alongside then whacked the hood with his fist, "Park it, Savannah."

Now that made her mad. Telegraphing the emotion was easy until Ennis fell in behind Seth. She noticed her expression at least backed *him* off a step. Seth wanted the car parked? Well, okay... She clicked the transmission into Drive and revved the engine which panicked Ennis. His brand new truck sat less than ten feet from her front end. Releasing the brake, she squealed her displeasure by racing the ten feet then slamming on the brakes. Jamming the gearshift into Park, she quickly killed the engine and jumped out. She squared off with her brother, staring up at him with the same heat she'd felt most of the day, "I'm sick of people telling me what to do."

Seth suddenly smiled then swung his arm around her shoulders, "Then stop acting like a baby."

Savannah pulled from his embrace, pissed off that he took her anger so lightly, "I'm not kidding, Seth. This is the week from hell and everyone's treading on thin ice." She glanced at Ennis whose eyes had squeezed tight and his face faded lily white. "Ennis, your truck is fine."

His eyes opened cautiously to peer at his prized vehicle. Upon sight of the whisper of space between it and her Camaro, they widened to saucers and he swallowed audibly. She stalked past him then the sound of her car door slamming spun her to once again face her brother.

Seth held up the bag of donuts, amused, "Aren't you forgetting something?"

After three determined strides, she ripped the bag from his hold, "Thanks to all of you I've fallen off the wagon. My last one was in June. I've had two today already and I'm seriously thinkin' about polishing these off." She stomped toward the front door. The sight of the lock stopped her, "What the hell is this?"

"A deadbolt," Seth said. "I installed it while you were gone. Ennis let me in."

Savannah heard Ennis swallow again. One thing about Ennis – he knew her well enough to realize when the shit was deep enough to drown in. He'd opened the door to hell for her that morning and it hadn't let up since so no, not even water wings would save him now.

She didn't bother to turn around, "Well, he's mighty handy, isn't he? He makes decisions for his dimwitted partner quite often lately. Surprised he lets me out alone." She gave the deadbolt a brief inspection, "Did he also tell you the guy came through the *window* and not the door?"

"Yes, but the insurance of a deadbolt won't hurt." Seth sidled up behind her, whispering, "You realize Ennis is only trying to help, right? Don't smack him upside the head for caring."

This coming from a man who, before his marriage, told his fiancée to stop hovering around him so much. The remembrance lingered on her tongue for a second before she swallowed it, "I'm not but I'm not five years old either. We're partners, Seth, not spouses."

His large hand covered her shoulder to tug her closer, "He's thinking with the right head, Van. That should count for something. He's the only one I'd give my stamp of approval on."

She turned to him, blinked a few times but said nothing. Hers and Ennis's relationships – professional and personal – were their business alone. She didn't interfere with his and Leah's so she expected the same courtesy. Yeah, right… She could expect whatever she wanted. Truth remained both her siblings not only tried to commandeer the train but reroute the tracks to their liking.

She'd absconded to the bathroom for the long awaited bubble bath while her brother and partner conversed in the living room. More likely they conspired, Savannah thought darkly. And it frightened the living hell out of her to wonder what they conspired about.

At least the bath gave her a slice of time to think about the murder in Augusta, Roy's involvement (if there was one), and her attack. Her hand lifted to her throat to gingerly inspect the bruises. Little bolts of pain traveled to her brain making her cringe. She finished washing up then proceeded to towel off. Halfway through she heard her cell phone ring. It rang a second time until someone answered it. A moment passed when a soft knock rapped on the bathroom door. It was Ennis, "It's Rose Austin Psychiatric."

Savannah wrapped the towel around her, thoroughly puzzled, "What do they want?" She sincerely desired an answer before opening the door. Once it opened, the serene atmosphere and her sanity would take a nosedive for sure. Lately, reality had that effect on her.

"They're not in a chatty mood with me. What'd you do, reserve a room?"

She yanked the door open then gasped as a blast of cold air swept through the once cozy room, "Hush up and hand me the phone." She palmed it, noticed Ennis had muted it then finished, "And turn up the heat, okay? I'm not a polar bear."

"No," her brother called from the living room, "but you *are* a bear today."

"You can shut up too," she declared then slammed the door shut. Why the hospital would be calling her stumped her. She knew no one in Rose Austin but if things didn't level out soon, she *would* reserve a room for herself. She lifted the phone, un-muted it then answered it,

"Savannah Prince."

"Detective Prince, I'm Amber Wilson, a nurse at Rose Austin Psychiatric Hospital. I'm sorry for bothering you this evening but one of our patients has requested we contact you."

Finally, she breathed. An easily correctable misunderstanding, "I don't know anyone at Rose Austin."

"Do you know a Roy Carlson?"

So much for a misunderstanding, "Roy's in the psych ward? What happened?"

"The police brought him in earlier today when he was delusional and uncontrollable. We've sedated him but he keeps repeating your name and phone number. I thought I'd give you a call. I was hoping if he saw you, he might calm down."

Savannah gripped the towel harder, "You want me to come see him." *No chance in hell of that, lady. Not unless,* "Is he restrained?"

"Oh, yes. The police said he'd assaulted another officer and considering Mr. Carlson's condition, we had no choice." The nurse sounded perfectly apologetic for some reason. Savannah intended to put her mind at ease, "*I* was the detective that was assaulted. From what I understand, Roy has bipolar disorder but I didn't think he was delusional." *He sure seemed coherent to me – if that was his hand around my throat.*

There was a silence on the other end. Savannah assumed the nurse contemplated what to say next. Thinking she heard something, Savannah listened closer. A steady racket in the background continued. She heard a voice yelling something, repeating it over and over. "Is that

Roy?"

The nurse answered quickly, "Yes ma'am, it is. He's been like that since eleven this morning. I'm sorry, I didn't realize you were the officer attacked –"

"I'll be there in about thirty minutes. I'll do what I can to calm him down."

A relieved sigh heaved over the phone, "Thank you, Detective. *Thank you...*"

15

As usual, she didn't travel alone. Ennis made sure of it. Seth insisted on going as well except Savannah ran to the Camaro and started out of the driveway before he could leap in. Ennis, though, knew her well enough to follow close – in case she bolted. He succeeded in hauling the door open and planting one foot inside before she shifted into Drive. Savannah refused to look at him, instead settling for a brief instruction, "Buckle up. This ain't no Sunday drive." Yes, she still fumed over the day and Ennis fully recognized it, especially when she pressed the accelerator.

Now, walking the semi-quiet halls of Rose Austin Hospital, she wracked her brain trying to remember the nurse's name that had called. Amber was all she recalled. Men and women dressed in perfectly pressed white attire passed with momentary glances at the two striding toward the nurse's desk, but none appeared to expect them or seem curious enough to address them. *It's no wonder*, she groused. *We look like veritable hobos.* They shed their coats upon entering the hospital and now she took stock of their apparel. She'd thrown on the first pair of jeans in sight and a cherry red Atlanta Falcons sweatshirt that had seen better days. Ennis seemed right at home in his faded, practically torn jeans and an old blue Dallas Cowboys sweatshirt. They couldn't have made a more conflicting pair of hobos if they tried.

The two stopped at the nurse's desk where Savannah introduced herself and asked for Amber. Upon hearing the name, the woman sitting behind the desk slumped temporarily, her features awash in relief, "Thank you again for coming, Detective. Mr. Carlson isn't settling down like I'd hoped. We've medicated him as much as safely possible. I told him you were coming but I guess he doesn't believe me."

"He still tied down?" Ennis asked only to receive a jab in the gut from Savannah's elbow.

The nurse nodded, her brow furrowing as a sign she didn't appreciate the outburst either. She pointed down the hall, "I'll go with you." Nurse Wilson held Ennis back, "I'd allow you to go however Mr. Carlson isn't receptive to anyone, especially men."

"Wonder why," he mumbled. He jerked away from a second assault from his partner's elbow.

The two women walked the hall's brilliantly waxed floor in silence. The walls were bare and painted a clinical white, and everywhere she looked, the interior exuded the charm of a pile of dirt. Every door they passed was closed and, she assumed, locked. Only a card with the patient's name broke the visual monotony.

The place was quiet with the distinct exception of a voice repeatedly yelling, "Detective Savannah Prince, Atlanta Police!" then her cell number – for all the world to hear. Well, all the world residing at Rose Austin.

Savannah paused before stepping in. Roy's tone sounded panicked and pitiful at the same time. Peeking around the corner, she noticed he was indeed restrained to the bed. She released a long breath and tried to calm her pounding heart. She took a step inside, amazed at the fight Roy gave the leather restraints. Roy thrashed wildly against them, giving the bed a generous rattle. She worried it might not survive his flailing thus giving him the freedom he fought for – she looked at her watch – nine hours to gain. His body was soaked in sweat, his hair and face glistening. Lines of tears streaked his anguished handsome face. The sight almost made her tear up. Almost.

He arched on the bed, pulled at his wrists and yanked at his ankles. He looked like a giant railing against the bonds as he yelled, "Detective Savannah Prince, Atlanta –" then suddenly the yelling magically ceased. Amber released an audible sigh upon the abrupt silence. Savannah didn't move.

"Kitten," he called, his voice hoarse from shouting. Roy's relief surfaced in the way of more tears, his body finally relaxing, "Please help me."

Savannah stayed put and also remained quiet. Roy pulled against the restraints to gain a better view of her, "Help me."

"What do you want, Roy?" The fear in her voice startled her. She sounded scared out of her mind which she wasn't. Tentative and jumpy, yes. Peeing her pants scared, not yet.

"I didn't do it," his voice pleaded. More tears fell, "I didn't do it. Help me."

She guessed he spoke of her attack. Despite his efforts to draw her near, she refused to for fear he'd bust the restraints and finish the job. "From what I saw, the man looked very similar to you."

Roy's body stiffened, the muscles strained and bulged beneath his moist skin, "I didn't do it!" he yelled. His fingers splayed in a futile attempt to reach her, his tone a jumble of imploring and anger, "A DNA test."

Making sense of the conversation was like baking a cake without a recipe. She uttered a prayer and hoped she mixed it together right. Savannah ran her thumb across her fingernails remembering the scrapings forensics took. "What are you saying? The police didn't get a sample of your DNA?"

A swell of rage overwhelmed Roy, sending him into another battle with the restraints, "Bastards!"

She stepped back in response to his temper, "I take that as a 'no'." She knew for a fact they had, though. Mathis said they were awaiting the results. Roy either didn't remember or the delusions set in worse than she thought.

Roy saw Savannah edge backward and displayed his most pitiful expression, "Kitten, please help me."

"Then calm down," she stated frankly. Savannah barely knew dip about bipolar disorder. Most of her experience came from the job. Without medication, people suffering from bipolar disorder became delusional and sometimes violent. She witnessed the effect of delusions on its victims. Roy's wild flailing and anger rang a bell with her, his limited vocabulary didn't. Her interactions with delusional bipolar individuals proved they had a profound knowledge of the English language – even profane – and some used it until it ran on rims. Roy barely strung a sentence together and from that, she had to form an intelligent idea of his ramblings. Between swings in his personality and mood, he struggled to tell her something he thought important.

Before her very eyes, Roy metamorphosed again by sinking to the bed, his arms and legs falling limp. He placed his head gently on the mattress, "Please don't leave me."

Savannah shifted her vision to Amber who whispered for her to be careful. The detective baby-stepped forward, still wary of his demeanor. "Roy, I'm here. You called for me and here I am. Tell me what you want."

He inhaled slowly, looked at her. Savannah swore she stared down at the old Roy, the sweetest, kindest gentleman aside from Ennis she'd ever met. The hardness left his eyes, the tension melted from his jaw and neck and the vein across his forehead disappeared at last. He opened his hand in offering to her. She did not partake. Eventually it drooped to hang loosely in the restraint. "A DNA test," he answered quietly. "I didn't do it." Lifting his vision again, tears welled and a shaky smile crossed his lips, "I love you so much, I couldn't hurt you."

She stood, searching for words that never came. His sentiment went straight to her heart. She knew she'd cut him deep by refusing his marriage proposal years ago. It was the first time she'd seen a man cry. It was also the only time a man had taken to begging her for anything, and Roy merely pleaded for her not to leave him. Back then she gave little thought as to the damage a woman could do with one little word. With time, she'd grown mentally and emotionally. She loved him but her love differed from his as she now realized. He'd loved her wholly and in her haste to leave Augusta and R.J., she'd broken Roy's heart. Staring into his eyes that once again pleaded with her, the realization brought tears to her eyes.

Roy again offered his open hand to her, "I've always loved you, Savannah."

She glanced down at the trembling fingers. Her head told her one thing – her heart told her another. Roy was innocent and that Ennis had been right. Way down, she believed Roy Carlson. And she took his hand.

Tears fell from his eyes as he held on tight. Savannah covered his hand with hers and to appease him, said, "I'll have a DNA test run. But Roy," she said, bringing his eyes open to meet hers. She continued, "You have to settle down while you're here."

His eyes sparkled, his lips curled into a weak smile, "Thanks, Kitten."

"If you'll behave in here, I promise that DNA test."

As though a moment of clarity hit him, he nodded obediently even while tears streamed his face, "I promise too."

Roy hadn't exactly kept his promise but, in his condition, she hadn't expected him to. Consequently, he incessantly serenaded the ward with his thunderous ritual of repeating her name and phone number again. Most of Rose Austin had no choice but memorize the information considering they heard it 24 hours a day – at one volume or another.

After one disturbing visit, Savannah questioned them about medicating him with anti-psychotics. Roy's delusions graduated from them being old flames to them marrying and having a little boy. The moment she'd walked in, Roy questioned where her wedding ring was. She failed to pull her mind into that particular gear. Hadn't they discussed this, oh, about thirteen years ago? Before her lips moved to reply, Roy interrogated her about their son, Mark. How was he, how was school, did he make the soccer team... Still too stunned to react, Savannah merely stood with a blank expression. To know someone personally with a mental disorder – a person who she'd cared deeply for, it brought her to her knees. Seeing Roy babbling about their next anniversary – and his promise not to forget it, the fact she needed to retire from the department to raise Mark at home, and the goal to buy them a bigger house was all too much. She approached a nurse to inquire about anti-psychotics and lithium, "He's getting worse. We aren't married and we don't have a kid." Savannah realized she sounded more alarmed than she intended. All the years as a cop neglected to prepare her for this. She'd hardened herself to a point but watching Roy lose his mind was disturbing her in ways she'd never thought possible. If she wasn't careful, she'd lose hers too.

She came to that particular conclusion when, after arriving home, she found herself rummaging her jewelry box. The beautiful Maple Burl jewelry box had been a gift from her mother on Savannah's eighteenth birthday. Charlene presented each daughter with one and inside tucked another priceless treasure – a ring of Grandma Culberson's. Savannah kept that ring stored beneath the tray in its own special box.

The six pound jewelry box was polished to a shining piano finish and had a tassled key for locking and unlocking it. Lifting the lid brought back fond memories of Charlene as the tune "What a Wonderful World" began to play. Her mother, always the optimist, loved to sing and always found time to sing that song, no matter how difficult times got.

Savannah opened the lid and as the song played, her eyes grew moist with memories of her smiling mother. She consciously pushed those aside, knowing if she mired down in tears, the old depression would return. Instead, she concentrated on the various pieces of jewelry including her class ring and St. Michael pendant. Georgia enlightened her to the fact St. Michael was the patron saint of police officers. Savannah dangled the necklace from her fingers and made a mental note to wear it more often.

With a tad more scrounging, she located the little box she searched for. With it in hand, she opened the velvet box to reveal a delicate silver band with a single diamond in the middle. She'd kept it for thirteen years though she doubted Roy intended for her to. At the time he proposed, she offered the ring back to him only to have him close her fingers around the box, "Keep it and think about my proposal. Please, Kitten. Just think about it."

Savannah sat on the bed, leaving the ring in the box, her mind adrift in a sea of melancholy. Reminiscences of high school with Roy and speculation of "what if" she'd accepted his proposal? Would their marriage have survived his illness and the trials associated with it? She tried to imagine what Roy's wife thought and did while her husband's personality changed so drastically before her very eyes…

"That looks ominous. In fact, it looks like an engagement ring."

Savannah gasped and hastily closed the box while Ennis rounded the bed and sat beside her. He held out his hand. Reluctantly she plopped the velvet box into his palm. Ennis reopened it, studied the ring inside, "So he wasn't bullshitting me, after all. You really were engaged."

"No, we really weren't," she corrected. "He told me to keep the ring and think about it."

Ennis considered that. He tilted the diamond toward the light until a beam of a multi-colored prism shone in his hand, "Are you still thinking about it?"

Savannah slanted him an "are you kidding?" glance, "If I was going to marry Roy, I should be into my, oh, twelfth or thirteenth anniversary by now, don'tcha think? I wasn't sure when to return it to him. First, I'd like him to remember we're *not* married before I give it back."

He removed the ring and placed it on the tip of his index finger. It barely slid to the first knuckle, "Sorry you didn't get hitched?"

"Ennis, don't," was the weary plea. She hadn't the patience or energy to reassure his ego. Hard as he tried, Ennis's jealousy cropped up at the most unexpected or inopportune times. She watched him angle the diamond to her left hand and for the pure sake of his entertainment, allowed him to slip it on her finger.

Ennis admired it and a tiny smile played at his mouth, "Looks good on you." He placed a gentle kiss on her knuckles, "But mine will look much, much better."

16

Morning found her wide awake even earlier than usual. The whole situation consumed her throughout the night whether in dreams and total consciousness. Various questions plagued her like an itch she couldn't reach. At five o'clock, she rolled out of bed to prepare for a little trip. She grabbed a quick breakfast and by the time she leaned down to kiss Ennis goodbye, his eyes popped wide as though sleep never graced them, "Where are you going?"

"Augusta to poke around."

"Need a lookout, Snoopy? I'm all eyes and ears."

She smiled then pecked him on the lips, "Nope, I think I can handle it. Thanks anyway." She began to straighten when Ennis palmed the back of her head and drew her down for another kiss, this one longer and deeper. The heat of his kiss toyed with the idea of leaving, especially so early. She *could* hang around to delight in further pleasures. She'd made no appointments, no commitments. No one expected her anywhere.

His hand slid beneath her blouse to caress her back gently. Savannah heard herself release a small moan. Then the world spun...

Ennis's arm snaked around her waist and pulled her atop him. The moment vanished swiftly, however, as pain registered in his features and he muttered an expletive sharp enough to make her blush. Other general abuses of the English language followed then, "Blazing hell, I didn't know you had your gun."

Savannah winced as Ennis's hand raced to his lower regions to cradle them. Nothing like crippling someone to make a person feel like a rat, "I'm sorry, Ennis. I didn't know you were going to do that or I'd have braced myself."

"S'okay," he squeaked. "My fault for surprising you." He threw the covers back to inspect himself, "It all still functions, I think."

Feeling a tad naughty (and bad about his near life-altering incident), Savannah pressed a kiss to her palm then reached down and cupped the injured site. Instantly, Ennis's body went board stiff, some places stiffer than others as his arousal regained momentum. His eyes rolled back and his fists clenched in the covers, "You minx. You're trying to finish me off."

Giving him a gentle squeeze, she winked into his pained vision, "Well, I just proved your equipment is fully operational."

"And," he gasped when her fingertips brushed along his arousal. "And you're leaving me in this condition. Your cruelty knows no bounds."

She bent to kiss his pursed lips, "I promise not to leave you in dire straits again."

He smiled rather miserably, "At least cure me of this affliction before you go. Otherwise I won't be able to walk."

Savannah tickled under his chin, "Then I'll know you're safe and sound waiting for me in bed."

He captured her hand, kissed it softly, "About that. For future reference, just remember I'm the only one allowed to bring a loaded weapon to bed."

She hadn't left Ennis in a world of hurt. It took little encouragement for her to fall into his embrace, this time without wearing a gun or anything but a big smile. Her partner certainly had a way that promoted thoughts of marriage. At the strangest times she found herself thinking about it or glancing at her left hand. Ennis put up with a lot from her, she knew that. He tolerated her temper, her moods and her claustrophobia and still wanted to marry her. On her way to Augusta, she again found her thoughts wandering toward the matrimonial state of mind. After the situation with Roy wrapped up, she decided maybe she should think about their relationship.

After the long two hour drive, Savannah nearly dropped off at her house for a breather. She decided against it when her father's pickup stared back at her from the driveway. She didn't feel like another confrontation so she proceeded with her original plan. Her watch displayed the time as eight-fifteen. Someone, somewhere would be open by that time. Initially she planned on visiting Roy's landscaping business. At the last minute she hung a left on Haynie Drive. Her goal – Augusta Police Headquarters. She drove down East Robinson Avenue until pulling into the building's parking lot. The building looked aged enough the cops would probably start asking for a newer, bigger building and higher salaries. Since she was a kid, the place only got new paint and new windows. To her it looked kind of quaint, like it belonged in a small town. But to the local cops, she knew it seemed small and cramped.

She clipped her badge to her belt – just in case ol' Vincent Price made trouble for her. After inquiring about Owen at the front desk, she meandered down one hallway then another. She passed empty offices, careful to note the names as she went by. Evidently Vincent was out or in another office. At the end of the hall she found Owen Dunne's tiny office, the door closed. Through the blinds she saw him hunkered over his desk, reading from a report. She knocked softly on the door then waved at him.

He motioned her inside. She opened the door just enough to slip in then shut it behind her, "Hey, Owen."

"Hey, Savannah, how's life treating you?"

"Like a bucket of paint. All mixed up."

"Anything I can do to un-mix the situation?"

She paused, unsure of his reaction to her upcoming request, "May I look at the Maria Saxon reports and crime scene photos?" She held up her hands to ward off any negative response, "I'm not interfering in your investigation. This is just one cop to another, looking things over."

Owen peered past her, out the window. She figured he looked for Vincent. When he saw the coast was clear he shrugged, "Sure, why not? A fresh pair of eyes might help."

She whipped out her glasses and slid them on. Perhaps this visit might produce hope for Roy. Restraining her excitement became difficult since she'd love to walk into Rose Austin to exonerate her friend. She pulled up a chair to face Owen's desk and thanked him.

Owen thumbed through a few files, finally settling on one. Before handing it over, he inquired, "How's Roy doing?"

"He's been better but haven't we all?" she replied noncommittally.

"Yeah," he pointed to the bruises on her neck, "how's that feeling?"

"Sore as hell." She took the thick file and opened it. Numerous witness interviews along with a generous thickness of photos greeted her. "What all did my dear neighbor tell you?"

Running it past Owen seemed more political rather than skewering him with leading questions. It seemed best to find out what the nosy old lady said first. He shrugged, "Just that Roy was at your place most of the night. She saw him leave for a while then come back. Said he sat in his truck for a while before going back in."

"According to Roy, that's when he went after the beer." Momentarily she skipped the interviews and went straight to the photos. The first picture showed Maria Saxon lying on the floor of her house, on her stomach, her dark hair splayed wildly across her face and the floor. From what Savannah could tell about the woman, she had a dancer's body, long and lithe and legs that went forever. *Not only beautiful*, she thought, *but shapely*. "How tall was she?"

"About your height. Five eight, five nine. Why?"

She shook her head, still in thought. Maria was fully clothed with one added, very unusual accessory. An electrical cord around her throat. "Any usable prints on the cord?"

"Nope, just smudged partials. Most matched her."

Savannah glanced up at Owen, "How did the guy get inside? Front door like she knew him and let him in or forced entry?"

Owen leaned forward on his elbows. He studied her until she lifted her vision to him. "Broken window in the back bedroom."

She swallowed, and the resulting ache in her throat reminded that hers and Maria's attacks began the same way – with a broken window in the back bedroom.

Owen evidently sensed her thoughts, "That's how Roy broke into your place, isn't it?"

"That's how *someone* broke in," she corrected. Unlike the rest of humanity, she wasn't entirely ready to lynch Roy yet. "If Roy and Maria had been a couple, he should have a key to her place, right?"

"They broke up."

She chuckled, "And how many people are honest about giving back a key, Owen? Only safe way is to change the lock which I assume she didn't. Have you interviewed her current love?"

"We've searched email, mail, credit cards, phone records, everything, and there's no indication of a new boyfriend as such. There are plenty of calls to and from Carlson Landscape which raises a question. Obviously she and Roy still spoke to each other."

"Roy's not the only person in that building or the only one who uses the phone there."

"Now don't get defensive, Savannah. This is our investigation so far. Even her friends said she tried for months to ditch him and he wouldn't take no for an answer."

Savannah looked away briefly. She'd had to basically threaten him off of her that night he stayed at the house. But, her brain interjected, he probably wasn't on medication either. Bipolar behavior included aggression, increased sexual drive, poor judgment and impulsiveness. Those certainly fit into his insistent nature the night they were together.

She returned to the photos. The next one showed the broken window used for entrance. A few jagged shards hung from the top but most of the glass peppered the carpet, some bigger pieces but mostly smaller, crushed shards. Her mind cranked out a visual of a man Roy's size trying to squeeze through the broken window without slicing himself up. "He couldn't have fit through that window, Owen. Roy's a big guy. His shoulders," she indicated with her hands, "are that wide."

"Well, the photo was taken after a rookie lowered the window. It was open before the photo, like the killer smashed the window then reached in, unlocked it, raised it then entered."

The new information lit her temper. The first two things she instructed rookies to do at a crime scene were one, keep their hands in their pockets and two, make like a statue with their hands in their pockets. In other words, she'd say, don't friggin' compromise an already chaotic scene. Sloppy and incompetent police work deserved nothing short of instant dismissal, in her opinion. Hiding those feelings took effort, "This rookie, is he still on the job?"

Owen shied from her anger and shrugged, "Don't rightly know."

She let it drop but not because she wanted to. With her question, she managed to put Owen on edge without intending to. She referred to the folder again and another critical clue caught her eye, "Muddy footprints…"

Owen answered quickly to diffuse any rant she may have, "Detailed photos of them *and* impressions. The shoes were Nike Shox NZ. We matched the soles from the FBI database. The prints are size thirteen. Over a hundred dollars a pair."

Mental note. Find out Roy's shoe size… She'd call the night nurse at Rose Austin for a favor later. Unless, "Do you have Roy's shoes?"

"Every pair we could find. All of 'em Nike, all size thirteen."

Deep down, Savannah felt her heart break a little. The evidence began piling up on him while he was strapped down in a mental ward. Fighting for his innocence would do no good if Owen kept bashing every gem of hope she held. He'd basically deflated her with his last statement and his expression revealed he knew it, "Savannah, I'm not ganging up on Roy. We don't have all the evidence analyzed anyway. The shoe prints aren't done and the DNA we found isn't back. It's not an open and shut case but, honey, you're gonna have to face it. He could be guilty."

She screwed her mouth to the side to avoid agreeing with him. Until the evidence buried him, she wouldn't. "What about glass shards? There should be some in the tread of his shoes if he broke the window and walked through it. He'd have to walk through some of it."

He shrugged, his tone remained soft, "Like I said, still haven't analyzed them. I'm gonna tell you something that Pierce would have my ass over if he heard me."

"Yeah, about him. What's his beef with me?" The words tumbled from her lips freely and recklessly. As she spoke them, her brain scrambled to grab them back or at least stop her tongue from flapping. Attacking a cop's partner was a nice way of cutting off the supply of information. And she'd just jumped on with claws bared.

Owen, thankfully, didn't seem to take offense, "He knows where you came from. The money, I mean."

"Ah, the silver spoon routine. Thought I outgrew that in Atlanta."

"Hey, *I* know you're a good cop. This is his rub, not mine. I'd be honored to partner up with you any day."

She smiled easily at that. As a kid Owen had a slight crush on her that lasted until Roy dominated the picture. She gave him a wink, "Same goes for me, Owen. If Pierce doesn't set me aflame with his searing stares, maybe you and I can work together on this."

He nodded a bit in agreement, "I'd like that. I'd better tell you before Pierce gets back. Maria Saxon was pregnant. It was a boy."

Savannah's mouth went dry. A baby twisted the plot even tighter. A dead woman was a priority to police. A dead *pregnant* woman became an obsession to them. Detectives tried keeping a wide scope during the investigation. Truth was, if someone looked good, they tended to gravitate to that person. Roy evidently looked like a pot roast on Christmas Eve and every cop in Augusta licked their chops. "Was it Roy's baby? Do you know for sure?"

"We need results of the DNA test. It'll take a while to return.

Savannah, I understand why you're defending Roy but fact is, if the baby was his, maybe he didn't want the kid. Some guys are like that."

Not likely with Roy, she thought. He seemed partial to the idea of having children, at least when off his medication. Mental disorder or not, she doubted a person could fake such sincerity about kids. If he knew about it, Savannah wondered if Maria's pregnancy played a part of his fantasy life with herself and their little boy "Mark".

"Did Roy know about the baby?"

Owen nodded. She chewed on that one a minute then, "You're already leaning toward the baby being his, Owen. She may have hooked up with someone else after ditching Roy."

"Not according to friends and family and neighbors said the only stray vehicle they ever saw was a Carlson's Landscape truck. They're all sure the baby is Roy's because she told him about it before their breakup."

"Did they say he was pissed about being a daddy?"

That inquiry made Owen pause. Savannah watched him mentally review the interviews which she intended to read and verify later. As if a light bulb went on inside his brain, he shook his head, "No, they didn't."

Since she managed to derail his train of thought temporarily, she forged on, "How about maintenance workers? Gardeners, lawnmower guy, plumbers?"

Owen dismissed it with a wave of his hand, "Checked 'em out. She mowed her own lawn, did her own gardening and the last plumber she called was two years ago."

Great. She was beautiful, shapely, green-thumbed and rarely used the bathroom. If Savannah tried to maintain her lawn and flowerbeds plus keep a successful job, they might as well bunk her in with Roy. Not only did juggling everything drain the sanity, it sapped the energy to zero. And if she added pregnancy to the equation – whew... Savannah just shook her head at the hideous scene taking place in her mind. "How in hell did she do everything herself while pregnant? The first trimester is a bitch or was she past that?"

"According to the medical examiner, she was about four, four and a half months."

"She either had the constitution of a horse or her baby made fewer headaches than I did. Mama said she barely dragged herself out of bed because I made her so sick."

Switching gears again, she tended to the nagging in her brain. It nettled her for the past few minutes as she perused the pictures, "Maria was a stockbroker, right? No offense but those people are as high on my food chain as lawyers and dentists. I assume you've questioned her clients?"

To her disgust, he nodded, finishing, "We've also checked her computer. In fact, she was a damn good broker, seemed like. Wish I had someone that good."

So she was beautiful, shapely, green-thumbed, hardly went to the bathroom, <u>and</u> successful. Chances are she has another boyfriend tucked away somewhere... For mere fodder she threw out the possibility, "No insider trading going on, was there? Every broker tanks once in a while." She smiled at Owen's comically sour frown, "Just asking, just asking." She scanned the pictures methodically, searching for proof of a statement Roy made.   She looked at every wall in every picture, "Your people take pictures of every room?"

The question perked Owen's interest.   Instead of tossing back a defensive reply, he strained to see the photos, "Yeah, and we've got double prints. Why?"

Had Roy lied to her? Or had the mental disorder scrambled his recollection of that one night? The walls looked clean and in tact. No holes from Roy's fist that she could tell. "How about behind pictures and taller furniture?"

"Ah, the holes in the walls. We found four. Her friends told us where she hid them. She hung pictures over them. The photos of them are further down in there."

Well, shit...   She was half hoping Roy had lied or at least stretched the truth and in a way he had. He said he punched three holes. There were four. The next photo sucked the breath from her. Maria Saxon's nude, lifeless body on the silver autopsy table. Her neck sported the stripe marks from the electrical cord and, now that she lay on her back and not her side, Savannah saw a gentle, subtle rise at her lower belly. *The baby...* "My God," she whispered more to herself than anyone. Death and abuse of babies and children literally turned her gut. Being a cop hardly seemed worth it at times like that.

The following picture showed Maria from above. The purplish-red lividity highlighted her body from her right cheek, down the front of her torso and the tops of her thighs. Even a fool would have noticed the darker oval spots sporadically scattered over her chest and belly.

Savannah's vision traveled the body then returned solidly to the stomach. She'd seen fist marks plenty of times before. The knuckles were perfectly outlined to indicate a man with big hands beat the woman to a pulp.

Owen appeared to be in tune with her thinking, "That photo gets to me too."

"A rage attack," she mumbled. "Tried to kill the baby and decided two for one sounded better." After viewing the photographs, her mind still tripped at the fact Roy, sick or not, was incapable of such heinous acts. The person set out to kill the baby then, horrible as it sounded, finished Maria as an afterthought. The unborn child bore the brunt of that person's rage.

Without closing the folder, Savannah rummaged her purse for a Tums to settle the nausea. She doubted it would work but any help was better than tossing her cookies. She glanced up at Owen, "Did anyone *hear anything* that night? *See* anything? Any helpful neighbor like I've got?"

"Woman across the street saw a man that matches Roy's description running from the house around the time of death. Saw him running west." Owen left it at that. Savannah didn't, "Toward my house. Great. Explain how this witness saw anything? Pitch black, no street light close by and the lamps on these houses are more for decoration than actual security. The most I could give this woman is the 'he was a big man' description."

"She'd seen Roy numerous times before in daytime and nighttime."

This "neighbor" grated on her nerves. Unless the woman had

night vision equipment and a propensity for staying up all night, a positive identification was improbable. "What was the man wearing? Did Mrs. Fletcher notice?"

The corners of his mouth lifted at the reference, "Just jeans and a green jacket is all she could see. I'm guessing it was a Carlson Landscape jacket."

Yeah, well, she wouldn't. Not until more solid evidence came along. Prodding a fellow detective never created a Disneyland relationship however Savannah wanted to cover all the bases, "Have you got the employee list from Carlson?"

Thankfully not offended, he nodded, "We've collected DNA from them all and I'm running background checks on them."

She built up the nerve to ask for a copy of the list only to be refused with an apology, "I know you're trying to help but I expect your superior would question any unauthorized computer access, unless you can tie Maria's death to something in Atlanta."

Savannah smiled sickly in response. The Tums certainly hadn't cured the stomach upset and now Owen began shutting her out. The latter puzzled her somewhat. In his younger days, Owen Dunne possessed the mother of all crushes on her. In second grade, he hung out at the living room window, forcing Seth to always shoo him away. Her brother finally told him to either speak to Savannah or leave her alone. The few times Owen tried to converse with her, he grew so tongue-tied all that ultimately surfaced was a nervous giggle and a hasty "Bye," as he ran away.

Now, the shy little boy found his voice and used it to say "no" to her. It was then that a twinkle of an idea hit her. She casually flipped through the photos again, "Owen, darling," she fluttered her lashes in her best Southern Belle manner, "may I at least have copies of these?"

Her friend flushed red from his neck to his scalp. She sensed another refusal developing. Nervousness poured from him as he fiddled with his tie, "Savannah, you know I'd love to but..." He winced like she'd punched him, "Not just Pierce would skin me but my lieutenant would too. I – I'm sorry..."

"Owen, stop apologizing," she waved it off as dispassionately as possible, considering she felt angry enough to bend steel. "I understand your position. I just thought I'd ask." She returned the folder to his desk, "You don't mind if I pass along any information I come across, do you?"

"Of course not. Uh, Savannah, you know I would help you if I could, right?"

She nodded, not trusting herself to answer sweetly. What did Owen think she'd do? Flagrantly interfere with the investigation or try to muck it up somehow? The request wasn't unheard of. Detectives shared information and photos during a murder investigation. Sometimes they *had* to when searching for results.

Owen smoothed his tie, his vision unable to meet hers, "How about dinner sometime? We can review the case, share info and insights, if you want."

Owen, you dog. That's a hell of a way to ask for a date. A genuine smile curved her lips and she winked, "You've got a deal."

17

"They have names for women like you," Mathis announced when she walked by his desk. Savannah waited for the punch line but like a good little pest, Mathis out-waited her.

"What?" she asked.

"In Biblical times, didn't they stone women for what you're doing? Yeah, I think so. I mean, I'm not judging but someone will and his name is Rutherford."

"Mathis, stop pecking at me and tell me what you're talking about."

"You're committing adultery. Aren't you married to the Carlson guy? And you're making eyes at Rutherford at the same time. I'm not standing next to you anytime soon. Lightning may strike."

Well, that gem of news traveled like wildfire. God only knew which culprit started it and she was too drained to find out.

Mathis leaned back, enjoying every minute, "How's the young 'un, anyway? As fiery as his mama or as nutty as his papa?"

Savannah sighed, "Now I know why they make us check our weapons at the door. So we won't shoot each other." Waving tiredly, she bid Mathis good-bye.

"Doesn't Mrs. Carlson want to know if her hubby drew the lucky number?"

She wheeled, genuinely annoyed now, "Mathis, it's hard enough without you adding your brand of humor –"

"His DNA didn't match. Neither did the fingerprints on your gun. Someone else threw the Half-Nelson on ya."

Stunned by the news, she migrated back to his desk, wondering if Roy hadn't attacked her, then who had? Mathis saw her quandary, "If it helps, they said it was a relative of his. They mentioned so many yin and yangs matched but not enough for an ID. What'd you do, piss off the in-laws?"

Still it didn't help. "Roy's an only child and I never met any other family except his parents." She made plans to visit Roy again later in the week. This time, however, she'd ask who Mark was. The name was important enough to him to incorporate it into their imaginary marriage. Maybe it was important enough to fit into the convoluted puzzle from the last week.

A call from Rose Austin woke her at six. The dayshift nurse asked yet another question she had no answer to. What medications did Roy take? The situation escalated into the dreaded, "But you're his wife, you should know" area. Shoving a hand through her hair, she fell back to the bed with a sigh, "He's hallucinating. We are not married."

Finally Savannah managed to accomplish what everyone did to

her lately. She thoroughly confused another individual. The nurse hemmed and hawed then settled for, "Could you find out what his meds are?"

"That I can do," she replied. So, after a quick shower and breakfast, she found herself back on the road to Augusta. Savannah planned to stop by the landscaping business then by the police department. She'd ensure Owen had access to the DNA results of her attack. At least it cleared Roy of one criminal act...

She arrived at Carlson Design & Landscape just after the morning rush hour wrapped up. The high schoolers were deep into first period classes and Joe Blue Collar had been clocked in less than thirty minutes. It shouldn't have surprised her when Carlson's parking lot stood empty of work trucks. Mostly it peeved her since she hoped Nate might be around. Since he wasn't, that forced her to deal with Mr. Stephens, the iceman. Her spirits had seen better days. Savannah braced herself, took a deep breath and pushed the store's door open.

"Can I help you?" a woman's voice asked.

Savannah turned, shocked and grateful for the female intervention. Maybe, just maybe, she could avoid the Abominable after all. In his place came a cute bubbly blonde that practically bounced up to meet her. When she smiled, she looked like Jessica Simpson – but when she moved she looked like Jessica Simpson on uppers. The petite woman, aged not a day over twenty-two, thrust her hand out, "Hi, I'm Candy Douglas."

Savannah hadn't felt so out of place since high school. Nothing like youth to bring out the old lady in her. Savannah was not only older but taller and slightly heavier than Stick Girl. Her shoulders were wide compared and her hips hadn't seen a size 6 since junior high. She wasn't fat but women like Candy sure made her feel like it.

She extended her hand, "Savannah Prince, I'm a friend of Roy's."

Candy's hand suddenly became energized and she gave Savannah's hand a frenetic shake, "Oh, *you're* the detective! Roy's told me *all* about you." She bobbed her brow knowingly, "He's really sweet on you."

"We were high school sweethearts," she replied uneasily with an attempt to diffuse any more marriage talk.

Candy emphasized her words with an occasional hearty shake on her captive's hand, "Roy *told* me. He *also* said to look out soon – that *you'd* be part of our *family*! Oh, Savannah – you don't mind if I call you Savannah, do you? Savannah, it's going to be a *hoot* having you here!"

Her hand began losing its feeling. A distinct tingling migrated up her arm to her elbow by the time Candy mercifully released her. Giving her hand a discreet shake to return blood flow, Savannah smiled quaintly, "Well, thank you, but the wedding date's not written in our family bibles yet."

Candy happily waved her off, "Just a minor detail. What brings you here? Need advice on showers, registries, wedding chapels? Roy said you've lived in Atlanta for years so I imagine you're a little lost around here now. He said you'd marry here in Augusta then transfer to the Augusta Police."

The situation sped toward bizarre faster than a runaway train. Problem was, Savannah couldn't seem to locate the emergency brake.

She opted to play along for now, "He's been awfully chatty about this to you. When did he clue you in?"

"About a week ago," then Candy winked, "but don't worry. I won't tell a soul."

"I'd appreciate that. As for why I'm here, he's kinda tied up in Atlanta on a job and wanted me to bring him some clothes and his meds. Do you have an extra set of keys to his place?"

The blonde unexpectedly turned positively despondent. She twisted a long lock of golden hair around a finger, "He, well, hmm... How do I say it?" She rolled her eyes, "I can't believe he didn't tell you."

"Tell me what?"

"Oh, honey, I'll just go ahead and say it. He lost his apartment months ago. It was a nasty dispute with the landlord. He's been living here ever since." She grabbed Savannah's hand again, covered it with her own, "I'm so sorry to tell you. I thought he already had."

Savannah grimaced when the girl took her hand. Thankfully she didn't squeeze or shake it like she tried to kill it. "It's okay, really. He's probably trying to save money for the," she gritted her teeth and forced herself to say it, "wedding."

"That's exactly right," Candy gleefully agreed. "You have a great attitude. I know you two will be perfect little lovebirds."

Disregarding the cheery comment, Savannah merely grinned, "Mind if I grab his clothes right quick?"

"Not at all," Candy finally released her hand and started toward the back of the establishment. "His room is back here," she pointed. "Second door on the left. His meds are in the bathroom. I'll get them for you."

And since you're such a helpful little elf, "Oh, and could you run a list of employees for me? I'll want to invite them to the wedding, of course."

"No prob," the girl replied. "I'll get that too."

Savannah thanked God for the brief breather. Candy's spring was wound entirely too tight. She also realized playing the fiancée wasn't the cat's meow manner of finding information however Roy planted the idea in everyone's brains for some reason. She'd ride the ride as long as possible.

She opened the door to Roy's room to discover her claustrophobia still held strong. The tiny cubicle he called living quarters stifled her just looking inside. He'd taken up residence, literally, in a storage room. He kept it neat – maniacally orderly, in fact. The small cot he slept on had the blankets folded and placed on top. The walls hadn't been painted in forever except there was one obvious plaque or picture missing. The years of hanging on the wall outlined the small five by seven frame like a sore thumb. To her left stood a rustic, well worn chest of drawers. She pulled the top drawer out to find Roy not only painstakingly folded his socks and underwear but categorized them in order of age. The older, more worn pairs went to the right of the drawer, the newest to the left. Just when she thought he'd sprung all the surprises on her, she found as she pulled the drawer out further, her ex-boyfriend still possessed plenty of revelations for her. The discovery certainly reinforced why their marriage would have failed miserably. Savannah attempted to keep things neat but fanatical she wasn't.

She grabbed a couple of pairs of socks and underwear to make her visit look legitimate. The second drawer revealed his shirts, folded equally as precise, only categorized in colors, not age. The third drawer contained jeans. A tiny smile surfaced on sight of the newest pairs lining the left side, the older ones on the right. Roy was well-organized if nothing else. She was convinced of it until the fourth and last drawer. His junk drawer looked like a storm blew through. Old watches and car magazines mingled with compact discs and spare tools. So much so that the drawer creaked and refused to shut when she pushed on it. Hunkering down for a better look, she peered to the back of the drawer. She reached back and felt a picture frame wedging the drawer open. Gingerly she tugged to dislodge it. What emerged amazed her. The five by seven frame sported a crack in the glass across the middle. Upon holding it against the aged outline on the wall, she guessed it could be the missing photo. That possibility itself didn't stun her, the picture itself did.

One look at the photo and Savannah's knees went weak. It was a picture taken at the senior prom. The two standing in formal dress – Roy and Savannah. Roy still looked centerfold sexy in his dark blue suit. *So young, sweet, and gentle,* she thought, tracing the line of his jaw.

At the time she'd hated the long robin's egg blue dress Charlene made her wear. In retrospect, Savannah saw why her mother insisted. The two did look perfect together. The image seemed to suck the air from her. He'd kept it, framed it and just lately taken it down. Flipping it over to the back, she noticed yet another shocking detail – her current address in Atlanta written on the back.

"Here you are. Lithium, Thorazine and a list of employees." Candy's too-close high-pitched voice made her jump like a kid caught stealing a cookie from a cookie jar. Candy's attention immediately swung to the contents of Savannah's hand, "Oh goodness, it's broken! And what a lovely picture of you too."

Savannah felt a hand on her arm while another tried to remove the broken frame from her possession but failed, "I'll get another frame. It'll be good as new, I promise." Candy flustered around, her words sounding far more dire than Savannah thought necessary, "Roy loves this picture. He's had it hanging up forever. Did it fall off the wall?"

She watched the blonde closer now. Candy stared at the photo, pain filling her expression. Trying to follow her line of vision, Savannah sensed the girl worried more about Roy's side of the photo than his date's, "Actually I found it in the bottom drawer, stored away."

The girl's blue eyes darted upward to meet hers, "In a drawer? Why would he do that?"

The question was met with a shrug. Silence might draw out any pertinent information Ms. Douglas had. The importance of her answer was negligible, "He hasn't really been acting right lately, maybe that's it. The stress of the wedding..." Then her eyes popped, "Not that I'm blaming you or anything. But people with his disorder don't handle stressful situations well." She sat the prescription bottles on top of the broken picture, "It's really sweet of you to think of these. Sometimes he skips a day or two and we have to remind him to take them."

"We?"

"Mr. Stephens and me. He's like the vice president of the

company. Very genteel and proper though not like Roy. Roy's more of a," Candy's expression went, as Savannah would say, dreamy, like a teenager with a crush, "He's like your big brother but not. More like your big, sexy boyfriend who could protect you like a big brother."

Savannah knew exactly what she tried to say. She'd felt it all through their school years together. Candy's eyes widened, "Oh my goodness, I hope I didn't upset you. I realize he's a married man, or nearly a married man. Men like that are strictly 'hands off' for me, I swear."

"No worries," was the response as Savannah tucked the medication bottles into a baggie and zipped it shut. She tucked the employee list under her arm and picked up the picture again, careful to avoid the broken glass, "Roy's a friendly guy, I know that. So how did Mr. Stephens become vice president?"

Candy's jaw dropped in an exaggerated reaction, "You don't know that either?"

"You'd be surprised at everything I'm learning."

"My goodness sakes, Roy really has left you out of the loop. Mr. Stephens is his brother. Well, half brother. He stepped in after Mrs. Carlson passed away. She left the business to Roy but left a little clause in the will for her other son to have an involvement in the company."

"Mrs. Carlson owned the business?" That was news to her. All that time she figured it was his father who owned it.

"Oh yes. She changed the name years ago." Candy thought a moment, "I guess when she married Mr. Carlson. Evidently she'd had a son before that because when the will was probated, Mr. Stephens showed up." Candy leaned in close, whispering, "He was none too happy that their mother left the company to Roy. Madder than an old wet hen. He thought the oldest should have been in charge."

Savannah took that into heavy consideration. As she suspected, things weren't black and white as Ennis and the others assumed. There was a giant shade of gray named Mr. Stephens to consider, "When did Mrs. Carlson pass on?"

"Three months ago but don't mention her to Roy. He's real touchy about it. Gets red hot mad when anyone mentions her."

"Why does he get mad?"

Candy's vision lowered, "It's his way of dealing. Later I'll find him in the back crying his eyes out. Poor, poor man." She brightened to beaming again, "That's why it's so fantastic that he found you! He's been so energetic since he's engaged."

If stressful situations and bipolar didn't mix, no wonder he began exhibiting symptoms again. He was very close to both parents and with Mrs. Carlson's passing, Savannah couldn't think of a more stressful situation than that.

Besides learning a prospective answer for his relapse, she also put Detective Mathis's voice with another piece of information. Her attacker was a relative of Roy's. *"They mentioned so many yin and yangs matched but not enough for an ID,"* Mathis had said. A half brother definitely fell into the "relative" category.

Before she literally doubled over from pain with the thought of marriage, Savannah asked, "Does Roy have any other siblings I should be aware of? Don't want to leave out anyone on the wedding invitations."

"Heavens, no. If he's got others out there, I don't know about them."

"Sure would like to meet Mr. Stephens. Know where I could find him?"

"Yeah," a heavy, deep voice resounded from behind, making her jump. "I'm right here."

Savannah slowly turned, making sure to note if he fit the description of her attacker. Unfortunately, he did. The Abominable was back and shooting daggers just like the day she met Nate. The man standing in front of her forced a tense smile. Dressed in an emerald polo shirt reading appropriately enough "Carlson Landscape", Savannah noted he possessed arms indicating a very powerful man. Thrown over one muscular arm was a thick down coat. Mr. Stephens visited a gym regularly – probably even too regularly since the bulging muscles seemed exaggeratedly toned. Even through the denim she saw the outline of thick thigh muscles.

She tilted her head back slightly to meet him visually. Her hand extended, "I'm Savannah Prince and I hear you're Roy's half brother, Mr. Stephens."

His rough hand slid around hers in an oddly snakelike way. Or maybe it was just her remembrance of how quickly he struck in her kitchen. The cold, hard grasp, however, was as real as the danger she felt when he answered, "That I am."

"And your first name would be..." she hinted, trying not to show her discomfort from his handshake.

"Mark." He released her to turn his attention to Candy, "Take the afternoon off. I'll be here."

The order tickled the woman who launched into a hug around Savannah, "It was great meeting you, Savannah. I can't wait to have you in the family!" She then proceeded to launch herself in the opposite direction to leave. "Bye!"

Savannah rolled her shoulder and popped her neck to realign her spine. The girl hugged like a bear climbing a tree. "How is she part of your family?"

"She's not," Mark replied, his answer as cold as his hand. "She's a ditzy, meddlesome blonde who insinuated herself into our business." A harshness spread across his face, "And what can I do for *you*?"

"Did you know Roy is in the psychiatric ward in Atlanta?"

He breezed past her to Candy's desk, tossed the coat onto a nearby hook on the wall then sat down, his fingers purposefully pecking at the keyboard, "I heard something about it."

"Candy said you both have to ensure that he takes his medication."

"Miss Prince, if you know anything about bipolar disorder, you realize that a person with it does not want to take medication. They don't believe they're sick."

Savannah held her tongue. Being addressed as "Miss" basically stopped the moment she acquired a badge, at least in most circles. Mark Stephens tried to irritate her with the title for some reason. She caught the corners of his mouth lift slightly as if enjoying a private joke then they curled downward, back to the same sour expression he held before. He glanced up from the monitor and nodded toward her, "That's a nasty bruise on your neck. What caused it?"

Nice of you to notice, asshole, considering you put it there... Still, she touched the lilac turtleneck, drawing the collar up to hide the bruise, "An unfortunate accident," she replied. She added with finality, "It won't happen again."

Mark deliberated over her words a moment, "Yes, I'm sure it was unfortunate but one can never safely say it won't happen again." He leaned back in the chair, relaxed. His hands clasped behind his head, "Let's cut to the chase. I know you're not engaged to Roy because he's too busy bouncing off the walls in his rubber room. What do you possibly expect to gain by lying about your relationship?"

Savannah nearly laughed. If he'd been her the past few days, he'd realize there were no perks being associated with Roy Carlson lately. Instead, she pulled up a nearby chair and plopped down, "Now how could you possibly know we're not engaged?"

"Number one, no ring. Roy's a stickler for tradition no matter who the woman is or what she does for a living. Number two, you're a cop and he's a nutcase. With your schedule, managing to feed a stray cat regularly is difficult so keeping *his* meds current is impossible. Number three, just before he took a dive from normality he mentioned you keeping company with your partner – a Finus something or other."

"Partners spend a lot of time together, true."

For the first time Mark genuinely laughed, "Miss Prince, stop being demure." He'd said it in a manner suggesting she'd never known a demure moment in her existence. "We both know you're sleeping with your partner and we both know you rebuffed Roy the last time he saw you."

"We do?" she inquired convincingly enough despite the uneasiness slowly growing in the pit of her stomach. The man knew quite a bit about her but how? She gave him the part about Ennis as commonly recognized facts. She hadn't hidden hers and Ennis's relationship – she hadn't touted it either. But the tidbit about rebuffing Roy... She hardly believed he'd confide in Mark. Roy had his pride like every man. Men didn't share intimate details unless they stroked their ego, not wounded it.

Mark's brow drew downward. His attention fully on her, he answered, "Roy and I are close enough I notice when his mood freefalls. He told me he was going to meet you since you were back in town. The day after, he begins to regress into his depressive state. I tried to increase his medication but he refused to take it. It's no wonder he's railing and flailing in the nuthouse right now."

"Sounds like you're blaming me for this episode." And it did. The man dripped with venom. She stood her ground but for safety's sake, made quick exit plans in the back of her mind.

He shrugged, "A woman is always the downfall of a man. This is no different. Roy has always gravitated to loose women."

It took every ounce of self control not to fire her fist straight at him. Instead she tried to turn the conversation around, "What glowing praise you bestow upon the female population. Are you saying Maria Saxon was a whore?"

Mark grunted lowly, "You give her too much credit. A slut who thought she was a great stockbroker. Mediocre is still too complimentary. Tried to warn Roy about her. Did he listen?" He leaned forward, "No. He went on investing and sleeping with her until the bitch got knocked up with his kid. She's not stupid, she knows his family has money so she's not about to abort the thing."

She found herself gripping the armrest way too tight. Referring to a baby as a "thing" nudged her close to the edge. Still, "When did he find out she was pregnant?"

He smiled an unfriendly smile, "Why don't you ask him yourself since you're the bride to be."

Savannah leaned forward to stand when something caught her attention. If the light hit his cheeks and forehead just right, she could see a few raised marks streaked across them. They could have been her defensive scratches. "What caused those marks on your face?"

"You've obviously never tangled with a Cabana rose bush. They have more thorns than a brash, intrusive woman. This conversation is over."

He certainly didn't mind getting personal, she thought. First time in her life she was compared to a rose bush. It figured that her first wasn't a flattering statement. If Stephens refused to play nice, she would too, "Where were you on the fifteenth?"

"Maybe you didn't hear me. This conversation is over. I know what you're trying to do and it won't work. I'm a respected citizen of Augusta and targeting me is a dangerous idea."

And on that inhospitable note, she walked out without looking back. Stephens wouldn't be winning any awards for charm, that was for sure. That preyed less on her mind than the fact was hiding something and enjoyed flaunting the fact. Looking up the term "bad apple", a person would likely find his picture plastered beneath the description. The chill that ran along Savannah's spine settled about the location of her gut when he rolled the word "dangerous" off his tongue. Had there resided a doubt in her mind, he cleared it up with that vague warning.

She slid the key in the Camaro's lock, still deep in thought, when she twisted it to unlock the car.

"Hello, stranger," a voice directly behind her spoke.

Savannah jumped, the imminent prospect of an earsplitting scream poised on her tongue. She spun on her heel and stepped back to face a person she'd hoped to see earlier, "Nate, you scared me."

Unlike the day they met, today the stud in his mid-twenties dressed in charcoal khakis and slate crew neck sweater. *Sharp*, she thought. *Must have a hot date.* Nate leaned against the Camaro, conveniently blocking her entrance. The idea of startling her tickled him according to his chuckle, "Sorry. I saw the car and felt it my gentlemanly duty to say hi to the beautiful driver. Took a couple of days off and thought I'd pick up my check. It's destiny, Savannah. We're meant to have dinner together tonight."

Okay, so no hot date. He just naturally looks gorgeous no matter what... "I'd love to but I'm only here for a couple more hours."

He took the news easily, "Then back to big ol' Atlanta, huh?"

Savannah nodded, a bit uneasily. He'd closed in on her, causing her claustrophobia to threaten a return trip.

Nate sensed her apprehension, "Mr. Stephens told me you're helping Roy out with the investigation."

"Trying to but not very fruitful as of yet."

"He said you're a detective. Now that's a cool job."

Mere seconds away from asking him to move, Savannah noticed he also had scratch marks on his face. Was it an epidemic? "What happened?" she pointed to his face.

His boyish features blushed deeper, "Good deed gone bad. Tried to help my friend bathe her cat. You ever tried that?"

She shook her head in response. Nate bent down to show her, "Well, take my advice and don't. Look here, that's where her back feet nailed me. Those critters bite too. You'da thought we were trying to boil her in oil instead of freshen her up." His vision stumbled across her bruises, "Hey, looks like you've been in your own battle."

Again, Savannah tugged the turtleneck up, "I'd like to say it was a cat but it wasn't."

He stepped closer, his hand lifting to pull the sweater's collar down. Savannah moved back, against the car. Nate smiled, "You're not scared of *me*, are you?"

"Not so much scared, just edgy these days."

Nate waved it off, "That's understandable. Someone made marks on me like that, I'd be damn careful myself. Who did it?"

He was friendly and nice but the question required no truthful answer, "It's a mystery, Nate. A complete mystery."

Her reply brought a burst of gentle laughter, "Well, then it's a good thing you're a detective. Say, what's the picture?"

She held it for him to see, "High school prom picture. The glass broke and I'm going to reframe it for Roy."

Nate nodded, impressed, "High school, huh? You sure haven't changed."

That's what you think, she told herself but thanked him anyway.

18

She headed out across town to home. She spent a few moments appraising the house, gauging whether R.J. had returned and finally drove off. Her life was miserable enough without another showdown with him. Instead she pulled into Riviera's Restaurant parking lot. She hadn't had a decent Mexican dinner in forever. The place served authentic Mexican cuisine by genuine, authentic Georgia Mexicans, at least that's what the owners called themselves. Their food was nothing less than ideal though Savannah could not attribute the same to their English. The front door to Riviera's stated the business hours and a disclaimer to any roaming thief. "This door is alarmed 24 hours a day" it read. The place certainly wasn't lacking in entertainment.

Today, Riviera's enchiladas and salad called to her now. The spicy aroma drifted in through the window, bringing on a long passionate growl from her stomach. With her mouth watering, Savannah glanced at her watch, praying for enough time to eat. Reality sent her hopes swirling down the drain. Indulging in the anticipated feast would have to wait. When she glanced out the window, the brightness of the sun had given way to a softer light that dipped behind the treetops. Nightfall approached in a mere few hours. Businesses would close, leaving her to wait another day and no place to stay overnight. Going home to do battle with her father was as taboo as consuming a plate full of beef and cheese enchiladas with a side order of salad and huge glass of sweet tea.

Torture as it was, Savannah remained parked in the scent trail of heavenly Mexican cuisine while removing the prescription bottles from her purse. According to the date, Roy's medication had been filled just a week prior. Examining the amount remaining, she tried guessing at the number then opted for dumping the contents into a tissue to count them. Just as Roy stated, he'd been faithfully taking his medication. The bottle was missing the exact number of pills from the refill date to the current, telling her that… well, that she was back to square one.

Carefully she poured the pills back into their respective bottles. The pharmacy was located close by – though nothing in Augusta was very far away – so she pulled the Camaro into Drive and headed down the road.

When she drove past the Richmond County Courthouse, she chose to stop there first but gave Ennis a call to update him on her revelation called Mark Stephens. By his tone she'd hit a nerve with him – a good or bad one she wasn't sure. Anything involving Roy irritated Ennis like a jealous spouse. His attempts to hide his feelings failed miserably even when he offered to help her sniff out clues. She vowed to continue working on this as long as possible, with or without Ennis and whether anyone approved or not.

Five o'clock approached fast and working on another hunch, she decided to get a copy of Mrs. Carlson's will. She'd take it home and study it that night. Candy proved to be a fountain of information however reading the actual document might open up different possibilities. Right now she'd bet a hot plate of Riviera's enchiladas that Mark Stephens was up to no good.

Perhaps luck played a part. Perhaps the fact the day's work approached its conclusion and the pharmacist was tired and desired a big piping hot meal and long hot shower – like she did. Whatever the case, the fatigued expression James Hagins displayed evaporated upon seeing Savannah. Then he couldn't stop smiling. She stepped up to the counter and the instant his weary vision met hers, he broke into a bashful grin. Mid-thirties and very married, the pharmacist preened discreetly in a mirror then rounded the corner with an overtly genuine, "How can I help *you*, ma'am?"

Savannah sized him up the best she could. He was attractive enough though not a knockout. Everything about Mr. Hagins spelled anal retentive. Each short brown hair combed in place, and his white coat starched and ironed to a degree it shamed the military. When he extended his hand, even his nails were manicured, "I'm James Hagins, the pharmacist."

She shook his hand and noticed his rather limp grip, "Detective Savannah Prince, Atlanta Police."

His grasp tightened slightly though his smile merely widened. Describing his smile as "warm" would be stretching it. It bordered on predatory, however the knowledge of her profession backed down the wattage, "And what brings you here, Detective?"

In that instant Savannah decided to can the official stance and go casual. He obviously considered her decently attractive or she wouldn't have caught the grooming ritual in the mirror earlier. She presented her prettiest smile, "Call me Savannah, please. I'm just here for a friend..." Then she went on to explain that she and Roy were friends all the way back to grade school and a brief history of their relationship.

After hearing her out, Hagins studied her face, "I do believe Roy's mentioned you before. The name does strike me as familiar." He leaned across the counter to her, "Now what is it you needed again?"

"Well, James," she smiled again and watched him blush. "I was asking if you remembered who last picked up Roy's medication." She retrieved the bottles and placed them on the counter.

The sight of them wrinkled his brow, "I remember it wasn't that blonde that normally comes in. This was a big guy." He reached around the cash register for a clipboard, "I have everyone sign for prescriptions when they pick 'em up." James thumbed a few pages until settling on one, "Yeah, here it is. Good luck deciphering that signature."

Indeed, the chicken scratch scrawled on the page resembled the flagrantly distorted style her physician used for signing prescriptions. Only a sample of handwriting could confirm the name and that itself took a trained eye. In the brief seconds she studied it, the signature could have been the name Mark Stephens, in a roundabout way. Savannah merely shook her head, "Was it Mark Stephens?"

"I don't believe I know him. This guy was tall and beefy if that helps. He hadn't shaved in a while either. If he hadn't been wearing a company jacket, well, I would have hesitated to hand over the medication."

Savannah took a mental note on the appearance. She reached in her jacket for the notepad to write down the description for what it was worth. Beside it she added a notation with a question mark. She'd seen plenty of Carlson employees fitting that description. A landscape company needed well built men for the heavy lifting and required work. Savannah looked up, noticing the pharmacist's brow trenching a worry line between his eyes. He picked up one bottle then the other to examine them.

"What's wrong?" she asked.

James the pharmacist now focused his attention on the contents in the bottles. "This isn't right at all." He rolled one pill into his palm and studied it, "This isn't Thorazine and I filled this prescription myself – with Thorazine."

She leaned in now as his stoic demeanor cracked slightly. Methodically he examined each of the bottles, "These are not his pills."

"Do you know what they are?"

He shook his head, "I'll look at them closer but Thorazine is darker orange and larger." James reached beneath the counter to retrieve a book. Thumbing through it, he finally laid it on the counter for her to see. He pointed to a specific pill. "That's what Roy's taking."

Savannah took a hard look at the picture then at the "Thorazine" in the bottle. Sure enough, the difference was substantial. It struck her that the stuff in the bottle looked amazingly like, "Baby aspirin."

The pharmacist rolled the pill in his hand again, examining it closer, "I believe you're right." His vision swung to hers, his brow still wrinkled, "But why would he substitute? He's had them refilled on schedule and I've not heard that he's been having any troubles. If he took baby aspirin instead of Thorazine, he'd definitely have problems."

"He's having them now. He's in Rose Austin in Atlanta."

Hagins swallowed hard. The glow of her attractiveness must have faded because he stepped back in a defensive stance. His features resembled a frightened animal convinced his breathing days were numbered, "I filled those prescriptions correctly, Detective. I'd never substitute anything and I'd surely never go so far as to –"

"Relax, James. I'm only trying to help Roy. Crucifying someone comes later and I'm highly doubtful it'll be you. Is there any way to tell about the Lithium?"

Her spiel slackened his shoulders, and the tension in his jaw and eyes released. The old James returned, his smile tentative now, "Not easily since they're capsules."

"But replacing the contents would only take patience and a steady hand."

Barely a nod of his head. Mr. Hagins flushed but Savannah blamed it on something other than guilt. For now. She nearly felt bad for him when he offered a soft but unwavering, "I didn't do this. I like Roy."

That's all it took for her to make the drive to the Augusta Police Department with a brief prayer that Owen's partner was AWOL. She followed the hallway past occupied offices until finding Owen hunkered over his desk, reading a file.

"You readin' or sleepin'?" she asked.

Owen jolted to an upright position, his eyes trying to refocus and hardly succeeding. He blinked, rubbed them with his thumb and forefinger and managed a smile, "Hey there. You caught me reading on the case."

Reaching into her jacket, she withdrew her glasses, "Need to borrow them? Close as you are to that page, you're gonna get ink on your nose like I used to."

He respectfully declined, "I might get more dates if I look like Rudolph."

"Trust me, you won't and if you don't get glasses soon, you won't even know if your date *is* Rudolph."

Owen chuckled at an obviously humorous image in his mind, "So what brings you to my humble shoebox?"

"I stumbled onto something disturbing," she said then updated him on the visit to the landscape business and the medicine discovery.

Owen listened intently, giving her time for details though she stopped short of accusing Mark Stephens of switching the drugs. She wanted to see his reaction to her findings first. To her surprise, he lifted one thick, auburn brow to ask, "How about the Lithium?"

"The pharmacist couldn't tell since they're capsules."

"Does the guy look good for tampering with Roy's meds?"

She shook her head, "Not from what I saw. The fella doesn't seem the type to deviate from much, not even a shorter haircut in summertime."

Owen smiled, "Anal, is he?" He leaned back in his chair and motioned to the medication bottles on his desk, "So I'm guessing you're wanting these analyzed."

"If you could swing it, yes. It's got something to do with the murder, I just feel it. Whoever's messin' with Roy, they aim to finish him off."

"You're his advocate now? He nearly killed you."

"See," she edged gently into her thoughts, "that's just it. Roy didn't attack me. I never got a solid look at the guy. Our lab did a DNA test and it cleared him. I'm having those results sent to you personally. In case it comes in handy for the Maria Saxon murder." She felt as smart as a turnip having to admit to the mistake in identity but figured anyone in her position at the time probably would have done the same. Plus, Owen didn't seem to hold any questionable feelings about it.

He answered, "Don't see how it could but thanks for the info."

She waited a beat then mustered the nerve to ask, "How well do you know Mark Stephens, the fella that works with Roy?"

"His brother? Don't know him personally. My ex-wife had our lawn landscaped and he was in charge of the job. Runs the joint and the men like a Nazi from what she told me. No wonder Roy lost his mind."

Mulling the information over, she clammed up about Mark Stephens for now. She'd take Mrs. Carlson's will home and study it. Mark's name lurked in the pages of it and she wanted to know exactly in what capacity.

19

Legal mumbo jumbo always confused her. The terms and sentence construction baffled her mind, much like the King James version of the Holy Bible. Being a high school graduate, Savannah prided herself on some decent knowledge and a solid, well rounded education. However she suspected that even the majordomo of ego, the master of intellect at Cross Creek High, their valedictorian Howard Baker – Howie for short – would mire down in the legalese of Mrs. Carlson's will. With every edict followed an exception to that edict, with plenty of sub-exceptions to the exceptions. No wonder lawyers got paid the big bucks, she thought. It took a double-talking genius to weave such a convoluted tapestry.

She sat at her dining table, hunkered over the mass of a will, frustrated that the supposed English would have made more sense in Greek. To top it all off, her new glasses continually slid down her nose – something to add to her already maddening day. She began to regret the trip to the optometrist. Reading wasn't entirely important to life, as the will painfully pointed out. But, like a good little soldier, she shoved the glasses back into place and read the paragraph over again despite the fact she'd read it twenty times already.

After another ten minutes she found herself on the phone to her brother, "You know anything about wills? I mean, the language of how they're written?"

"Yeah, they're usually written so everyone gets the gold mine and I get the shaft."

Savannah flinched at the reference.   Grandfather Prince promised each grandchild a portion of acreage of the orchards. The exception to *that* particular edict was only the grandchildren who, at the time of his death, resided in the state of Georgia. That left out plenty of grandkids, including Seth. The only beneficiaries were herself, Georgia and two others. She and Georgia offered to share the inheritance with their brother only to have him throw it back at them with, "You were always the favorites anyway. You should have it."

"Seth, I'm sorry about Grandfather's will, okay? I didn't write it. Hell, I couldn't even *begin* to write it, obviously. I need help interpreting Roy's mother's will."

"Why, do you inherit from her too?"

"You know, being a smartass isn't your calling. Are you going to help or not?"

"Yeah," he sighed, "give me fifteen minutes. Just remember I'm not a lawyer. My interpretation may be pretty loose."

"At least you'll have an interpretation. All I have now is a headache."

The instant he sat at the dining table, she presented him a peace offering of a Budweiser. Ennis kept the beer in the fridge like she kept her Yoo-Hoos. They both became a staple of the household at her house and his apartment. Seth eyed the Bud warily, "Plying me with alcohol? Are you planning to take advantage of me later?"

"Only that encyclopedia socked between your ears." She popped the top and sat it next to his right hand.

Her brother gave the place a brief inspection then put his reading glasses on, "Ennis not here?"

She nodded toward the bathroom, replying sheepishly, "He's taking a shower."

He peered over his specs, "I'll refrain from asking why he's in *your* shower. I do, however, want to know why you're helping this son of a bitch," his finger tapped Roy's name on the will before him. "He nearly killed you, remember?"

Savannah eased into the seat next to him, "Obviously Ennis didn't tell you. Roy didn't attack me but I think I know who did." She saw Seth's arms tense, his hands clenched into fists. She covered one with her hand, "And no amount of blustering will make me tell you so calm down. Point is Roy didn't hurt me." Self-consciously, she slid her glasses on, "I had a DNA test run."

"Still doesn't mean he can't hurt you." He looked up from the will briefly and did a double-take. Savannah rolled her eyes, waiting. Sure enough, he craned his neck to fully see her face, "Welcome to the club. You look good in them."

"Thanks. It's definitely a club I could've lived without. I have plenty of crap to keep track of, now I have to remember my damn glasses."

Seth snickered, "Need one of those old lady chains around your neck?"

Not taking kindly to the comment, Savannah popped the back of his head with her palm, Italian style, "No, and if you buy me one, I'll kill you myself."

Gifting her with a gentle smile and wink, he then took a generous swallow of Bud, leaned forward and dove straight in to reading.

The bathroom door creaked open and after a waft of steam billowed out, Ennis appeared wearing a fresh pair of jeans and ash colored sweater. He stopped short upon sight of Seth who momentarily shifted his gaze to him then back to the will. Her brother spoke calmly, evenly, "You're safe, Ennis, it's only me. If our mother had caught you, she'd have taken a broom to your head. If Pops catches you, he'll take a shotgun to your backside." To Savannah's scoff, he answered, "Don't test the man, sis. You two had words but you're still his baby."

After a brief nervous laugh, Ennis joined Seth by opening his own beer and sitting next to Savannah. He planted a quick kiss on her while Seth continued reading. He spent a few minutes wading through the legalese, his brow alternating between sinking and lifting, depending on what he found. Savannah tried not to stare. It was like watching surgery – fascinating but sickening at the same time. She knew Mark Stephens was up to no good but couldn't prove it. The key had to be the will. Seth's expression appeared to concur. He questioned two names circled in red, "Who are Alicia and Nate Stewart?"

"Evidently mother and son. Nate works at Carlson Landscape. I just thought it odd that he was mentioned in Mrs. Carlson's will."

"Yeah, along with these other names, John Pruitt and Thomas Dawson. What connection to Mrs. Carlson do they have?" He shook his head, "Nevermind. I probably don't want to know." Another run through the document later, he removed his glasses and pinched the bridge of his nose as he winced, "I hate lawyers."

Savannah wholeheartedly agreed. She waited for him to slug down the rest of the beer then noticed he eyed her with a seriousness that tightened her gut. "What made you think to get a copy of the will?" he asked.

Her voice sounded low, unsure, "Hunch."

"I gotta hand it to you, Tiger. You did good. From what I can tell, Mrs. Carlson knew the possibility Roy's bipolar disorder might develop when she had this written. Either that or knew he had the possibility of losing control."

Savannah sorta figured that part out. From mulling over the words and phrases meant for a doctorate holder, she'd surmised that Roy's mother wrote the will to protect her money and business more than her son. What she didn't realize was to what length Mrs. Carlson went...

Seth thumbed through one page of the will, then another. He slid his glasses on to review one particular section. Finally he enlightened them, "If one son is incarcerated, the other inherits automatically. No questions. So Roy's pretty much screwed. He was given the business so it's his to lose."

"Yeah but..." her voice trailed temporarily. She regrouped

quickly, "But he didn't kill that woman. I still don't believe that. Maria's pregnancy didn't push Roy into killing her. He loves kids. He wants kids." She made a point of lowering her turtleneck to show the bruises, "Mark, however, wouldn't bat an eyelash about killing."

"Okay," Ennis joined in, his tone skeptical, "so you're saying Mark's framing Roy."

"That's what I'm saying," she replied, decisive in the words.

"Ohhh," he feigned elation, "that's every boy's dream. To inherit a lawn-mowing business."

Savannah slanted him a warning look, "I agree it's not exactly IBM but it's a successful business, even lucrative in Augusta since it's a military and tourist town. Maybe Mark thinks it's more successful than it really is."

Seth leaned back in his chair, "Nope, I think he wants the money. If you read closely," he rubbed his eyes, "and I mean with a microscope, you'll see that nail in Roy's coffin. The Carlsons have more money than anyone thought, obviously. Enough to have a tiny clause about stocks, gold, bank accounts and real estate, some of which went to the Stewarts and Pruitt and Dawson, whoever the hell they are. I don't see a motive with these people. They stand nothing to gain if Roy goes bonkers. The plum real estate went to Roy with seconds being doled to Mark. That's why Mark Stephens might want to frame him for murder. There's no telling how much money's tied up in all that by now. Read the back page. They own enough of Augusta to make the town leadership flinch if the Carlsons pinched them."

Indeed, when she glanced over the back page, the details merged with the land descriptions. The Carlsons owned land in Woodland, a ritzy addition where homes cost a million dollars or more. The homes were decisively larger than her family home on Walton Way. Then there was the land where Lakeview Country Club now stood. Homes brought a cool half a million on their worst day.

Savannah perused the document with a clearer vision of what Mark's plan probably was. In the grand scheme of life, the landscape business meant nothing. The money and real estate Mrs. Carlson willed to Roy (with a minimal amount doled to Mark) added up to major big bucks. If Mark could somehow tilt Roy off balance with the fake meds, and get him thrown in prison for murder, that served up a retirement plan anyone would envy.

Savannah cursed and made it count. Georgia always threatened to slap her when she uttered that particular expletive. To give her words teeth, Georgia added, "Mama would thrash you for blasphemy if she heard you right now." Judging by Seth's features, the expression, coming from her, came as a shock. She tried to soften the blow, "I'll hang that bastard with my own rope. I gave Owen some evidence that's key in this whole mess. I think Stephens tampered with Roy's meds. He replaced one medication with baby aspirin. Owen promised to have the other analyzed."

Her brother glanced over the top of his glasses, "We *are* talking about the little fat kid who had a serious crush on you, right?"

The blood rose to her cheeks but Savannah nodded. Seth gifted her with an easy, genuine smile, "I had to roust that kid from the living room window dozens of times. He'd tap on it, trying to get your attention. Maybe it's time you gave it. At least a small amount."

Savannah shook her head, visibly uncomfortable revealing the truth, "Already tried, already failed. I don't have the charm Georgia has. Eventually maybe Owen will warm up to me enough to enlighten me about their investigation. That's all I can hope for."

20

Despite what her brother believed about lack of motive, Savannah decided a quick call to Owen couldn't hurt. She explained the contents of the will and asked if he'd questioned John Pruitt, Thomas Dawson *and* Mark Stephens and Nate about their alibis the night Maria died. Owen answered with a "Yep" to all. He explained that all were Carlson employees and described the following alibis – or lack thereof. Pruitt was out of town on vacation with his family, Dawson was home with a sick wife and their two kids, Mark noted he was home alone that night – which didn't set well with Savannah. Nate, on the other hand, swore he was at the Roadhouse, a local dive, until four that morning.

She couldn't argue with someone on vacation since Owen affirmed he double-checked the story. That left family man Dawson, loner psycho Stephens and barfly Stewart. Savannah knew the Roadhouse well. Her father roosted there quite often when she was younger. The place's reputation scraped bottom because of fights and a couple of killings. The fights became so regular that the owner installed surveillance cameras to cover his ass from lawsuits. She mentioned the cameras to Owen, "Check with the owner. He should have a videotape of the crowd the night Maria was murdered. If Nate was there during the hours he said, those tapes are his alibi."

Owen agreed to do it, despite the grumblings he still thought she barked up the wrong tree. Savannah begged to differ. Roy didn't kill Maria which only left the rest of humanity as suspects. As detectives, she and Owen owed it to Roy to cover every base, however remote.

Shortly after Seth left, Ennis ran an errand. She thought it odd he refused to elaborate on the errand but was too tired to grill him too much. After all, they weren't married so his comings and goings were supposed to be off limits to speculation. Too bad her brain hadn't received the newsflash. Ennis mostly tended to be a homebody so when he picked up and left without a real reason, it ruffled her feathers somewhat. Maybe marriage wasn't a bad idea... Ennis was one fine looking man with a killer body, manners that put any true blueblood to shame and a genuine heart of gold. She couldn't trust a female within sight or hormone range around that treasure. She trusted Ennis but she did not trust her own gender. Savannah glanced at her left hand with the ultimate decision that a ring would look good there. A ring, however, would split them apart professionally and that she couldn't stand right now. Ennis would eventually return from his mystery mission, the wanderer would soon be home, she assured herself.

With an empty house, it gave her time to think – a gift that she considered the equivalent of a frying pan for Christmas. She didn't need it and didn't want it. The day measured up as the others lately. Long with many painful revelations. Thinking about Mark Stephens made her red hot mad, that's why she opted for a long shower. Nothing ever came of hissy fits, her mama always said. Savannah added the postscript "Especially when the other person's bigger, stronger and probably committed murder."

A shower helped a great deal, relaxing her tense muscles, relieving her weary mind. She toweled off and opened the shower door. Once the fog began clearing, the image appeared of a man leaning against the sink. The memory of Mark slithering his way inside her home hadn't completely disappeared as evidenced by her audible gasp and automatic defensive stance. So much for relaxation.

With her heart pounding relentlessly in her throat, she looked directly into the eyes of her partner who seemed surprisingly entertained by her show of panic. If her throat hadn't closed, she'd have screamed at him until he tucked his tail and ran. That and the fact he stood half naked in front of her. One thing about Ennis – he had a habit of looking damn sexy, especially with his mischievous smile. To most women, they might mistake the look as lecherous. To Savannah it meant hold on tight for a long, long night.

Indeed, when he presented her with the sly expression, it became nearly impossible to resist him. That and his flawlessly sculpted physique. His strong shoulders flexed when his hands pushed off the cabinet. Dark wisps of hair sprinkled the span of his chest, wisps that thickened slightly at the taper of his flat abdomen and narrow waist. The line disappeared into the waist of his jeans, giving Savannah a jolt of excitement – a rare commodity lately.

She watched his humorous expression quickly transform to one she'd rather see. The ravenous look he displayed telegraphed one important message. The word "no" would not be accepted or tolerated in any respect that night. Not even wrapping the towel tighter around herself managed to dim the glimmer in his eyes.

"I'd swear you're one of the seven deadly sins. You cover three of 'em for me." He hooked his finger in the towel and sent it to the floor, "Lust, greed and gluttony."

"Ennis, you're impossible," she smiled and bent down to pick up the towel. The distinct velvet sensation of a kiss on the small of her back brought her upright with a gasp. Her partner just grinned, "Just sneakin' a quickie. Proceed."

Reaching for her panties, she gave him a sideways glance when he snatched them away with the suggestion, "Let's forego the undergarments tonight."

"And render myself vulnerable to potential attacks from a certain detective?"

"Well, that's why they call it copulation. Intercourse between two consenting police officers." He caressed her cheek with his knuckles, "Come on, sugar. Let's participate in some down and dirty debauchery. You'll feel better, I promise."

Savannah chuckled but didn't commit. It frustrated him, she could tell, however it only told in his words, "Did you hear about the man who got sex almost every night?"

Savannah knew better than to answer. Whatever she said wouldn't matter anyway. She patiently waited for him to finish which he did, "He almost got it on Monday, almost got it on Tuesday…"

"Ennis, I'm sorry. This whole situation with Roy is a mushroom cloud. Plus, if I intend to keep my job, I'd better be coherent in the morning to actually show up. I promise we'll have time together."

"Oh, I know that. Because tonight's the night." He wrapped his arm around her waist and drew her near, "I turned both cell phones off and hid yours. No interruptions, misunderstandings, or disasters allowed. Tonight is ours."

Ennis could charm the igloo away from an Eskimo. Unfortunately, this Eskimo wasn't buying tonight and he knew it. "Okay, mule-headed," he shrugged. "I'll make you a deal. I'll try to convince you to say yes while you keep telling yourself no." He slid down her body, his hands gliding down her back like warm silk. The resulting shiver only encouraged him to continue.

The words "not tonight" poised on her lips until she suddenly gasped. Ennis enveloped one breast in the wet heat of his mouth and drew gently on her. His tongue rasped her nipple and, despite her best efforts, she felt her fingers threading his hair to hold him close. A throaty moan emerged when his hands flattened on her back to refuse her escape. Not that she wanted to. The sensations he created made her deliriously happy. Damn him.

Ennis sensed a rejection on the tip of her tongue. He'd fight tooth and nail to avoid another night of blue balls. His body reacted to Savannah the way a kid's eyes lit up on Christmas morning. There was no ignoring it. He'd unsuccessfully dealt with the hard-on from hell for days. Work suffered as well as his reputation for his good nature. After the third day of celibacy, their colleagues refused to speak to him unless forced to. He couldn't exactly explain that walking with a spear in his pants didn't make for comfort or good moods.

So after seeing her brother off and tying up a few loose ends at work, he'd plotted and planned to get her into bed. He dropped by Kroger's for some double fudge Yoo-Hoos. The second stop consisted of a six pack of Budweiser for him. He'd drink to success or drown his sorrow either way. The third stop was the flower shop. Most people might have labeled him nuts for buying the flowers. Savannah radiated a hard aloofness in public but he knew better. In private, however, she was all woman and every woman loved flowers. He asked for a special bouquet of purple iris, purple asters and lavender freesia. His mama didn't raise a fool. She told him to take notice of a woman's preference of flowers. It might not win her over right away, she'd said, but it's always a good start.

The vase bursting with various purples overwhelmed Savannah's dresser. If anything, she'd see them and it'd tip her off-balance enough he'd finally win his sex argument. She wasn't one to brush him off or normally say no, but when the stress reached a certain level she'd hem and haw about it. The secret was catching her before that level was surpassed. For weeks her stress scale glowed red so it would take some work to break down the defenses. But, of anyone, Ennis was more than willing to try.

The instant his tongue curled around her nipple, he felt her resolve weaken. He drew her into his mouth and pressed her body to his. Her trembling hands clasped the back of his head and she moaned. Resolve officially splintered. He wasn't foolish enough to assume he won the fight. And it was a good thing he didn't...

Savannah's fingers tightened slightly in his hair and tugged him backward. Ennis revealed his displeasure by capturing the tender nipple between his teeth. Consequently when she urged his head back, he took her with him. The sound of her moan was priceless. He flicked his tongue over the imprisoned flesh and suddenly her pushing away reversed to pulling him closer again. "Ennis," she breathed, her body trembling with every movement of his tongue.

He released her breast momentarily, "Surrender to me. Then the torture will stop and the pleasure will begin."

She tilted her chin down to face him. Ennis sensed her gathering her wits faster than a kid searching Easter Eggs. She smiled into his features, her voice soft, "Respect your elders, young man. You will not tell me what to do and get away with it."

His hand, flat of her back, caressed the tiger beneath it, "You may be older than I am, but I'm bigger and I will sling you over my shoulder, haul you into that bedroom and make you sorry you delayed this."

"You wouldn't dare because I'd –" her declaration fell short of completion as Ennis wrapped an arm across the back of her legs and rose to his feet with her literally over his shoulder. "Ennis!" she cried, startled at his actions. Her hands grasped for a handhold and settled for holding to his belt. "Put me down."

"No, ma'am. Not until I'm good and ready." He turned halfway to view them in the mirror. Her bare ass stuck temptingly in the air. Unable to resist, he drew a finger down her crack that brought a gasp and frantic wriggling from her. Then she spanked him, telling him again to put her down.

Ennis smiled while she wriggled on his shoulder. The smile broadened at the heart-shaped ass and long legs in his current possession. Oh, she kicked mildly here and there, wiggled like a worm and protested vehemently at the barbaric treatment but he suspicioned this was the first time any man attempted to wrestle power from Savannah Prince. He also suspicioned if any man besides him tried, she'd stomp them into oblivion. Her objections to this handling were mild as a kitten. Just enough fight to make *her* feel better. Just enough fight to make *him* hornier than a dog.

He could barely move because of the totem between his thighs. With her open hand repeatedly banging on his butt, life became quite unbearable in his Levis. So he swatted her bare ass to show her how it felt, "Quiet down back there, woman."

There was a significant flinch when his palm came down on her cheek. Her whole body tensed to the point Ennis feared he'd overstepped his bounds. His vision locked onto the scars across her bottom and lower back. Suddenly he felt lower than a snake. With her childhood even the most playful swat could ruin the night. He swallowed hard, waiting for her reaction.

"Ennis," she called, her voice light, quiet.

"Yeah," he answered tentatively.

"You'd better pray you can keep me beneath you tonight."

By her tone, she didn't sound upset. In fact, she sounded challenging. He'd interpreted her correctly when she finished in a much stronger tone, "If you don't, this old lady's gonna show you a thing or two about corporal punishment."

21

She didn't get a chance to show Ennis about corporal punishment. He kept her well worn out all night, so worn out she overslept by two hours which forced her to sneak into work. She recalled Ennis bending over her sometime during the morning, kissing her awake to the words, "I'm headed out. I'll tell Josh you're under the weather and will be in later."

He sounded so smug, she thought. Of course she hadn't fought him off once that night. Not one peep about "no" or anything to the effect to stop. "Under the weather" didn't come close. She was dog-tired exhausted. However many times the young buck managed to revive himself, it surprised her that he hadn't literally drained himself dry. For a man his age, didn't the plumbing rust up even slightly? She wasn't ignorant in the ways of a man but hell, even the stoutest appetites sated at some point. He brought a new meaning to the term horny.

She managed to stumble into the shower – at a liberal 10:05 a.m.. Washing herself proved a great way to wake up. The washcloth grated tender nerves and tender flesh. Even her breasts ached a little from his attention. She softly washed the nipples since any contact at all nearly sent her through the roof. Ennis definitely made his point. He'd branded her as his from top to bottom. She had the love bites to prove it. The little teeth marks here and there still blushed pink in places. One or two would take a while to fade. Those, along with the bruises still adorning her neck, would alert any authority to probable abuse but her smile told another story. The more awake she grew, the clearer the memories of their lovemaking became. While dressing, she relived a few to assure herself of a good day.

The time read eleven o'clock when she stepped foot inside the police department's building. Like a thief in the night, she ducked past the dispatch quarters, the sergeant's desk and down the hallway past other detective's offices. Savannah's lungs released the pent up air when she stylishly tiptoed past the doorway of Detective Mathis without a playful remark or biting comment from the burly cop.

She waved at Ennis as she ambled across his open doorway, giving him a smile and a wink. Yes, so far so good. If she retained this good luck, she'd invest in a horseshoe and mount it on her front door. She'd made it to work without a major crisis crumbling the universe – finally.

Crossing the threshold of her office felt like winning a race two steps ahead of a rabid pit bull at her heels. It felt good to prevail but she couldn't relax. For the past few weeks, Savannah convinced herself there were evil spirits at work in her life. Those spirits frolicked and played with her once uneventful life. They ironed it then folded it three ways from Hell.

No more than she'd locked her purse in her desk than the phone rang. It was Owen, "The DNA from your attack matches the DNA from Maria's fingernails. Problem is we don't know who it matches."

They conversed a little longer, and Savannah mentioned she planned to be in Augusta later that day to do more snooping. Owen seemed just fine with the idea which surprised her.

Sitting down in the semi-comfortable office chair should have provided her a bit more comfort. All it did was bring her closer to the day's new round of battles. She made the mistake of looking down at her desk...

Staring back at her laid ten messages fanned across her already overburdened desk. Each pink slip of paper read the same in the "You've got a message from" area then the message taker filled in the name. On nine the name read simply, "RJ." The tenth held a degree of anger in not only the name given but the handwriting that penned it. The last slip read, "You've got a message from Robert Jefferson Prince."

Savannah took a deep breath. When her father used his name and not initials, his temper glowed as hot as he did when drunk. The last message was taken yesterday, ironically when she was in Augusta. She entertained dropping by – but entertained it about as long as sticking her hand in a fire. After the fiasco in that very office, she'd blocked his number from her cell. Thankfully he hadn't the forethought to use a different phone to harass her. No, he just prank called her workplace until people probably vowed to strangle her upon sight. The last note, along with his given name, was a note from Lily, the woman who answers the phone. The large, mostly hassled cursive read, "Please call him back."

So Savannah made plans to do exactly that. At least to get him off Lily's back. She palmed her cell and dialed. R.J. answered on the third ring. "Robert Jefferson Prince?" she asked incredulously. By now everyone at work knew who the hell R.J. Prince was without the theatrics of dragging out his entire name. She hoped by inquiring in a tone as to question his sanity, maybe he'd get the idea he'd screwed up.

"Oh, so you finally decided to call your old man back," was the indignant, nearly hurt reply.

So much for knowing he'd screwed up. Savannah found herself battling a sigh. Instead she grabbed the nearest *safest* object to clench in a fist – the pen on her desk, "If memory serves me correctly, you disowned me in front of Georgia, Bobby and Ennis. Plenty of witnesses can attest to the fact so it escapes me why in hell you'd want to talk to me."

R.J. released the sigh she wanted to. Long and loud. Silence dominated a few seconds – no doubt while he fortified himself with scotch. Sure enough, she heard him swallow then, "Hellfire, Savannah. You ever gonna cut me some slack? You know you're my baby. You got my eyes so there's no denying it."

"I also got your godforsaken temper. Only I'm younger than you and it takes me longer to cool down. You specifically told me I was dead to you."

"Well, ya sure gabbin' like a live woman to me. Why don't you get off your ass, drop by the Boll Weevil for some chicken and biscuits and we'll have dinner together?"

No, thank you for the lovely offer but no... "Which one put you up to this? Georgia or Seth?"

R.J. groaned and indulged in another drink, "Hell, kid, nobody can order me around, you know that. Georgia could nag a monk to suicide but I hold my ground. And Seth, well, he just ignores me. But you..."

I what, she wondered. If he got weepy on her, or melancholy, she needed to prepare herself. R.J. reverted to a temperamental baby when he teared up. He cried a little but mostly yelled until getting his way.

"You leave me be," he continued in a reserved, almost hushed tone. "You don't crawl on me for drinking like Georgia does and you don't cut me out like your brother does. You come when I call on you. Always there for me."

The pressure on the pen mounted. R.J. wasn't above flattery to weasel his way. As sincere as he'd sounded, she needed more. Normally Savannah would tiptoe around the subject but not now. If he was serious about mending fences, he'd admit it or she'd hang up. "Are you saying you were wrong to disown me?"

He waited only long enough to brace himself with another belt of scotch, "That's what I'm sayin'."

"And you're apologizing for hitting me?" Now she was pushing his buttons. She'd gone nearly two weeks with his slicing words wounding her heart – he'd have the balls to apologize too, or else...

"Savannah, baby, you know I didn't mean to hurt you. I lost my head..."

She remained silent. Giving him more time to think about his actions wouldn't destroy the world. If he refused to outright apologize, however, it would be a decent beginning to destroying hers.

"I'm sorry for hitting you."

She searched for bitterness in his voice, the unrepentant tone she'd heard numerous times before. This time she heard none. Savannah didn't believe the abuse would stop. She merely believed it would stop for one day. Maybe. "So what did you want to eat? Your usual?"

"Yeah, and don't forget the cole slaw or fried pie."

"Okay. And you want a Coke, Dr. Pepper or Sprite?"

His answer was quick, "Johnnie Walker Blue."

Savannah audibly choked, "Aren't *you* the one apologizing? You could buy North Atlanta out of Yoo-Hoos for the price of one Johnnie Walker Blue."

"Okay," he capitulated, "Johnnie Walker Gold if they got it."

She shook her head despite the fact he couldn't see it, "Still not hearing you. Going from two hundred a bottle to sixty doesn't compute on my salary. I can afford Red Label."

"That'll do."

"Be there in a few hours." She ended the conversation relatively happy with its outcome. If the rest of the day went as well, there was hope for the rest of the week.

Before she left, she informed Ennis of her plans. He rose from his desk and plucked his coat from the back of the chair, "So what are we having for dinner?"

Savannah's hands plopped tiredly on her hips, "Daddy and I are having fried chicken. Ennis, I'd invite you but he's finally in a nice mood. Even if Georgia went with me, he'd freak." She watched his mouth thin to a razor sharp line, his eyes following close behind, "Ennis," she warned softly.

"I don't trust him. There, I said it."

She nearly laughed. He'd announced it defensively as if she'd bolt for the door or rear back and slap him. His seriousness prompted her to smile which handily disarmed him. "Join the club," she whispered. "I don't trust him either."

"Then let me go. Having me around will remind him to behave."

Finding a way to explain without hurting him couldn't be done. Ennis's chivalrous demeanor demanded he protect her. She stepped closer and put her hand to his cheek, "Baby, you don't understand." She felt his jaw relax with her touch. His eyes, however, met hers with flaming determination. Time to get semi-brutal with him, "You represent a threat to him. He's backwards from every parent on earth. He doesn't want his kids to find someone. When they do, he blows like an atom bomb and the results last just as long."

Her partner inhaled a deep breath, no doubt with the intention to debate the issue. He held it a moment then released a heavy sigh, "Okay."

Savannah rocked to her toes and kissed his cheek, thanking him. Ennis caught her by the elbows, holding her to tip-toe, "But you promise to call me every two hours or so. If you don't, I'm hauling ass to hurt someone."

She gave him a quick kiss, "I promise."

22

She spent a tentative meal with her father. They conversed about benign subjects initially, the weather, the town, and past and current neighbors. Half an hour into the meal R.J. poked into a meatier topic, "Good thing you didn't marry that Carlson boy. Turned out to be a loon *and* a killer."

Savannah stopped eating. The word "loon" grated on her. It gouged her personally because she still had feelings for Roy. Despite the fact they'd basically been engaged in high school, he was still her friend and she didn't appreciate the label her father – and everyone else – kept slapping on him. "Daddy," she warned.

"Don't get all flustrated. I know you two planned on weddin' and leaving your daddy to fend for himself."

She tossed her napkin beside the plate, "You don't know any such thing. Besides, Mama was still alive at the time, if you recall. You weren't alone."

R.J. tipped his glass of scotch to his lips, emptying it, "She left me soon after. It woulda been just you and me but you ran off and joined the police." He tilted the Johnnie Walker to refill his glass.

Savannah leaned back. She closed her eyes and rolled them so he wouldn't see. "My job has served you well. You call me and I get you out of jail."

"You don't have nothin' to do with it. I get one call, I use it for you. To remind you you got a daddy. My name gets me outta jail."

"Your name?" *What, that you're a hopeless drunk and, that unless the department is willing to see you through withdrawal, it's no use to lock you up?* The words danced precariously on the tip of her tongue, begging to be spoken. It forced her to purse her lips to prevent their escape.

"The name Prince carries weight here. If you'da been smart you'da got your job here. People respect our name."

She sincerely doubted that. Most of the Prince family migrated to other parts of the country. A slight chance remained that *part* of her immediate family were respected but only to a degree. Mostly, when people weren't busy displaying jealousy over the Prince's wealth, people pitied R.J.'s wife and kids. Absolutely no one with a scrap of gray matter respected Bryan Prince or his youngest Randy, the grand demon of the family. The only Prince in town anyone probably respected was Bobby, Bryan's oldest.

"So," she began slowly, deliberately. "If your name carries a 'get out of jail free' pass, you won't be needing my presence the next time you're locked up."

R.J. leveled a glare that could melt glass, "You may be a cop but you're still my daughter and you'll speak to me respectfully. Got it?"

She met his stern expression with one of her own, "The road

should go both ways, Daddy. Calling me stupid for not hanging around Augusta and calling Roy a 'loon' isn't very respectful either."

R.J. puffed up, ready for an argument. Savannah already decided to leave if he continued the same line of conversation. To her surprise he leaned back, like her, and took a deep breath, "Yeah, well, you're probably right." He poured another round for himself then splashed a thimble full into a shot glass and nudged it toward her, "Go ahead. You bought it. Oughta indulge."

"Thanks but no," she nudged it back. "Don't much care for scotch."

"That's good. Leaves more for me. But drink that anyway. It'll be a gesture to our reunion."

Savannah hated scotch. It represented the reason for her miserable childhood, the painful scars on her back, arms and ass but it symbolized more painful memories, mostly of her mother's suffering. She'd drink antifreeze over scotch if given a choice. Both did about the same thing. They killed a person for making the mistake of ingesting it. She had to balance her intentions. Not drinking the small amount he'd poured would piss him off and they were back to square one. Drinking it at least might salve the wound temporarily, giving them both a respite from fighting.

She lifted the shot glass and studied the contents. R.J. lifted his glass, "Here's to us, kid. Just you an' me." He threw back his portion and she followed suit, ensuring to hold her breath before allowing the stuff to register with her senses. The instant it hit her stomach, the scotch threatened a return trip. Holding her breath, Savannah waited a beat then swallowed tentatively, and followed it up with a healthy gulp of Coke to cut the taste.

R.J. found the scene humorous, "Still can't hold liquor, eh? I used to wonder if you were my kid. Other two can drink with no problem. You, you smell it and heave."

"Oh, I'm yours, alright," she grumbled and ran her tongue around her teeth as a last ditch effort to expel the bitterness. "Like I said before, I've got your temper in spades."

"Yeah, I know. Least attractive thing about you." R.J. tilted the bottle toward her glass again but her hand covered the top, stopping him. His eyes lifted to hers to see her shaking her head. One drink was too many, especially of that nasty crap. To soften the refusal, she offered, "I bought it for you."

R.J.'s expression softened. Odd what touched people, she thought. Most men might offhandedly thank a person for the booze but her father seemed literally moved by the idea she bought a bottle for him. He gifted her with a wink and a compliment, "Besides your pretty face, that's the *most* attractive thing about you."

Well, she now knew the most and least attractive attributes of herself, at least according to her father. To save herself from answering, she bit into her last piece of chicken. Before she was able to chew thoroughly and swallow, her phone rang. Savannah rolled her eyes. Naturally when grace and manners were required, bad timing forced her to wing it. Swallowing the half-chewed chicken, she wiped her hands on her napkin before answering. It was Owen, "I know it's kinda late but have you had supper?"

He's got something new on the case, she hoped. And since dinner with Daddy swung back and forth between uncomfortable and total nightmare, her reply was simple, "No. What'd you have in mind?"

"Nothing much, I guess. Burgers and Cokes, if that's okay."

About the time she planned to answer, he threw in a hook to see if she'd bite, "Thought maybe you'd like to see the crime scene. Pierce is off with a family emergency."

"I can meet you in ten minutes." A person could meet another *anywhere* in Augusta in ten minutes, no matter where they were. Assuming her agreement might settle his nerves, she was surprised to learn it only heightened it.

Her answer seemed to please him, "I was headed to Gary's. You have any special requests? No tomatoes or onions, something like that?"

"The second one," she said, hoping not alert her father to anything suspicious.

"Got it. Meet me down at Maria's place then. I'll be there in about twenty."

"Okay. And, Owen, don't forget a crime scene kit."

23

It was something about cops, she finally decided, that none of them could eat slowly or at a normal pace, especially when working an active case. They stuffed food in for energy, not bothering to taste it on the way down. But a burger from Gary's demanded patience. Its juicy, savory meat, delicious tomatoes and toasted buns commanded that the person slow down and enjoy the experience.

Evidently she was the only one heeding the advice because Owen plowed through his burger in record time. They sat in his Toyota 4Runner scarfing food for a solid fifteen minutes. Owen appeared amazed at how slow she consumed her food but didn't mention it, "According to company records, besides Roy, four employees made service calls to Maria's house since she bought it six years ago." He reached in his suit coat for his notes and held it for her to see. She recognized three names – Thomas Dawson, Mark Stephens and Nate Stewart. The rest she'd tried to investigate quietly and nothing emerged as questionable. Of course, Mark and Nate came out squeaky clean too.

Savannah swallowed then took a sip of Coke, "Every one of these guys drives a Carlson truck?"

Owen nodded, "Roy convinced his mother to buy eight new trucks a couple of years back. Since then, two have been in accidents, one totaled and the other's out of commission until repairs are done. The wrecks happened about year ago or so."

"Well, what do you think about Stephens?"

"I think he'd be a perfect well digger. Limited association with other human beings and less chance of being hogtied and left for dead."

Savannah nearly squirted soda out her nose she laughed so hard. She couldn't have said it better herself.

"That's why I wanted you to look over the crime scene with me. Maybe we missed something. You could be right. Maria might have had another boyfriend she kept secret from her family and friends. She sure never left indications of it on her computer or anywhere else."

Savannah wadded up the Gary's wrapper and stuffed it in the sack their supper came in, "Well, let's get busy."

They casually meandered up the sidewalk. The two suppers began wreaking havoc on her stomach and she should have known better than to chase chicken with a humongous Gary burger.

Maria's house looked Southern Beauty sweet against the towering trees behind it. Spruces, Hemlock and Magnolia trees framed the two story clapboard like a postcard. They would also trigger her damn allergies. Between that greenery and the pathetically healthy cedars bordering the porch, she'd be positively miserable before long. Winter in the South didn't bring a welcome vacation from withering sneezes and watering eyes. She sighed. Just another trip to the pharmacy...

After Owen sliced through the crime scene tape with his pocket knife, he unlocked the door and opened it for her. Savannah crossed over the threshold into a stark black and white world. Literally.

The walls were a warm cream color and the carpet, much to Savannah's surprise, was basically the same color. She could only imagine a scene from "Psycho" if the killer had knifed Maria instead of strangled her. The furniture could've risen the dead it was so drastically bright. The long, brilliant white couch dominated the living room while on either end sat midnight black end tables to break the monotony. In front of the couch sat a black coffee table with old issues of Architecture Magazine and Vogue.

"Very modern." Personally she preferred the warmer feel of wood furniture. She stepped further into the room. A table lamp once resided in the corner – the only hint of its existence was a ring of dust where it sat. Forensics collected the lamp, shade and glass from the busted bulb. Muddy footprints still spotted the carpet and she sidestepped to avoid disturbing them.

Savannah recalled seeing the photos and mentally reconstructed the scene. Maria's body had been found behind the white couch. There were signs of struggle according to the coroner. She clawed her attacker much like Savannah had so the DNA beneath the dead woman's nails would be the key to solve this case. Savannah glanced around the immediate vicinity. Maria had no impromptu weapons she could have used to help save herself. She'd kept the room to a minimum of furniture and trinkets. All she had was her own strength and that clearly wasn't enough.

"Careful of the glass over there," Owen warned. "I'm sure there are still shards."

She nodded. Giving the area a general but thorough going over, she resigned herself that the forensics team had done well in their recovery efforts. Not a shred or hint left behind. Savannah visually perused the remaining rooms, she noticed an open "country" type kitchen that led to a smaller quaint dining room. Maria hung abstract art prints throughout the living room and dining room, the only hint of the woman's personality she found thus far, besides the modern look.

The bathroom provided no new clues and neither did the guest room. Owen followed behind her room to room describing what they did and what they found. Interestingly he never provided an assumption of what might have happened or who might have done it. Had Savannah's tenacious campaign to exonerate Roy paid off? With any luck she'd at least cast doubt in Owen's mind.

They ventured down the long hallway and veered right to the master bedroom. Her brain stripped a few gears upon viewing the room. The environment transformed, from stark modern to a flower garden. Savannah turned back to Owen, confused. He merely shrugged.

The window had been boarded to secure the scene without displacing possible evidence. A trail of large muddy footprints began from beneath the window through the hall into the living room. Again, she stepped around the prints as a precaution.

She made the tour, her latex gloved hands opening drawers to inspect the contents and feeling behind and beneath furniture.

"Are you looking for something specific?" Owen inquired, clearly puzzled by the gyrations she went through.

"I'm not sure." After visually perusing the bedspread, Savannah threw it to the floor. Owen mentioned not finding any evidence of sexual activity on the sheets. As though she'd barely heard him, she kneeled by the side and lifted the mattress. Nothing. She did the same with the other side. Still nothing. She rummaged the bedside table only to find notepads and allergy medication. It was no wonder she needed the latter with all the trees surrounding the property, Savannah thought.

Next she moved to the closet and switched on the light. Maria had fine taste in clothes. Only high end suits and blouses graced the small enclosure. Stuff that Savannah refused to indulge in because they were just threads hanging together. Walmart was more her style. "Your people searched and documented the closet, right?"

Owen was so far off base with her actions, he wasn't even in the ballpark now. He just nodded at the question. Savannah took it as a green light to dive in. Using her arm, she shoved the choking amounts of Armani aside and began inspecting the walls with her flashlight. Besides the usual nicks and scratches closets endured, nothing seemed out of place. She aimed her flashlight beam upward, to the top shelf, "They looked through all those boxes?"

Again he nodded. Savannah directed her attention downward now. The houses along Walton Way built in the fifties and sixties were built with shoe racks in the closets. Maria's proved no different. While some people removed them during a remodel of the bedroom, some left the rack as a convenient way to store shoes. Lining Maria's wooden shoe rack were brands like Prada, Bruno Magli and Gucci. Savannah still preferred Walmart.

Taking her time, she removed every shoe then pointed the flashlight's beam across the rack. Halfway down the length of the board, there was a crack as though two boards were used to create one long rack. Savannah knew that was wrong. The racks in her parent's house were all made from one board. She decided to bring Owen into the picture now, "Bring the camera."

Delighted to finally be included, Owen rushed to prepare the 35mm camera and flash, "What did you find?"

"Maybe nothing but take some shots of it anyway. The footboard where the shoes were. See that cut from top to bottom? That's not normally there."

Owen snapped a few photos of the entire shoe rack and two with her pointing to the demarcation line she mentioned. She offered to dust for prints but he shook his head, his cheeks flushed and eyes wide with hope, "I'll do it. That'll give you time to stretch your legs."

Savannah didn't mention that her legs were fine. She merely backed out of the closet and allowed him to take over. She opted to hand him the bi-chromatic powder and brush, then kept the lifting tape handy in case he needed it. Owen worked with the diligence of a rookie detective afraid of screwing something up. He took a few snapshots then his hand extended for the lift tape. By the time he finished, they had four good, solid prints. "What do they look like?" Owen asked, repacking the brush and powder.

Borrowing the magnifier from the kit, Savannah shook her head, "All the same, from what I can tell but the computer's a better judge. Now let me back in there."

They traded places and she searched the kit for a knife. Owen produced his pocket knife, "What do you need it for?"

"Thanks to my sister's cleverness as a kid, I have a suspicion something's in here." She unfolded the knife to the longest blade. Tapping around the edge of the shoe rack, she finally found the spot she searched for. She slid the blade down between the wood and the sheetrock and lifted until getting a solid finger hold. After more wrangling, the wood groaned then gave way and pulled out.

Owen stuck his head around the corner like an eager kid, "What'd you find? Anything?"

Since, due to his excitement, Owen seemed to forget protocol, Savannah took the camera and snapped a few pictures of the contents. "It's a book. Looks like a journal type thing."

"Dear God," he sighed. "How did you think to look here?"

"That's the joy of having a neurotic sister. She hid her diary from me – she thought. But she had a secret compartment in the closet and I found it too."

Owen laughed now, "You must have been a real pain in her ass."

"And a few other places as well."

His spirits rose further, "Let's take a look at it. Maybe it tells us something."

The journal-looking notebook covered in a multicolored plaid design had a dust free cover indicating recent use. Savannah wanted to check for prints first. After they dusted the cover and collected several solid prints, she removed the book. Once she slid her glasses on, they both ventured into Maria's private writings. Maria began writing several months earlier, documenting hers and Roy's relationship. As with most couples, they ran across bumpy roads but from her writings, their relationship sailed pretty smoothly. In fact, the writing contradicted the interviews from friends and family who spoke so negatively of Roy.

While flipping through the pages filled with kind words for Roy, she and Owen stumbled onto an awkward piece of the puzzle. Maria – as Roy said – found another man, except she quickly discovered the guy was too possessive.

"Let's take this to the dining table," Owen rubbed his neck and shoulder, "My neck's cramping."

Savannah wasn't sure how a neck "cramped" but then she used phrases like "seize up" when it came to her back. Her own quirky descriptions usually brought a smile to Ennis's handsome face.

The two settled at the modern dining table and the moment her bottom hit the black lacquer chair, she realized Maria obviously never sat in there long, if at all. Her body would, no doubt, create a riot to rival the Revolutionary War. Owen appeared to have the same problem. She watched him adjust then readjust then squirm in his chair.

"Careful," she cautioned with a half smile. "Your tailbone will etch a trench into the surface."

He glanced down at the uncomfortable stick of furniture, "Is that what that noise was?"

They shared a laugh then decided they'd better return to reading. Maria wrote about the new man in her life without naming him for some reason. The more they read, the more it became evident she feared her new boyfriend and tried numerous times to break off the relationship.

He followed her wherever she went, she said. "If I go to the police, I'm afraid he'll hurt me or do something worse."

Savannah turned the page, reading aloud, "He's called me 24 times today and it's only 8:30 p.m. Roy's been a blessing throughout my ordeal with this maniac. He wants to help but I'm afraid to involve him."

They read on until Maria mentioned the baby. "Roy will be brokenhearted it's not his but he'll go ballistic if he knew who the father was."

Savannah continued reading – this time, however, she felt her brow sink with every word, "Roy's slipping again. His symptoms are barely noticeable to others but I know him. Something's wrong and I wonder if he's off his meds." Savannah noticed the date: A week before he'd come to her door with pizza and Cokes. The medication had plenty of time to filter from his system. By the time she saw him that Thursday, he seemed okay until stress entered the picture. The higher the stress, the wilder his behavior became. Threatening him off of her unwittingly raised the stakes for both of them and she hadn't known the possible consequences at the time. Now that she did, a shiver worked through her.

Savannah began reading the journal again, silently bemoaning the fact if the cops had found this piece of evidence earlier, Roy might not have been pegged as the likely suspect. At least he wouldn't have suffered as much. He'd run away from the police then been betrayed by her (with the gun) then accused of attacking her as well. Now he resided at Rose Austin while he attempted to collect all his marbles. No, life certainly hadn't been fair to Roy Carlson lately.

"This is the day before she was murdered," Savannah told Owen before journeying into the book again. "Dropped by All Point Security today. They come Friday to install a full alarm system. I'm terrified of him and I can't involve Roy because Roy might kill him." Maria carefully omitted the father's name but why? With a journal hidden as well as hers (Georgia would have admired Maria's craftiness), the fear of naming the father shouldn't have caused hesitation. After all, the manner it was written sounded like she purposefully documented every step in the relationship, especially afterward.

Elvis broke her train of thought by cranking up with "A Little Less Conversation". Her cell phone rang again and she answered it.

"This is the Atlanta Police," the voice said. "We're looking for a woman, thirty years old, about five feet nine inches tall, answers to the name Savannah Prince. We're afraid she's been abducted or just plain run away from home. Can you give us any assistance in this matter?"

She stole a glance at her watch. It read 9:15, "Ennis, I'm sorry. Owen and I are at Maria's house looking over the crime scene and I lost track of time."

He sighed, "Figured that. I called your charming father and he informed me that you were on a date. He obviously thinks you're still sixteen."

"Still treats me like it too. I'll head out shortly."

"I'll wait for you," Ennis growled seductively. "Even if we don't do anything, at least we'll be together."

24

They hadn't done anything, probably because she felt like death warmed over by the time she stumbled in the door. It was just after midnight and she barely possessed the energy to strip her clothes off, much less get frisky.

She basically slept naked but with Ennis wrapped around her like a hotdog bun, she stayed warm enough. Dragging herself upright the following morning was the trick. At one point she swore she heard the raucous clatter of the alarm clock. She decided it was all in her mind when the noise suddenly stopped. What drew her from deep slumber was a soft kiss on her cheek, another on her lips. She groaned. Surely morning hadn't the audacity to slink in like a thief, not yet. To guard against facing another grueling day, she did what self-respecting human does when ignoring reality. She turned over and threw the covers over her head.

A deep, gentle laugh registered and the covers were peeled back to her waist. Another warm kiss, this one on her shoulder, then Ennis spoke, "C'mon, Princess, it's a new day."

Savannah groaned again, "I was afraid you'd say that."

"Rose Austin called early this morning."

The mere reference brought the covers back over her head with a pitiful, "No, no, no…"

Ennis laughed again, "This time it's good news. Roy seems to be responding to the meds. At least from what they can tell."

She hooked a finger over the blanket and dared a peek over it, "Really? This isn't a ploy to entice me out of bed?"

He leaned down and kissed the tip of her nose, "If you recall, my choice is enticing you *into* bed. Oh, and Owen called. Something about test results on the Lithium."

Savannah heaved the covers back, nearly burying Ennis in the process, "When did he call? What time is it?"

Ennis watched her basically flail a robe around her shoulders, "7:30 and 9:00, respectively."

She felt wide awake for someone without their morning caffeine. Ennis side-stepped to clear the path into the living room. She slid on her glasses and glanced at her watch. 9:01. Good God, how did she sleep that long? "Did he tell you the results?"

Her partner took a slip of paper in hand, "Contents were sugar."

Savannah stared momentarily at Ennis's hen scratch, "Good thing Roy isn't a diabetic. Did he have a clue as to who tampered with the meds?"

Ennis shook his head. He followed her to the kitchen and she smiled when she saw the cup of coffee waiting for her. The steam rose from the cobalt blue mug emblazoned with "Police Officer" in silver block letters. She held the mug gingerly between her hands, warming them then blew the steam off to take a tentative taste. The moan escaping her lips sounded downright sexual, even to her, "How do you make this stuff? It's not normal coffee."

"Sorry," he shrugged. "Some secrets require the bond of matrimony to reveal."

"Well, I don't feel like getting married today so maybe I can keep bribing you to brew the coffee in the mornings."

"I might be persuaded to continue, especially if I go with you today. I told Josh I was taking a vacation day."

"Then you'd better hurry up because I'm heading out as soon as I regain total consciousness."

Worry about his partner commandeered most of Ennis's time. She tended to bull into situations without fully analyzing them first. When she described Mark Stephens and Nate Stewart, he decided alone wasn't how she'd approach this case. A break in their own case surfaced so he asked Josh for a day off. So far she'd spent the lion's share of her time in Augusta and, while there, meeting people that may be capable of murder. He intended to get his own take on them today. No matter how intelligent a cop was, there was a criminal trying to deceive them. Ennis worried that Savannah wrapped her emotions entirely into exonerating Roy while the real murderer lurked in a shadow she couldn't see.

In less than an hour they hit the road to Augusta. Today they rode in his Dodge truck. He'd traded in his Acura for some muscle – a move that Savannah loved at first, until she rode in his truck the first time. She spent most of her time staring down at traffic, the reverse of riding in her Camaro which made *him* nervous staring *up* at everyone as they drove. "It just gives my neck a new position to try," she'd said.

Interstate 20 ran smooth for the most part. The few bumps and valleys that her Camaro's suspension overlooked were unfortunately magnified by the big Dodge Ram. From the corner of his eye, he saw Savannah instinctively grasp her travel mug like a toddler holding its cup. She knew the road like the back of her hand and sure enough, a short two seconds later, the right front wheel plunged into a dip that jarred the truck.

"Sorry," he offered.

"Don't worry about it. This is better than you speeding around corners at fifty miles an hour like you did with that Acura."

Ennis laughed quietly. Unbeknownst to him, he'd made her plenty sick a few times with his driving. After one particularly wild excursion around Atlanta, Savannah simply removed herself from the car, her cheeks pallid and her hand on her stomach. Her words were still etched in his brain, "I'm never ridin' with you again, Rutherford. Not until you get a vehicle that doesn't belong at Six Flags. Join NASCAR and get this shit out of your system."

They drove another hour, mostly in silence since she'd nodded off in the passenger's seat. Even with the occasional bouncing and rough roads, she snoozed right through to the outskirts of Augusta. As though she smelled the city limits of her hometown, her eyes slowly blinked open and she yawned. "Didn't mean to go to sleep," she said.

"You were pretty tired. My coffee didn't even keep you awake."

He'd never tell her how he blended two separate coffees to make her favorite. Ennis thought twice about that. He'd tell her on their honeymoon. Eventually, he'd break her iron hold on single life and walk her down the aisle. He'd already made serious progress since they met. At least now she didn't threaten bodily harm at the mention of marriage…

They pulled up to Carlson Landscape before noon. Savannah grabbed the travel mug and gulped the rest of the cold coffee without a flinch. Ennis stared in amazement since she literally hated cold coffee. She caught his stare, "Believe me, cold coffee is nothing compared to meeting Mark Stephens. You'll either leave the building charred or frozen."

"Sounds like a charming bastard."

They walked in and Ennis saw a man resembling a lumberjack size Norman Bates at the front desk talking on the phone. "Where's the family resemblance?"

"They're *half*-brothers by Mrs. Carlson."

"Was she ugly as a mutt?" Seriously, he could see getting jealous over Roy. The man could pose for magazine covers. Ennis could nearly hear the women swooning over him. But Mark? The only magazine cover he measured up to was Fido Monthly. His train of thought derailed when Savannah's elbow mashed itself into his side.

"Mrs. Carlson was pretty," she scolded with a whisper.

"Oh, then Stephens gets his good looks from his daddy." He prepared himself to get mashed again but she smiled instead.

Mark's vision went from the computer to the two visitors at the front door. His shoulders slumped and he sighed, "I'll call you back." Before the receiver hit the cradle, he began speaking, "What's your problem now?"

Ennis noticed the man's cold stare fixed on Savannah. She chose a more diplomatic route instead of bashing him over the head with a sharp response, "Where's Candy?"

"Not here, as you can plainly see. If your business is with her, I suggest going to her home."

"It's her day off?"

Mark's temper wavered at a threshold Ennis considered a warning. Stephens possessed little to no patience with Savannah – now Ennis understood why she thought he was her attacker. Stephens scribbled hard and fast on a slip of paper, "Here. Go." He thrust the paper at Savannah in a way that set Ennis's teeth on edge.

Savannah plucked the note from him, "Is it her day –"

"Miss Prince, you're not required to know her schedule so spare me the inquisition." He rounded his desk to take his jacket off the wall hanger. Ennis noticed the green Carlson logo embroidered across its back.

"Are you always this generally pleasant?" Ennis drawled in his Texas twang. "'Cause my mama would take me to her knee with a switch if I spoke to a lady like that."

Stephens harrumphed as he shrugged the jacket on. A cynical smile crossed his pursed lips, "And you have to be Finus Rutherford, the good ol' Barney Fife she's doing now. Before you take the chivalrous route, remember you found *the lady* camped out with my brother when it should have been you."

Ennis puffed up at the reference. He'd twist this mealy-mouth punk into a pretzel before taking this level of shit, especially unprovoked. His hands balled into fists and the usual little twitch emerged in his right eye. His jaw tightened, his teeth gnashed so hard they literally hurt. Then he detected a soft brushing against his left fist. Savannah's hand secretly stroked his as a signal to calm down. When his hand refused to relax, she wrapped her fingers over the bulk of his fist. He wanted to deck Stephens for implying Savannah was anything but a lady. Ennis wanted to grab him by the hair and smash his face into the keyboard of that fancy computer until "QWERTY" was stamped permanently on his forehead.

Savannah's touch made that impossible. The more she stroked him, the gauge on his rage meter descended from "insane" to "pissed off". Semi-confident he could speak calmly, Ennis returned her calming motion by clasping her hand in his, "I'm lettin' that foolish statement slide not because I want to but because this is Roy's building and when he comes back, I don't want him freaking out when he sees your worthless carcass littering his floor."

Ennis watched the muscles in Mark's jaw tighten much like his had moments earlier. The man's eyes shifted between Ennis and his partner, maliciousness and hatred pouring from him in waves, "Been doing your homework, I see." He centered strictly on Savannah, "And I suppose you believe I ran Roy nuts just to inherit this crap-ass business." He zipped the jacket in one swift motion and stepped closer to her, "You're nothing but trouble. Ever since Roy saw you nine years ago, he's been walking a tightrope with sanity." He stalked closer still, "All because you said 'no' to him in high school. *That's* what I meant about women being the ruination of men. The best thing that could happen to Roy is if you…" he suddenly clammed up, his fists jamming in his jacket pocket. "I have to go. Go harass Candy." Mark sidestepped her only to have Ennis block his path. Stephens rounded on him, "What are you going to do? Teach me a lesson about talking to ladies?"

Fury drowned out most of the man's rant. Ennis knew damn well what lingered precariously on Mark's tongue. He felt Savannah's touch again, this time in the form of an insistent grasp on his wrist. From the corner of his eye, he saw an almost pleading expression crossing her features. He'd listened the first time. This time was his. "Finish what you were saying. The best thing that could happen to Roy is if what?"

"Ennis," Savannah begged in a whisper.

"Not now," is all he replied. "Go on, Stephens. Finish it."

Mark either suffered a mental disorder like his half-brother or he delighted in spooking people for a living. The man remained stone still and non-blinking, practically deadpan, "You already know what I intended to say."

"Savannah," a cheerful male voice broke the thick air of tension hanging around them. All but Stephens turned. Ennis rotated on his heels, careful to keep Stephens within pounding distance. The man who interrupted the unpleasant conversation possessed strikingly handsome features and a body rivaling Michaelangelo's work. Ennis instantly didn't like him. No one was that perfect, at least he hoped not.

His partner, though, brightened and threw out her hand when the new guy extended his. Ennis watched the young man's large hand basically swallow hers and give it a gentle shake. The guy shoved a lock of dark hair back from his forehead, "Guilt drove you to accept my dinner invitation, I can tell. I know just the place."

Savannah blushed and it gut-punched Ennis. She never blushed for anyone but him – well, until then. Suddenly he was positive he disliked this guy. She shook her head, "I'm sorry, Nate, but I'll have to pass. Unless my partner can come along, that is."

At that moment, Nate's vision swung to the side to see Ennis who forced a smile and a 'hi'. Savannah introduced them but Ennis still stung over the blush. Common sense slapped him with the truth. She might be playing Nate. But how did a person blush on command? Could they? Ennis realized Nate's hand extended to him and he gave the young man a solid handshake. *To let you know this woman is mine,* "Does the dinner offer include Savannah's partner too?"

"Don't bother, Nate," Mark squeezed between them to leave. "She's sleeping with him. Oh," his mood strangely lifted, "but she might be open to a ménage a trois."

Ennis's temper spiked only to have Savannah put a hand to his chest, "Ennis, he's baiting you, remember that."

Nate agreed, "It's hard to find him in a good mood." And to Savannah said, "I don't think he's fond of women. Don't take it personally."

"I don't," she replied. "Because I'm not fond of him either."

The response brought a roll of gentle laughter from her young admirer, "What can I do for you today? I'm guessing dinner is pretty much out of the question."

"We just dropped by to check on the business for Roy."

"Yeah," Ennis added, "and make sure Stephens hadn't skipped town with all the profits. He's certifiable."

"Well, I'm taking Candy's job today so I'll watch the finances too." He winked at Savannah, "To make sure Mark stays on the up-and-up. Have you heard anything new on the murder case?"

They both shook their heads and Ennis spoke, "Not unless you've got some information to add." He didn't appreciate the wink Nate gave his partner. It looked suggestive to him. No doubt Savannah would label it "sweet". Sometimes he wondered about her intuition around men. She either didn't realize how beautiful she was or played ignorant to a man's obvious flirtations. Nate probably left the impression of a churchgoing, honorable man to most women. Ennis, on the other hand, could smell his interest in Savannah from the next county – and his intentions were less than honorable, guaranteed. He guessed Nate sensed this because the younger man's vision flicked occasionally to Ennis who also identified, along with the interest, another quality. Fear. Nate Stewart's anxiousness poured off in waves, piquing Ennis's interest.

Under the male detective's scrutiny, Mr. Stewart's confidence wavered, "*Should* I know something?"

Initially, Savannah appeared poised to reply then she held off. Ennis wondered if she gradually awakened to Nate's charming act. Ennis had no doubt it was an act. No man was that truly charming – not unless he was after something.

A muted sound of a guitar playing broke the moment. Elvis then began singing a tune most familiar to Ennis, "A Little Less Conversation". Savannah tended to her cell phone on the beginning of the second chorus. Ennis took that time to size up Mr. Stewart. He slanted Nate a sly grin, "Savannah tells me you're interested in her car."

The nervousness vanished from his expression and he reverted to the confident, carefree young man Ennis wanted to smack, "Yeah. I'd buy it in a heartbeat." He stepped closer, inquiring under his breath, "Could you convince her to sell?"

Nate had asked in a manner that reeked of a male conspiracy. He obviously assumed Ennis, being a man, could wheedle her on his behalf. Her partner planned to burst the guy's bubble, "I highly doubt it. Not only is she very partial to that car but Savannah's not like most women. She's immune to cajoling." Ennis glanced in her direction and caught the frown souring her features. Something was up and when her blue eyes shifted briefly to Nate, Ennis knew his intuition was correct. The guy was a snake. The exact species was yet to be determined but Ennis bet he turned out to be a sidewinder.

Savannah ended her conversation, waved Ennis over, and spoke in a hushed tone, "Owen spoke to the manager of the Roadhouse. Nate said he stayed until four a.m. but the manager kicked him out much earlier for being falling down drunk, rowdy, and finally starting a fight. The security video confirms it."

"Now *that's* a problem with our boy here," he whispered back, making sure not to look at Nate.

She nodded, "But when Nate was kicked out, he asked the

manager to call someone to pick him up. Any guesses who pops up on the outside security camera?"

At this point, Ennis found very little surprising. If Santa Claus gave the bum a ride, he'd just chalk it up to another freak incident in cop life.

"Mark Stephens picked him up. Mark told Pierce he was at home asleep the night of the murder."

"Don't know about you but I've never quite mastered the art of sleeping and being conscious at the same time."

Her lips curved into a tentative smile, "The wear pattern on Roy's shoes didn't match the crime scene either. At least Owen's taken him off the suspect list for now."

Ennis chuckled, "And you thought the day would end up in the crapper."

Savannah basically snorted, "It ain't over yet." She leaned closer to him, "Now, what do you think of our darling Nate?"

He'd really hoped she'd ask because his feelings fell freely from his lips, "He reminds me of a Stepford child."

25

Nate *was* a Stepford child, Savannah thought to herself. Her partner spoke the words just a day ago however something in the description rang true. It became clear as glass when Owen Dunne called at eight that morning with more astonishing news. The pharmacist, James Hagins, identified Nate Stewart as the man who'd last picked up Roy's medication.

The case quickly seamed together now but with no firm evidence of the killer, the police could only suspect certain people. Those people now began to narrow down to Mark and Nate. Maria's journal served only to open more of the mystery, not solve it. Once the DNA returned, maybe they'd uncover a motive and reveal a murderer. Owen expected the results by evening so she arose early for the trip back to Augusta. With any luck, it would be her last for an extended, she hoped.

As it turned out, the results were delayed which extended her day to the level of tedious and exhausting. The lab expected results by seven that evening, leaving Savannah, Owen and Pierce, to spend the day either discussing the case or twiddling their thumbs. To Pierce's credit, he attempted a fair effort at being pleasant but she defined it more semi-civil than anything. He peppered conversations with brief answers or opinions. She sensed Owen warned his partner to play nice and also figured it helped since Roy was no longer officially a suspect.

Savannah decided to go home instead of wait. She bid Owen and Pierce farewell at a quarter of seven with a promise from Owen to contact her about the DNA. This night she refused to leave without indulging in a feast at Riviera's Restaurant. The memory of the savory beef enchiladas smothered in spicy sauce practically melted the disappointment from her day. Recollections of the crisp salad generously sprinkled with chopped tomatoes seriously awakened her appetite. While waiting in line to be seated, she called Ennis to let him know she'd be later than she originally thought. Since she promised him it was her last trip for a while, she wanted to make the most of a less than fruitful day.

People overflowed from the restaurant's door and it took until seven thirty to be seated. By eight, her meal arrived – just in time for her phone to ring. It was Owen.

"DNA's back but it'll take some time to analyze the Carlson employees against our murderer. I'm getting itchy palms already."

Savannah nearly laughed while rearranging the enchiladas with her fork. The aroma got the best of her and she cut a small portion and chowed down. She nearly groaned with bliss at the scrumptious flavor, "Itchy palms?"

"Yeah, when a case is about to break I get itchy palms. They sweat too but I guess you don't need all the details."

She delicately stabbed the fork into her salad, "Well, don't break out the calamine lotion yet. If it helps, our lab narrowed the DNA down to a relative of Roy's. I gave you the results, right?"

Owen's tone lifted with hope, "Yeah, I remember. So how many employees are relatives?"

"Well, that's our problem. I only know about Mark Stephens. You could run Thomas Dawson and Nate Stewart since they inherited from Roy's mother. Run Nate first. There's something about him that doesn't feel right. My partner called him a Stepford child and that's a description worthy of further investigation."

"Okay. I'll let you know what comes of it."

After another fifteen minutes, one salad and two enchiladas later, she paid out to leave. Once seeing the line outside, she felt partially guilty for holding up traffic in the place. She'd been finished a while before actually paying the bill.

Savannah had a brisk one block walk to her car to look forward to. It would help settle dinner, she convinced herself. Down the sidewalk and around the corner she went, keys in hand. The Camaro waited faithfully as always, patient as ever. She opened the car door and slid into the seat, grateful the day was over. The clock read eight thirty so it would be around eleven or eleven thirty before she arrived home. Good thing she'd forewarned Ennis she'd be late. It allowed him to sleep in his own bed for the first time in weeks. Now she wished she'd left earlier. Remembering how he tossed her over his shoulder sent a tiny thrill through her. She hoped he'd do that again. Hell, she just wanted to curl up against Ennis right then and there, whether they had sex or not.

Dreading the long trip ahead, she slipped the key in the ignition and started the car. With the engine, the stereo also came alive with the oldies station she frequented. She reached to pull the car into Drive but movement behind her sidelined the plan. Before she could sufficiently react, something wrapped across her throat and pulled her back against the seat. The pressure meant to kill, nothing less. Savannah wedged one set of fingers between her flesh and the ligature choking her.

Savannah glanced in the rearview mirror and saw Nate Stewart grinning a purely malicious smile as he stared back, "Hello, Savannah. I noticed you neglected to bring your guard dog today. I'd say that was a mistake, wouldn't you?"

She yanked unsuccessfully at the thin cord as it bit into both her throat and fingers. It felt coarse against her skin, like regular rope. If she had something to cut it with, she could save herself. Unfortunately like Maria, she found herself weaponless.

Nate watched her struggle against his hold, twisting and writhing to draw a breath, to free herself. He pulled tighter, "'Fraid not, Savannah. You've proven yourself too much of a pest. You should have heeded my advice the first time. After all, I *let* you live."

In her panic, her elbow banged the horn, creating a short blast of noise. A solution to save herself finally dawned and she planted the heel of her hand against the horn. A long, loud torrent of noise filled the empty parking lot. Nate yanked the cord tighter, his composure disappearing quickly, "Can't kill you fast enough."

Well, she had no plans to die either. She intended to alert anyone in the vicinity to her emergency. Her feet shoved against the firewall with hopes of gaining an ounce of breathing room. When that failed, she groped for anything to break his hold. In her panic, her hand brushed against the answer. Wrapping her fingers solidly around the handle, she yanked on it, sending the seat backward into Nate's lap. Savannah used her weight and the added joy of leverage to flatten the bastard in her back seat.

He temporarily lost his grasp on the rope which she thanked God for. A loud gasp sliced the air as cool, welcomed oxygen filled her lungs. While he writhed in the back seat, she used the limited time to heave open the door and run. Gaining a hold on breath became particularly difficult through the fitful, laborious coughing that slowed her more than she anticipated. She gasped for precious air while inspiring her legs to carry her toward the front door of the nearest business. Despite the fact no lights illuminated the building, she banged on the door hearing the distinct sound of Nate's footfalls pounding across the parking lot toward her. One hand rapped on the door while her other migrated toward her gun. She felt Nate near but surprise still jolted her at the sight of his reflection behind her in the plate glass window.

Savannah pulled her weapon from its holster and began to turn. Nate struck quick and hard as his fist crashed into her jaw. The power of his attack staggered her against the glass door. Pain ripped through her head, dropping the gun from her hand. A sickness rose in her stomach from the ache. She'd been struck only a few times hard enough to practically buckle her knees and this time was definitely one of them.

Nate seized the .38 before she regained her bearings. From what she saw, he tucked her weapon into the waistband of his jeans. He fisted her hair, bringing her to her feet then forced her against the brick wall.

She felt him reach beneath the back of her jacket. Cool fingers touched the small of her back drawing a shiver along her body while he frantically searched her. "Nate," she began in a semi-pleading tone. She was fairly sure she could escape in the darkness if she could draw his attention from his actions.

"Shut up," then a stab from the barrel of his own gun were his only responses. His cold, shaking hand finally settled in one spot. He'd located her handcuffs. "Hands behind you."

She didn't readily comply, "What's going on, Nate? Why are you doing this?" Besides trying to stall for time, she truthfully wanted an explanation. She'd expected Mark Stephens to be the bastard who'd attacked her, not sweet Nate. He's a Stepford child, Ennis had said. Well, he was also an armed maniac who appeared hell-bent on killing her. The question was why?

"Don't play dumb with me," he growled. His large hand encircled her right wrist and jerked it behind her. Savannah swallowed a whimper of pain at the rough handling but still resisted him. Suddenly he spun her to face him. The darkness concealed the reality of what approached...

It felt like her head exploded. In response to the pain and surprise, her knees buckled this time, sending her flat against the asphalt. She blinked to clear the fuzziness from her vision and found Nate's fist still clenched at his side. He packed a debilitating wallop similar to her father. Nate's shadow closed in, enshrouding her in blackness. Still stunned and her brain still reeling, she lifted her hands to shield her head and neck, fearing another unforeseen attack.

The next sound was unmistakable to any human on the planet. He clicked back the hammer of his revolver, "Get up, Savannah."

Maneuvering to her feet became quite a trick with her instability and the darkness around them. A brief silver glimmer at his waist caught her attention. There was a metallic jingle then the next thing she heard was something clatter to the ground.

"Put 'em on," the shadow's voice commanded. "And quick."

She scooped up the handcuffs and locked them loosely around her wrists. She wasn't about to lock them behind her since he hadn't specifically said to. This way, slipping her hands through was a breeze and if forced to, she could use her bound hands to fight somewhat.

Nate reached out and squeezed each cuff, cinching them down, "My truck is parked around the corner. Get moving." He nudged in closer at the sight of a couple walking the sidewalk across the street and pressed the gun barrel snug against her back. "Don't get any stupid ideas either." He prodded her along the uneven sidewalk, climbing and dropping to the concrete's pattern. Savannah wished the damn thing was level. The pressure of the gun hurt like hell when they were out of step with each other. Her throat burned from his choking her, her neck ached and now her head and jaw joined the act. Added to that was the gun in her back so she basically conducted an orchestra of agony.

"To your right," he instructed. "Truck's there."

They reached the truck at which point Nate released her arm to open the door. She wasn't stupid (maybe a little *slow* at times) but her brain finally cranked out a possible reason for this encounter, "You wanted Roy convicted of Maria's murder, didn't you? And you wanted that because –"

Pure surprise stiffened her body as he spun her then flattened her against the truck's cab. He stared down at her, his dark eyes glimmering in the street lights. He thrust the revolver under her chin, "One more question and I'll blow your brains out right here, right now."

She saw the muscles in his jaw repeatedly flex. He hung on by a precarious thread – one she honestly didn't aim to sever. "Easy, Nate," she whispered, making sure to look him directly in the eyes. "I don't desire to expedite this process."

He leaned closer until she saw his enraged features clearly in the moon's muted light, "Then get in the truck and shut the hell up." Pointing to the passenger seat, he waited for her to climb in and afterward, slammed the door.

The Carlson truck rocked considerably when Nate climbed in. He was built like Paul Bunyan, her brain reminded. A physical struggle destined to end one way – in his favor. She had to find an escape that avoided any physical contest with him.

She gasped when he leaned across her, alarmed that he planned to kill her at that particular instant. Only when his hand drew the wide seat belt across her shoulder and waist did she take a breath.

Nate clicked the belt into place, "Don't want my precious cargo falling out. Or jumping out, for that matter."

They drove the streets of Augusta with minimal traffic impeding them. She took note of the directions, streets and turns they made, mentally mapping out their location. The city lights grew fewer and farther between, casting a faint glow on trees and homes outside the city limits.   They traveled along Highway 25 past North Augusta and Savannah knew the security of civilization would soon disappear, plunging them in a sparsely populated countryside.   She remembered lakes and big, expansive farms being out this way with land as far as the eye could see.

Savannah's cell phone rang, startling them both.   Nate let off the gas and palmed the gun once more, "Let it ring."

She kept her vision straight ahead, her voice calm, "Like I can answer it anyway."   And she couldn't.   Her cuffs hands were trapped beneath the waist belt, a move he purposely made when securing the seatbelt.

Nate returned to driving until he unexpectedly turned left off the highway onto a lonely, unlit, narrow dirt road.   Savannah searched for a street name but found none.   The further they drove the more she realized they were at a construction site.   As the headlights swept across the backhoes, bulldozers and front end loaders, she caught a faint glimpse of a sign.   Planted with one post on each side, the huge billboard type sign announced "Future home of Greenbrier Mall".

The lights of Augusta glowed behind them in the distance. Complete isolation surrounded them for miles.   When Nate cut the engine, panic rose in full force.   It finally dawned that this was where he intended to kill her – in the middle of Nowhere, Georgia.   For miles her mind raced for a possible plan of escape.   For miles she drew a blank. Now was the time for action – if she could possibly fathom what action to take.

Nate released the seatbelt, "Get out."

Strange how calm his voice sounded. Of course during her involuntary road trip, she discovered – she thought – why her once genteel companion changed to Mr. Hyde. "You stand a good chance of being released from prison before you collect Social Security. For Maria's murder, I mean. But you kill a police officer and it's the needle, guaranteed."

He got out, rounded the truck, threw open her door and forcibly jerked her from the seat, "If they find the police officer's body, you mean."

Savannah struggled to gain her footing momentarily then stood, watching him pace in front of the beaming headlights. She chanced speaking once more, "My problem is, why frame Roy for the murder? Why let him go to prison for your actions?"

His anxiousness slowly percolated to the surface. He paced nervously, his mind hunting for answers not related to her question, "*Your problems* are 'bout over so shut up."

No one ever claimed she possessed a shred of common sense, particularly in a dangerous situation. Her first partner regularly accused that she had one brain cell and it fought for dominance. "Sit down and give your mind a rest," he'd tell her. Riley Murphy was a good man and a great cop. He worked diligently with her to develop patience in a bad situation, to think through potential solutions.

Nate Stewart appeared confident of his position. He also appeared at a loss as though the road trip was a spur of the moment decision and now what did he do with her?

While he strode back and forth, she made conversation, "You're the fella Maria wrote about in her journal."

The words seemed to reach the recesses of his racing mind and he stopped, his vision lifting to meet hers, "What journal?"

"Maria kept a journal of her daily activities. You probably never expected her to, her being a busy stockbroker and all. The police found it and they studied it page by page. Maria loved Roy but you scared the hell out of her." She hit a solid nerve with the last statement. Nate charged at her like an angry bull, and she stepped back, hearing Riley's words echo in her brain. Her one brain cell really topped her shitty situation with a big, juicy cherry.

Nate's body connected with hers hard enough to send her back two more steps. His fingers clenched a fistful of hair and pulled her head back to meet his vision, "Shut up or I'll take more liberties than putting you down." A tense smile crossed his features, "And make no mistake. I'll ensure you go to Hell with plenty of unbearable memories."

"If you were smart, you'd let me go."

Nate's large hand took her arm and he dragged her past the headlights into the darkness. Savannah's eyes struggled to adjust, to gain a reference point. What registered put the fear into overdrive. Beside her was a giant rectangular hole she estimated about ten feet long by five feet wide. The depth measured out to bottomless in the night sky.

"Not so arrogant now are you, bitch?"

She felt him tense but before she could react, he'd shoved her with such force she couldn't fight back. Savannah's bearings somersaulted as she fell into the black pit. Only a sharp pain in her back brought her to the realization she'd stopped falling. She landed flat of her back against something large and curved. The force of the fall and the shape of the object arched her back to an agonizing degree. After a cursory inspection, she guessed her saving grace was a sewage pipe for the new mall. She never knew plumbing could be so damn hurtful. After saying a prayer of thanks that the fall hadn't killed her or knocked the breath from her, she heard an unknown object clink off the huge pipe. Her feet finally hit solid terra firma and she quickly she felt around in the dark for whatever Nate tossed in.

Above her, she saw him standing near the edge, gloating, "I'll be long gone by the time they find you. Unlike you, Savannah, I had a backup plan. In less than twenty four hours I'll be basking on a warm beach watching beautiful women pass by and you'll be roasting in Hell. Oh, say hi to Maria for me." His shadow disappeared and she heard his heavy footfalls pounding the dirt as he ran.

Soon after, a mechanical rumbling caught her attention. It was the sound of a large construction vehicle groaning to life. Knowing that the sound couldn't mean Nate was working overtime at Carlson's, Savannah scrambled to find the mystery object that clanked off the metal pipe while her other hand palmed her phone. Owen's number was on speed dial now, a result of their working together on the case. She ignored her voice mail prompt and called up Owen's number. Skimming the dirt with her other hand, she finally located what she hunted for. Nate threw her service weapon into the pit, intent on burying every trace of her existence. Obviously, the boy thought this war was won. Obviously, as Riley Murphy would happily tell him, he had grossly underestimated Savannah Prince. She holstered the gun just as someone answered the phone.

"This is Dunne," a voice yawned into the receiver.

"Owen, it's me," her voice teetered on trembling as she caught a whiff of diesel exhaust. There were only two or three different pieces of equipment on site but Savannah instinctively knew which one Nate currently operated.

"Hey, Savannah. Did you get my voice mail?"

"No. I need help, Owen. Right now. Can you call the sheriff or closest unit out to the Greenbrier Mall site?"

Owen sobered instantly, "Sure. What's wrong? What's that noise?"

"Nate Stewart, that's what. He's Maria's killer and now he's trying to kill me. He's going to *bury me alive*, Owen. I need help now." In the background she heard Owen speak to someone. She heard Pierce's voice in the near distance. He didn't sound as worked up as she did but then he wasn't about to be covered in tons of dirt either.

She climbed atop the giant pipe. By doing so, she barely saw over the top of the hole. Moving straight at her was the bucket of the bulldozer close enough to nearly touch her. Savannah backed off slightly but not so much to lose her balance. The bucket dumped an enormous load of dirt that knocked her off and slammed her against the earthen wall behind the pipe. She shielded her face and head from the onslaught of cascading dirt, yelling, "Owen, help!"

"We'll be there in a few. I'm calling out units right now."

By the time the bucket emptied, she stood, buried to her knees. After a laborious effort, Savannah pulled her legs free and waited for the next wave to come. "Savannah," Owen called, "you still there?" He now sounded as panicked as she.

"I'm here," she shouted over the growling engine and rasping gears.

"It wasn't Roy's baby," he flustered detective blurted. "The DNA finally came back."

Savannah tried to weigh the importance of the information against her current dilemma. She stood in a ten foot hole waiting for the sky to fall with hundreds of pounds of dirt. All because of Nate's glorious effort to silence her. *That little bastard*, she fumed while climbing the pipe again. *If I live through this, he surely won't.* She already knew from reading Maria's diary that Roy wasn't the father and thanks to Nate's present actions, she offered her take on the situation, "Nate was the father."

Owen didn't seem surprised she knew, "Yeah. Turns out he's Roy's cousin." He paused a second then, "Units are ten minutes out. Pierce and I are on our way."

"Ten minutes is a lifetime. Drive excessively fast if you can, Owen. I'm not sure I'll —" another load of dirt pummeled her, this time knocking the phone from her hand as she fell backward. Dust and soil choked her, sending her into a coughing fit while clawing her way free. The smell of damp soil reinforced the panic coursing through her.

She clambered atop the pipe again, this time seeing the bulldozer backed away to reload. The deafening noise receded enough that she heard Owen screaming her name from somewhere in the pile of dirt. Like a dog searching for a treasured bone, she frantically dug for her phone and luckily found it before Nate struck again. She brushed off the phone and said, "I gotta go. Just keep driving to the Greenbrier Mall location north of town. I'll either be above ground or below it." She clicked off and pocketed the phone.

Now she had use of both hands – albeit handcuffed – to fight for survival. The bulldozer roared as Nate revved the engine. She strained to peek over the top of the chasm to see the machine barreling down on her again. Savannah forced herself to stay still and calm herself somewhat, even through the raging claustrophobia engulfing her senses. Fear of a different nature flooded her system. As a rookie, the same bitter terror coursed in her veins. A fear no academy instructor warned her about. She doubted they could put it into words. She also doubted the gung ho recruits could or would try to fathom its debilitating depth. Experience was the only teacher. Stay cool under fire, Riley always said. Do that and your chances of going home alive increase dramatically.

Savannah repeated Riley's advice as a mantra. A level head, common sense and a boatload of good luck might get her home to her family and Ennis. She watched the bulldozer approach and after determining which end of the chasm Nate aimed for, she rushed to the other side of the pipe. If humanly possible, she wasn't spending eternity listening to everyone at Greenbrier Mall flush the crappers.

The bucket of the bulldozer blocked the meager moonlight as it towered over her. Savannah flattened against the earthen wall to allow the load to dump without burying her. Nate poured the heavy soil so fast she nearly didn't see a possible way out. When he backed away to refill, she could barely hear what she thought were sirens in the distance. Or at least she prayed that's what it was. Nate began working faster now, giving her hope that he'd seen the police approaching. The next haul came quicker and nearly hit her square on. She'd shielded her head for most of the load but when she sensed the torrent was over, she reached up, her hands grasping the edge of the bulldozer's bucket. The metal felt cold and slippery with damp soil and she cursed when both hands slipped off. *Next time*, she thought. *I'll get it next time.*

The next time came equally as quick. Savannah waited halfway through the load before grabbing the bulldozer's edge. She tightened her hold around a jagged piece of metal protruding from the once smooth edge. As Nate lifted the bucket, the metal dug into her flesh, slicing it, but she held true, allowing the machine to drag her from the dark, deep hole. Her knees hit the ground, giving her little time to celebrate her success or complain of the blood and pain from her hand. She got to her feet quickly, grateful Nate hadn't seen her yet.

He whipped the bulldozer around for another go. Savannah noticed the flashing red and blue lights on the highway, closing at an impressive rate. The sight would have inspired a degree of relief however when she glanced back, Nate stared over his shoulder at her. He jerked the bulldozer to face her, and shoved his foot against the accelerator. She stood her ground until he got a certain distance then ran toward the Carlson truck. He wouldn't want to destroy his only means of escape, she hoped.

The bulldozer followed obediently, like a rabid dog taking orders from its owner. Smoke streamed from its stack while gaining momentum and speed. Nate certainly didn't appear concerned about his future transportation. His primary goal remained simple. Kill her any way possible.

The bucket lowered even with her and the Carlson truck and the gears shifted sending the engine into a higher, faster frenzy.

Initially she had thoughts of hopping in the Carlson truck and taking off but the empty ignition dashed those plans. They were concreted when the bulldozer clipped the back of the truck in an attempt to run her down. She sidestepped and ran, afraid the truck might roll onto her.

A burst of noise immediately followed by a plinking sound redirected her vision to Nate himself. One hand controlled the bulldozer while the other held a revolver. Another shot clanked off the Carlson truck forcing her to cut a wide path around it and the treacherous beast on wheels, her vision keen on watching his gun hand. From the corner of her eye, she noticed the police units closing in now. They drove hard and fast down the dirt road leading to the construction site. She recognized Owen's Toyota 4Runner as one of the lead cars.

Nate saw them too but his intent to kill her overrode any ounce of rational thinking. The cars skidded to a stop at the perimeter of the action, lining up in a neat row. All the drivers left the headlights on, producing a nearly blinding illumination for all involved. Every cop opened their doors and hunkered behind, their weapons aimed at the runaway machine and its enraged driver.

Ignoring their visitors, Nate tightened the bulldozer's turning radius and it rounded on Savannah like a snake ready to bite. Taking the only opportunity offered, she grabbed onto the back of the machine, hearing Owen shout at Nate but she doubted the boy cared at this point, or maybe he did...

Surprising everyone, Nate turned in the seat and fired off three shots at the police. Savannah took advantage of the time by climbing up the back of the bulldozer. Nate wheeled, his revolver leveled dangerously close to her belly. Instinctively she kicked at his hand but the gun stayed securely in his grip. "I'm saving the last bullet for you," Nate yelled over the engine's roar.

With that threat, she doubled her fists, wincing at the pain from her injured hand and swung at the gun. Blood from her wound spattered his jeans when the handcuffs crashed against his knuckles but it produced enough pain to temporarily loosen his grip on the revolver.

Savannah pulled her own weapon from its holster, braced herself against the cab, and nestled the barrel under his jaw, "Drop the gun or I'll send you to St. Peter on the express flight."

Nate hesitated with the order, a decision that fully infuriated her. Even as her hand ached and burned from holding the gun, she applied generous pressure with the weapon, "Nathan, drop it. Even if you manage to shoot me, that mass of law enforcement will drop you in a heartbeat."

As if Owen heard her, he reinforced her words over the loudspeaker this time. Savannah nudged him with the weapon and finally he let the revolver tumble from his grasp. The instant it landed on the ground, a flood of officers converged on them, Owen and Pierce leading the pack. Savannah instructed Nate to slowly climb down from the cab. She suspected having ten weapons – eleven including hers –

pointed at Nate aided in his choice to follow directions. The officers forced him face down on the ground and handcuffed him.

Owen hopped aboard the bulldozer just as she switched the key off. "Are you okay?" he asked.

She nodded firmly but her shaking began already. In thirty minutes she'd be toast and in need of a painkiller for her nerves, not just her aches and pains.

He gave her a cursory inspection while unlocking the handcuffs, "You need a doctor. Your hand is bleeding."

Savannah managed a faint smile, "If that's the worst I've got, I'm thankful."

Owen helped her down, her good hand wrapped in his. Now that he'd mentioned it, her injured hand began stinging worse than ever. She holstered her gun which needed a good cleaning anyway so a little blood wouldn't hurt it for now. She was just grateful to be alive to complain about it.

Pierce and a uniformed officer brought Nate to his feet in a not-so-gentle fashion. Nate turned to her, still seething with rage, "You meddling bitch. All you had to do was keep to your own business like I told you to."

"Owen and Pierce had already cleared Roy as a suspect, genius. Why did you want him convicted of Maria's murder? You stood nothing to gain, not even her love."

The news sobered Nate like a good, hearty slap. He paused a moment then, "Roy wouldn't let Maria go. She'd broken up with him – she was with me but he kept nagging her." The anger resurged again,

"And that bitch planned to go back to him. Because she got knocked up with his kid."

"So you switch his meds so he'll what? Lose it and kill her? Roy's not a murderer."

Furious that she'd clearly missed his point, he enunciated very carefully, "I wanted her to see how crazy he was but all that did was bring them closer. That bitch! Throw me away for that nutcase? *No way...*"

He'd said it with such vehemence, such hatred, she pitied Maria Saxon during her last moments. Savannah stepped closer against Owen's caution. She studied Nate, trying to find a thread of decency somewhere. What she saw was cold and hard, nothing even remotely resembling Roy or his familial connection. "That's a fine way to talk about your cousin. No wonder Maria couldn't stand you."

To polish off her image of him, he leaned toward her, growling, "I wasn't gonna let her have that kid and live happily ever after with Roy. Not with everything I'd done for her. When I found out she was pregnant, I bought the cradle and shitloads of things, thinking it was my kid. Then she has the nerve to tell me it's Roy's. I'm not letting some bitch show me up for a fool, especially to *him*."

Refusing to back off, Savannah restrained the urge to strangle him herself, "No, you did that all by yourself."

A flash of confusion broke his mask of fury. She capitalized on it, "You killed Maria but you didn't kill Roy's baby. You killed your own." She turned to walk away with Owen. Stopping briefly, she glanced over her shoulder to see the news finally hit home with him. She finished, "From what I heard, it was a boy."

26

Soft lips pressed to hers, stirring her awake. Her eyes opened into slits to reveal Ennis leaned over her, a wide grin on his face, "Good morning, Wonder Woman."

After the previous day, Savannah felt like seven bags of watered down shit. Calling her Wonder Woman was way off the mark, at least for today. "Enough with the Diana Prince references," she groaned.

"Well, besides me there's another person here who thinks you're pretty wonderful."

She hadn't the motivation or energy to move or care. She'd spent two hours at the Augusta hospital having her hand cleaned and wrapped by Dr. Sadism. Pierce and Dunne hung around to make sure a uniform officer delivered her car to the hospital. In that time, Pierce tendered a startling declaration. He humbly apologized for being a jerk, finishing that he'd misjudged her as a cop. That itself nearly sent her ass over heels passed out to the floor. Or maybe it was the atrociously excruciating solution Dr. Pain used for her wound.

Owen contacted Ennis about the circumstances that night and against Savannah's wishes, her partner hit the road to Augusta at midnight to pick her up. She hadn't let him, of course. She was a big girl – or so she wanted him to think – and managed to drive herself home with him following in his Dodge Mammoth. They'd arrived home a few hours before the sun stretched and had its first cup of coffee. She showered and went straight to bed. Ennis curled around her, his body heat helping to settle her shakes from the cold and shock. She'd shivered until falling asleep in his warm, comforting embrace.

Ennis hadn't outwardly shown his stress but strangely Savannah picked up on it. She sensed he was wired for either total spontaneous combustion or total collapse. After her shower, she'd discovered it was the latter. His hands shook as badly as hers when he rewrapped the bandage on her hand and he'd dropped off asleep well before she did.

Now – she wearily glanced at the clock – at eight twenty in the morning, Ennis was forcing her into an upright position long before her bones thought necessary. "It's eight in the friggin' morning," she groaned pitifully. With that self explanatory statement, she turned over and tugged the covers over her head. Not even Ennis's chipper little laugh bothered her. All she needed was a healthy dose of slumber and she was good to go. Except...

A gentle swat on her bottom buoyed her consciousness to not-quite-dead-yet. She mumbled, "Go 'way. I'm tired. I'll get up when I'm forty."

Ennis sat next to her, peeled the covers back. He wisely stopped at her chin, "We've got company."

"Tell them I said hi." She tossed the covers back over her head.

"It's Roy."

Those particular words traversed the fog in her brain enough that she pulled the covers back down, "Roy? He's been released?"

He nodded, "He wants to see you."

Savannah's vivacity hovered around nil, even with the good news of Roy's release. She whispered, "Does he seem... You know, *okay?*"

Ennis curbed a teasing smile while bending to her ear, "He never seems *okay* to me but he's calm and talking rationally so that's a plus."

She sighed. This situation required her presence, and regrettably good old fashioned rest took a back seat. Dragging her presence from the warm, cozy bed entailed far more effort than it should have. That was when Ennis stepped in. A few seconds lapsed when the covers completely disappeared, leaving her curled in the fetal position. Thankfully she'd worn a pair of flannel pajamas to bed. The rude awakening, however, was received as well as a bucket of ice water over her head. "Ennis, you're the meanest shit when you put your mind to it."

He wrapped his hand around her arm to unceremoniously haul her from the bed. Savannah struggled to gain an ounce of leverage, "Ennis, *cut it out.* I'm up, I'm up."

"That's not sounding promising in there," a voice called from her living room.

"I'll be right in, Roy," she called, her voice missing on a few cylinders as she spoke. She yanked the robe from Ennis who couldn't halt the progression of a humorous smile. Savannah saw it, "Yeah, laugh it up, Rutherford. You'll get yours later when I'm conscious."

"Promises, promises," he teased and swatted her bottom as she passed by.

She jumped slightly but gave him a teasing smile, "Don't think I won't follow through. I hope you're taking your vitamins because when I'm caught up on rest, you'll be too worn out to yawn." No more than two steps into the living room, Savannah was greeted by a full cup of coffee in her favorite mug – served by Roy. He grinned sheepishly, "Ennis told me I'd likely survive the morning if I presented a peace offering. He said it's his special blend, whatever that means."

She rubbed her eyes, gratefully took the mug, and made sure to throw Ennis a covert wink, "It means a stay of execution for waking me so early."

Her former boyfriend pulled the dining chair out for her and waited for her to sit before planting himself next to her. "I wanted to thank you personally for getting me out of that jam. Those cops had their sights set on me from day one."

She sipped the hot coffee and savored the warmth coating her throat, "You're welcome, Roy. Just try to stay out of those jams from now on."

He took a drink from his own cup, "I'd have never guessed Nate. Hell, I didn't even know Maria was seeing him. She wouldn't tell me who the new guy was."

"Now you know why," Ennis added. "That was a rather difficult situation."

Savannah slanted him a quick look. Her partner evidently tabled his jealousy for the morning. So far he handled Roy's visit well.

She recalled one important piece of information, "Owen Dunne said he'd like to see you." Watching Roy recoil at the words, she tried to calm him, "It's only to explain the evidence. Since he's the detective in charge, it's his job."

"No worries?"

A tiny, weary smile curled her lips, "No worries. You know, on the subject of family. Far be it from me to judge, but your family tree needs some pruning like mine does."

Roy managed to set the cup down before bursting into laughter, "I don't think Home Depot has shears big enough for us, Kitten. We're stuck with them, nuts and all."

The coffee finally kicked in enough to remind her of the picture and ring. She fetched them from the computer table, "I'll let you take these back. I bought a new frame for the picture. The other one was broken. Oh, and you'll need to inform Candy our wedding is cancelled. She seems to think we're betrothed."

Roy's expression softened at the mention of her name, "She's a good girl. I might ask her out sometime."

"I'm almost positive she'll accept." The second subject was a little more difficult to broach, "I should have returned the ring years ago and apologize for not doing so."

Roy's hand extended to take the photo and the ring. The ring box still sat atop the frame. He removed the former and handed it back, "This is yours, babe. Do whatever you want with it." He then focused on the prom picture, "I will, on the other hand, take this little gem back and hang it in the respective spot." Roy stared at it, his thumb stroking her image, "On second thought, do you mind if I hang this on my wall of fame? You know, up front?"

The sentiment warmed her nearly as much as the coffee, "Of course I don't mind."

"Good. Yeah, another thing. Your flowerbeds look like crap."

Okay, sentimentality is officially kaput... "Your ability to flatter a woman brings me to tears," she said with a cringe. She slung her bandaged hand, trying to rid herself of the ache.

Roy and Ennis chuckled at her response which also neglected to strum her heartstrings. There was something less than heartwarming about a former boyfriend and the current one getting a laugh off her.

Roy shook his head, "No, you misunderstood. What I meant was, for helping me I'd like to pay you back somehow. Since I'm into landscaping and you already have a lawn guy, lemme do your flowerbeds. I'll plant whatever you want."

She took a sip of coffee, contemplating. "Money trees work for me," she winked at Ennis.

"'Fraid I'm not that good. How about hibiscus?"

"Remember who's caring for these plants. I don't exactly possess my sister's green thumb. She could've raised Lazarus from the dead. It positively wrecks me that she got Mama's talent."

Beneath the table, Roy nudged her leg with his and cast a mischievous grin, "But you got your mama's voice. It brings men to their knees. Right, Ennis?"

Savannah cut her eyes to Ennis again. That one hit the bulls-eye. Ennis's hackles raised, his vision narrowed a bit, "Trumps a green thumb with me, for sure."

"Hibiscus sounds great," she yearned to change the subject.

"Anything you think will grow and I won't kill."

"Your favorite color still purple?" Roy asked, obviously taking mental notes.

"Lavender," Ennis corrected with strong conviction.

Savannah really needed a refill. She made her way to the kitchen, sighing to herself that roosters had nothing on Ennis and Roy. She shook her head when the two began discussing the difference in purple and lavender and the reason why she liked one over the other.

She peeked around the corner, "Plant orange."

The declaration stunned the men into silence. *Good,* she smiled. No need in letting men think they know everything about a woman. "And pink, while you're at it."

When she sat down, she savored the heat from the heavy mug, and wrapped her hands around it, even though the heat managed to completely awaken the wound now. Roy watched her quietly then split a grin, "Trying to throw us off, aren't you?"

Whatever expression she held, she didn't know how Roy read it. He'd caught her dead to rights but she'd never admit it, "No, I really want orange and pink."

The two men stared at each other momentarily then said in unison, "Lavender." Roy stood up, "Well, I'm headed home. I'll be back Saturday to get started on your *lavender* flowerbed." He tipped her head back and planted a kiss on her lips, "Thanks again, Kitten."

"You're welcome, Roy. Stay out of trouble."

"Me? Don't worry about me, babe. You're the one headed for trouble. This fella," he pointed to Ennis, "he's got designs on a future with you." Roy grabbed up the ring box and tossed it to her partner, "Trade it in on a better model. This girl deserves the best."

J.L. Lemon lives in Texas surrounded by a loving and supportive family, two adorable and devoted puppies, and hordes of garden gnomes.

Before 2002, J.L. Lemon wrote opinions and product reviews for an online consumer guide. When fellow reviewers cited the author's knack for humor, she decided to return to writing fiction. To date, she's published 6 books with 5 installments in the Savannah Stories. There are 3 more in the works. For more titles from J.L. Lemon, please visit:

www.geocities.com/upatmidnightpublishing
www.geocities.com/authorjllemon

Savannah and Ennis keep the author busy taking dictation and making plenty of suggestions about their future.